VERNAL

A ROYAL PROTECTOR ACADEMY NOVEL

RANDI COOLEY WILSON

Vernal
Copyright © 2016 by Randi Cooley Wilson

Published by SECRET GARDEN PRODUCTIONS, LLC

Content editing by
Kris Kendall at Final-Edits

Copy editing by
Liz Ferry at Per Se Editing

Cover design © Hang Le

Interior Design & Formatting by
Christine Borgford at Perfectly Publishable

VERNAL (A Royal Protector Academy Novel, Book One)
Randi Cooley Wilson
Printed in the United States of America
First Edition June 2016
ISBN-13: 978-1519394194
ISBN-10: 1519394195

ROYAL PROTECTOR
ACADEMY

ALSO BY

RANDI COOLEY WILSON

THE ROYAL PROTECTOR ACADEMY
VERNAL
AEQUUS
NOX

THE REVELATION SERIES
REVELATION
RESTRAINT
REDEMPTION
REVOLUTION
RESTORATION

DARK SOUL SERIES
STOLAS
VASSAGO
LEVIATHAN

For those who are lost in the rain.

It is like the sun shining on the rain
and the rain falling on the sunshine.
Frances Hodgson Burnette
The Secret Garden

PROLOGUE

SERENA

WITH THE SPRING COME NEW BEGINNINGS.

Twenty years ago, amid the serenity of a winter snowfall, I was born into the London clan—a royal family of gargoyle protectors that for centuries has devotedly safeguarded mankind against evil.

There are many who would say it is a great honor and privilege to be Serena Elizabeth Vivian St. Michael, daughter of Abigail and Callan, princess and sole heir to the crown of the revered gargoyle protector race. My clan has fought darkness, overcome betrayals, restored balance, prevented a war, and solidified an honored place among the supernatural and divine worlds—all because the London clan of gargoyles carries a highly sought-after protector lineage: the dragon spirit.

You see, in the seventh century, a dragon named La Gargouille lived near a town on the River Seine in France. Legend has it that he was so grotesque to look at, his appearance alone would ward off evil spirits. But instead of protecting the town, La Gargouille terrorized it, until the archbishop of Rouen, St. Romanus, killed it.

Just before the beast was slain, the dragon sank his teeth into

Romanus's shoulder, a breath from piercing the archbishop's heart. Unbeknownst to both, the violent action caused their bloods to mix—a tying feat that caused the dragon spirit and a divine soul to become bound together for eternity.

At the time, no one knew that La Gargouille was a demon sent by the dark army. By attacking a man of God, Hell hoped to start another war. But in the end, they were unsuccessful.

By tethering the dragon—a demon of darkness—and an archbishop—a soul of heavenly light—together, Heaven created a secondary army: the gargoyle race. It is a lineage designed for one purpose: to protect mankind against evil.

Every descendent that has been produced from the archbishop's line since has been eternally bound to the dragon, including my family, the London clan of gargoyles. We proudly carry the bloodline of Romanus and the dragon, our clan's identifying mark. This in itself makes us the most powerful clan in existence. Yet my family's legacy extends beyond the normal good-versus-evil saga.

Before my birth, my uncle, Asher St. Michael, the king of our race, was assigned to protect a human named Eve Collins. She was created as a divine secret. The only one of her kind, Eve was born of a non-fallen angel and a human. To ensure her safety, the archangel Michael, her father, promised the Angelic Council that her continued existence would guarantee Heaven's gates were safe from Hell's dark army.

As a precaution, Michael designed the divination of redemption, preordaining the souls of the daughter of light and the prince of dark to join together; their sacrifice—love. In the end, their love conquered all, preventing another war between Heaven and Hell, and solidifying the connection between the dragon and the divine spirit for centuries to come, thus guaranteeing our race's existence.

As romantic as my aunt and uncle's tale may seem, growing up in the shadow of their epic fairy tale was never easy, and as the only child produced from any of the London clan's three couples, I have been bestowed the great honor of being next in line to the throne—an obligation I'm not interested in fulfilling. Alas, my oaths of duty, honor, and protection bind me to heed my vocation. As a protector, free will doesn't exist. Our lives are not our own. We were created only to protect.

My world is not filled with happily ever after. It's full of realism, treachery, and falsehoods.

When I was a young child, my mother and father would say that I was their piece of serenity in an existence filled with turmoil. The expectations that come with being a gargoyle born into the royal St. Michael family, and the London clan, are a heavy burden to carry. Those expectations chain me to vows, which are impossible to ignore.

But I am not them.

Their legend is not my ending.

This is *my* story. My beginning.

I am the next chapter of the London clan protector legacy.

My future was etched in stone until the day Tristan Gallagher swooped in, with his dark past and guarded secrets. The moment we met, I fell under his spell. It was a fatal mistake forcing us to choose between our hearts and bloodlines, trying to pull us apart with oaths and obligations.

Our love will ignite an ancient war.

Our pasts will collide with the present.

And one lie will destroy it all.

Welcome to the Royal Protector Academy.

ONE

LOST IN THE RAIN

SERENA

MY EYELIDS SLIDE CLOSED AS THE tiny drops of water cascade from the darkened sky. The warm beads hit my face, trickling effortlessly across my cool skin. The sensation of being alive wraps around me, as my spirit connects to the energy the weather bestows. Strength bleeds into my body, penetrating each layer until the energy drifts throughout my veins.

I ignore the dull ache making its way into my neck, a result of tilting of my face skyward. Instead, I lift my arms and, without thought, twirl and embrace each tiny droplet of water as the rain soaks the crenulated coastline around me in a fierce assault.

The elements heighten my supernatural powers, causing my core to hum with vitality. My lips form a small smile as I pirouette my way through the mist-shrouded, endless emerald hills. Each rise is crisscrossed by tumbledown ancient stone walls. My laughter floats in the wind. It's the only other sound encircling me, aside from the rainfall.

I loved doing this as a child. Spinning so fast I'd become dizzy and disoriented, until the earth around my feet would simply slip away, and breathlessly I would collapse onto the blades of grass. I miss the care-free days of my youth. There's something freeing—liberating—about standing in an open field, with your arms extended, allowing the rain to wash away your inhibitions. Not that I have many hang-ups, but the ones I do—they wrap around my heart like chains, squeezing until the simple act of breathing becomes almost impossible.

Another childish laugh escapes me as my body tumbles and collapses onto the soaked ground. I stretch my lean limbs and sink into the sponge-like soil, becoming one with the aged earth below my undressed body. My wet, auburn hair falls messily around my face and some of the long pieces stick to my dampened skin.

I don't care.

For the first time in days, I feel alive again.

Lying on the ground, I simply stare at the dark sky above, as the world spins around me. For a fleeting minute, the dizziness offers a brief reprieve from the musings that constantly cloud my head.

My free-spirited revel ends abruptly at the sound of a throat being cleared. I release a half moan, half sigh, knowing my moment of serenity has come to an end.

Rather than sitting up to face Rulf, the royal guard assigned to protect me, I pout like a child. My unhappiness overtakes the bliss I was feeling seconds ago.

It's not that I don't enjoy Rulf's company. It's just that his presence reminds me of my royal bloodline, my duties, and my obligations.

Knowing the gargoyle's temperament, he's probably standing with his arms crossed, aggravated by my lack of acknowledgment while he continues to get wet.

"Go away, Rulf."

"You're naked."

The statement comes from an unfamiliar, seductive, masculine voice, filled with an inherent confidence.

Definitely. Not. Rulf.

Unaware of who this stranger is, I remain still and strategize a plan of attack, should I need one. Though I'm without my weapons, I'm not concerned. Years of training with the best protectors have made me a skilled opponent. If all else fails, I always have my supernatural powers to help me kick this guy's ass.

I clear my throat and remain motionless.

"Your ability to state the obvious is mind-blowing."

The stranger releases a dark chuckle, unnerving me. I shiver in response, and my slight grin falls. My lips press together in annoyance at my reaction to something as simple as his enthralling laughter. It's like silk.

Cool.

Sensual.

Designed to pull you in and entrance you.

"I guess I missed the *clothing optional* portion of the Academy's handbook," he counters.

My stomach clenches in response as his velvety voice drifts over my exposed skin, caressing it. I swallow, in an attempt to keep myself in check and my tone even.

It is an epic failure.

"Something to work on, then." My voice is shaky.

"What's that?"

"Reading."

"Reading?"

"A prerequisite if you'll be attending the Academy."

A beat of silence passes between us before he speaks.

"Is nudity a habitual behavior of yours?" he questions, with an amused lilt to his tone.

At the sound of his deep voice, I roll onto my stomach, lift my gaze, and meet his curious expression.

He's breathtaking, in a dark and unrefined manner, if you're into that sort of thing. By the way my breathing has become erratic and my heart rate is spiraling out of control, I guess I'm into it.

"Yes," I reply.

A knowing smirk appears on his full lips. "Nice ass," he compliments, while his stare runs the length of me.

I don't shy away from his open perusal. I'm comfortable with my curves. Self-assurance comes with my title.

His eyes roam across my body, leaving imprints everywhere they go. I blush uncharacteristically at his heated intensity. My poise cracks as raw desire slithers inside me, crawling into the crevices, choking me.

Confused by the way my body is responding to him, I pinch my brows. He tilts his head to the side, watching my reaction. There's something captivating about the way he's looking at me. He's drawn to me, but can't figure out why.

I notice his self-confidence start to fade. Taking advantage of the fact that he's lost in his own thoughts, my focus shifts to his mouth, and I stare at a tiny, sexy scar on his upper lip. His breathing is smooth and soft.

Unlike me, with my unsolicited need to have him whisper dirty things to me, he seems unaffected. Cool and calm. Eerily controlled.

The stranger runs both of his large hands through his caramel hair, pushing the long pieces on top back in a sleek and sexy manner. The rain has soaked every perfect strand, and they keep attaching themselves to his sun-kissed face. It's almost as if they never want to let go.

I narrow my eyes at the wisps. They're eliciting a pang of jealousy within me. For some unexplainable reason, I feel an overwhelming sense of ownership over him. It's me who should be the one to touch his slightly scruffy, chiseled face—not those pieces of hair.

Wait, that isn't right. I don't even know him.

I scrutinize his thick eyebrows and attempt to compose myself. On most guys a brow piercing looks ridiculous. On him, it looks menacing and wild.

And hot.

So very, very hot.

I drop my gaze to the silver and hematite rings adorning his fingers. Like mine, every finger with the exception of his pinky is covered with them. I blink away the idea that our hands match, and instead concentrate on his broad chest, hidden under a white thermal.

The thin cotton is drenched, allowing me to take in his sculpted body. A pendant sits under his shirt, dangling from a black leather rope, which hangs from his neck.

Annoyingly, I can't make out what it is.

I sigh internally as my eyes trail over his rolled-up sleeves. They're pulled up to his elbows, showing off the leather-and-chain bracelets he's wearing on each wrist. At the sight of the familiar adornments, all my internal alarms go off, and something inside of me sinks. I attempt to hide the awareness that has fallen across my expression, and instead fixate on his worn jeans and heavy boots, while planning my escape.

This guy reeks of danger, and trouble. The air of cockiness he emanates is one I grew up with. It matches my father's and uncles'.

It all means this hot specimen is one hundred percent off-limits, and being near him is like being near a bullet that you never saw coming. It wounds you so quickly and deeply that you bleed out without even knowing you've been hit.

I meet his powerful cognac glare and a shaky breath escapes me. I'm startled by the way he's staring at me.

Like I'm all he's longed for.

A light chill brushes through me. I'm not accustomed to someone looking at me and seeing just me, not my bloodline. I need to get a grip on my erratic emotions.

Standing, I put my entire unclothed body on display, hoping to throw him off balance. Pushing some of my damp hair behind my ear, I lift a challenging eyebrow at him, daring him not to look at me.

Unfazed, he holds my gaze with an unwavering stare. A silent pause beats between us.

Who is this guy?

"Are you done assessing me?" he asks.

"You're a protector?" I point to the shaded Celtic tattoo on his right forearm.

The symbol binds him to the Spiritual Assembly of Protectors, allowing him to accept divine assignments.

Of course he's a protector—he's here at the Academy.

Why can't I think clearly around him?

The stranger's expression falls, as if my accusation hurt him somehow. He doesn't say anything, but dips his chin in response, confirming my theory.

I take a step back, empathetic to the heavy burden protectors carry.

Nervously, my fingers find and play with my own piece of protector jewelry. The silver bracelet sits on my left wrist and is intricately designed with flowers and vines around the band, hiding my smaller, identical Assembly tattoo.

My aunt Eve gifted the bracelet to me for my eighteenth birthday. It was something her deceased mother Elizabeth, a jewelry designer, had made for her. Aunt Eve had the emeralds, my healing stone, added so they hang off the sides in a pretty and feminine manner. A small watch face was set on top in the hope that I would become more responsible about time management.

Not one of my strong suits.

Along with rules, motivation, education—anyway, you get the point.

It's crucial that all gargoyles wear something containing their healing stone.

The mineral rejuvenates us, increases our powers, and heightens our restorative abilities.

It's a necessary evil in my book. I despise the leather bands my family wear. They feel more like handcuffs to me than required protector accessories.

"Tristan," he says, in a way that slices through me.

Another unwelcome shiver crosses my skin at the sound of his voice.

"Serena," I reply thinly.

Tristan's pointed look drops and travels over my body in a palpable manner, as he becomes intimately acquainted once again with my every curve.

"Are you always so . . . welcoming, Serena?"

When his eyes finally meet mine, my brow arches.

"Only to those I like."

"So you like me then?" He attempts to hide his smile.

I hold him with a glare. "Don't flatter yourself."

Tristan cocks his head and crosses his arms over his chest. My focus strays to the streams of rain dripping off his face. He steps closer to me, so close that I trap a breath he's exhaled in my lungs, when the bare portion of his arm brushes my own.

Why am I so reactive to him?

Slowly he bends down, piercing me with an amused expression. "And here I was, completely impressed with myself that I had a beautiful girl naked—and wet—within five minutes of meeting her," he seduces.

"That a record for you?" I quip.

I offer a shy grin, unable to stop myself.

"It would seem so."

"Maybe you're just having an off year," I surmise.

Tristan stares at me with an obvious sadness that stretches over us. "You have no idea just how off."

My eyes trace his lips. I start to speak, but he abruptly cuts me off when his hands lift to my face, cupping my cheeks. I stop breathing and my eyes widen at the unexpected motion.

At his touch, a warmth runs through my veins, igniting something foreign within me. His thumb lightly brushes a drop of rain off my bottom lip, and I watch with a rapidly beating heart as he brings the thumb to his mouth and sucks the bead of water off, watching me the entire time.

"It's been . . . interesting meeting you, Serena."

My name sounds like a test on his lips.

He releases my face and takes a step back, roughly sliding his hands into the front pockets of his soaked jeans.

I swallow, regarding him for a moment longer.

"You too, Tristan."

"See you around, raindrop."

TRISTAN

I SLOWLY BACK AWAY, WEARING A stupid grin, while holding her wide-eyed stare. The energy dancing between us is almost unbearable, and I have to force myself to look away from eyes that are bluer than any ocean I've ever seen.

Normally, unmated female gargoyles have gray eyes, highlighted with small flecks of color that match the clan they're born into. Of course the royal heir would defy the rules and have deep sapphire irises.

I look away from her and an unwelcome heaviness descends. Trying to appear unfazed, I turn my back and full-on walk away, before I do something stupid like storm back, pull her into my arms, and make promises I can't keep.

Then it hits me—I've left her unguarded. *Shit!*

Regardless of my assignment, I'm aware that Serena St. Michael can defend herself. Yet, the idea of leaving her out here, unprotected, causes my chest to tighten.

Why is that?

I press forward, reminding myself that her primary guard is close by. My nostrils flare at the thought.

Christ, she was dancing naked in the rain, with another male protector watching her. It's obvious she has no inhibitions, and that's both infuriating and sexy.

So. Fucking. Sexy.

A vision of her unclothed body hits me. The reminder causes me to growl like an animal. The photos in her file didn't do her justice.

Goddamn, she's beautiful.

I approach my Harley Davidson, digging my fingers into my front pocket to pull out the key. I'm drenched. Groaning, I straddle my Street 500 and bring her to life. The only thing sexier than my blacked-out, custom bike is the protector with the piercing blue eyes I just left.

In the split second that I laid my eyes on her, everything inside of me decided I wanted to be the reason she breathed. When a slight grin turned her mouth up at the corners, it was all I could do not to lean over and claim her lips.

Taste her.

Mark her.

Make her mine.

Something about the way she studied me, quietly considering me—in that instant, it became my mission to obliterate any space between us. Without thinking, I placed myself as close to her as I could.

A bad idea, because within seconds, my hands lifted of their own accord, cupping her cheeks. I became fascinated with the little bead of water that sat on her bottom lip, beckoning me to suck it off. I couldn't, though. Instead, I allowed my thumb to do what my mouth wanted to.

At the recollection, my heart thuds against my chest, and for a brief moment, I regret touching her altogether. All it took is that one time, damning me to hell. The moment I held her delicate face between my hands, my heart vowed to follow her to the end of all time.

Protect her.

Be her champion.

It didn't go unnoticed by me that at my touch, goosebumps immediately formed across her bare body, and her skin took on a slight pink hue.

Maybe I'm not alone in the inexplicable pull department.

I lick my lips and refuse to allow my mind to go there. To the place where I steal her away and permanently etch myself on her. The simple fact is that no matter what I want, at the end of this appointment, I'm the one who has to break her. Educate her in the ways of her reality.

Angrily, I take off out of the parking lot without a look back. It doesn't matter how hypnotic Serena St. Michael is. She's hands-off. An assignment. Nothing more.

I'm not allowed to want her because it's not about me.

It is about blood, oaths, and protection.

Loyalties and obligations that we're both tethered to.

If our pasts collide, our bloodlines would divide us. Acting on an attraction would trigger a shitstorm of darkness to fall over both our futures. I'll protect both of us from that fate, with my last breath if I have to.

I bristle as the scars and wounds etched deep in my psyche choose this moment to fester. I refuse to respond, instead tightening my grip on the hand clutch and pushing all thoughts of Serena St. Michael out of my mind.

TWO
BLACK AND WHITE

TRISTAN

THE PUDDLE OF WATER THAT I'M leaving on the rug is growing by the second. The rain finally let up halfway through the drive here, but the damage from this afternoon's encounter has already been done. Literally and figuratively.

I look down at my ruined jeans and shirt before exhaling roughly. The current state of my appearance is probably not the best first impression. Not that I'm trying to make one.

Agitated, I clench and unclench my fists, gaining the attention of the gray-haired woman typing on her computer. She looks up and offers a warm smile.

It does nothing to soothe me, but I wink in response, causing a blush to form under the lines etched in her aging face. The phone on her desk rings, ending our exchange.

"Mr. Gallagher?"

"Yes?"

Her tone is kind. "He's waiting."

"Thank you," I reply.

She stands, adjusts her dark skirt suit, and opens both heavy oak doors, allowing me to make a grand entrance into the traditional hunter-green, wood-paneled office.

The doors close silently behind me and I wait, rooted in my spot, observing the middle-aged gentleman staring out the window. Bored, I crane my stiff neck from side to side.

After a few moments of being ignored, I clear my throat, announcing my presence. At the sound, he turns to face me.

The skin at the sides of the protector's eyes doesn't crinkle. His smile is tight, almost as tight as the ridiculous plaid bow tie he's wearing with his brown tweed suit.

My gaze shifts, and I focus on the light filtering through the windows, casting squares across the rows of leather-bound books that line the shelves of several bookcases running the length of one of his office walls.

In four strides the salt-and-pepper-haired gargoyle approaches and motions for me to sit in one of the two chairs placed in front of the untidy, large desk between us.

Uncomfortable, I take a seat as he removes his glasses, placing them on a pile of manuscripts. I notice several of them strewn all over the piece of antique furniture.

The silence stretches between us while we consider one another, before he breaks it. "Mr. Gallagher."

"I prefer Tristan, Chancellor Davidson."

He dips his chin. "Your father and I are old friends, Tristan. I believe that affords you the right to bypass formalities. Please, call me Henry. In private, of course."

At the mention of my father, I shift. The elder gargoyle studies my uneasy movements before offering a sympathetic glance. In turn, I fixate my stare on one of the large windows and attempt to rein in my displeasure at the abrupt reminder of my paternal bloodline.

The doors to Chancellor Davidson's office open, and the woman from earlier steps in, carrying an elegant silver tray. She places it amid the chaos of papers and books dispersed on his desk. We both watch in silence as she pours the hot amber liquid into two dainty teacups.

"Thank you, Annabelle," Henry says, before she leaves. "May I offer you some tea, Tristan?"

I stare at the small cups with amusement. "No, thank you." Amber liquid in the form of brandy is more my *cup of tea*, but the Indiana Jones look-alike sitting across from me doesn't need to know that.

"I'd like to thank you for coming." His tone is polite.

"I didn't really have a choice. It was either this or stone petrifaction," I remind him of my sentencing.

Henry clears his throat. "Yes, well. Regardless of the circumstances surrounding your presence, I appreciate that you are here," he counters, ignoring any discussion of the offenses I've been accused of.

Within the gargoyle world, living out the rest of your existence as a marble statue is the worst punishment a protector can receive.

Stone petrifaction is more or less an eternity, watching and hearing everything around you, unable to live or to participate. I shiver at the thought, grateful to have dodged that particular punishment.

"Have you made contact?" Henry questions.

I motion to my damp appearance and his lips turn up into a grin, a clear sign of his fondness for the princess.

"Serena is a spirited young protector. It's the reason Rulf is having such . . . difficulty guarding her," he says.

Henry takes another small sip of tea, hiding his amusement behind the flowered cup. Small relaxed lines have now formed around his eyes. It appears that Serena's free spirit entertains him.

I shrug. "Maybe he's simply a terrible handler."

The leather of the executive chair groans under the weight of Chancellor Davidson's shifting body. "I'm quite certain there isn't a gargoyle in existence that could . . . *handle* Miss St. Michael. But yes, Rulf is finding Serena challenging now that she's older and more . . . defiant. This is the reason her clan has sought additional protection for her while she finishes her last year here at the Academy—given what her future holds for her."

"Makes sense."

"You've been briefed by the Spiritual Assembly?"

I nod. "I'm aware of the details in her dossier."

"Good." He casually places the teacup and saucer back on his desk. "The London clan is adamant that she is not to know who you are or why you are here. Are we clear?"

My jaw clenches. Living in the shadows is as easy for me as breathing.

"Crystal. No offense, Henry, but this seems like a black-and-white assignment. Guard the royal heir so she can fulfill her destiny, and all my previous transgressions will be overlooked. Ten months and I'm free of all charges."

My father made sure of it.

A humorless laugh emerges from him. "I don't envy your position. Miss St. Michael will be anything but a 'black-and-white' charge. I would think your brief encounter with her this afternoon would have alerted you to that fact." He arches his eyebrow in challenge.

I take a steady breath.

He's right. This isn't going to be easy.

A moment later, Henry pushes an envelope toward me. "Your living arrangements while at the Academy, Tristan. As well as your schedule and payment."

I remain silent as I open the package and go through its contents. My brows rise before I meet the gargoyle's twinkling stare. "Isn't this frowned upon?"

"Where the royal heir is concerned, nothing under the category of protection is frowned upon. If there are issues, come directly to me. And only me, Tristan," he adds firmly.

"This should be interesting," I mumble, forcing the papers back into the envelope before running my fingers through my drying hair.

The chancellor holds out his hand in a cordial manner.

I extend mine, allowing him to take it as I stand.

"I'll see you at the assembly. Until then, best of luck to you, son," he offers, with an amused expression.

"Luck is something I won't need, Henry."

His features turn compassionate. "I disagree."

He fails to remember I carry my mother's pedigree and lineage. To us, luck is just a four-letter word.

I turn and head toward the closed doors. Just as I'm about to pull one open, his softened voice reaches me. "You're different . . . than Gage portrayed."

The sound of my father's name causes blood to roar in my ears. "Probably because he doesn't know me well enough to describe me accurately," I bite out angrily.

He frowns. "You're a lot like him, you know."

Chancellor Davidson and my father met years ago at the Ecole d'Architecture in Paris. Gage Gallagher was on an assignment and Henry was his architecture professor, while simultaneously working to obtain his doctorate.

They became instant acquaintances, and recently their paths crossed again during another mission both gargoyles were assigned to. At least that's the account outlined in the paper file I'd read before taking on this assignment. I'd only found out recently that Gage is my biological father.

I shrug, unaffected. "I wouldn't know."

Henry's comment and my response linger heavily between us. I've been Gage's *official* son for all of two months and I'm already fucking sick of it.

I yank open one of the doors with more force than I intended. It squeaks loudly with the intensity of my pull, echoing throughout the small space.

"Please reach out if you need anything," he adds.

"I won't."

"Be in touch?" He pauses. "Or need anything?"

"Either," I throw over my shoulder.

I've never needed anyone and I'm not about to start.

Henry falls silent, and I do what I do best, walk away.

The moment I leave the building a shudder runs through me. Why do I feel like I just walked through Hell's gates and my life as I know it is about to cease to exist?

Taking in a deep breath, I make my way to the parking lot and attempt to pull my shit together by reminding myself of my mother's blood. We're not afraid of anything.

As I straddle my bike, waves of auburn hair, floating in the wind, catch my eye. Seeing her again makes the tight knots in my stomach unclench.

I watch Serena rush across the campus quad.

That's when it hits me.

I *am* terrified of something.

I'm scared of her.

SERENA

I'M LATE, PER USUAL. I REPRIMAND myself at my own tardiness and make my way across the sprawling open campus, toward the old castle that has been transformed into the main academic building on campus.

The Academy is located in County Kerry, Ireland. It's divided into two quadrants: the lower and upper schools. Each is built around a breathtaking jade quad, intricately woven with ancient stone paths, vibrant vegetation, and centuries-old trees.

Situated on the west side of campus, the upper school houses the academic buildings and training centers. It's protected by tall cliffs and miles of blue ocean. Located to the east is the lower school, which contains the student dorms and instructor housing, surrounded by lush forest.

The rain has let up, and thin beams of sunlight are breaking through the clouds, giving the sky a divine appearance. I inhale a deep brine-filled breath. The salty scent is floating on the light breeze coming off the ocean.

"You're late," Rulf states from the bottom step.

My attention remains skyward as I try to ignore Rulf's disapproving glare. "You know," I muse, "I've been training here at the Academy for two years and have yet to see an amazing, mind-blowing rainbow. You would think a country known for its rain, and its leprechaun folklore, could manage to produce at least one colorful arch." I sigh and motion to the lackluster rainbow forming. "These multicolored rainbow wannabes are dull and uninspiring."

Silence.

When I meet my guard's gaze, he rolls his eyes at my ramblings. He's used to them.

I shrug in retort, while his focus falls to the shirt my dad sent me in his weekly care package.

"My Sperm Donor Rocks," Rulf reads out loud.

The minute I saw the play on words, I fell in love with it and threw it on. My dad and I are gargoyles; we need stones, *or rocks*, to enhance our supernatural abilities.

"Dad sent it," I announce proudly.

"It has Callan's sense of humor written all over it." At the mention of my father, Rulf's face softens before my guard sighs heavily. "Serena, I'm here to protect you. I can't do that if you continually attempt to evade me."

I meet his annoyed expression. "It's not my fault. You should delve into your psyche to find out why you assume I'm being truthful when I claim demons are on campus. If you ask me, Rulf, I think you have a hero complex."

He studies my face, unimpressed. "You've been trying to ditch me since you were three. It was tolerable then, because you were cute. You are no longer cute, therefore it is no longer tolerable."

I wince.

He's right.

Since my birth, Rulf and I have had an understanding. I don't drool, bite, puke, or pee on him, and he lets me do whatever I want, so long as I don't get into trouble.

Or killed.

Lately, I haven't been living up to my end of our deal.

The trouble part, not the being killed part.

"Sorry," I offer sincerely.

He nods once and motions toward the doors. "Go in."

"You aren't coming?"

"I'm your royal guard, Serena, not your babysitter."

"I know. I just assumed—"

"You'll be in an auditorium full of protectors. I think you'll be safe without me for an hour or so. So long as you promise to stay in that room." He gives me a pointed glare.

I smile, grateful that he's giving me the chance to feel normal. Rising on my tiptoes, I plant a kiss on his cheek.

"Thank you."

"Don't make me regret it," he warns halfheartedly.

"I never do," I singsong, and step around him.

He grunts. "You *always* do."

Laughing, I sprint up the last few steps of the stone staircase and push my way through the stained glass doors to enter Domus Gurgulio.

A little over twenty years ago, this building housed the Royal Gargoyle Council of Protectors. That was before my family disassembled the corrupt ruling body. My father and uncles repurposed the castle and created the St. Michael family legacy—the Academy.

I make my way down the hallway, ignoring the intricate stonework on the walls and floors as well as the high, vaulted ceilings. I've seen them so many times over the years, they no longer impress me. The rich, colorful rugs decorating the marble floors quiet my steps as I pass by the numerous alcoves on my left, filled with the stone statues of my ancestors.

My interest shifts to the windows on the other side of the hall. The sun is now filling the sky. Its warm rays are bouncing off the droplets of water lingering from the earlier rainstorm. The effect causes the campus to glisten. It's truly beautiful.

Pulling me out of my moment of appreciation, my phone buzzes. I glance at the text from my roommate and best friend, Magali, scolding me for my tardiness.

I hit *Ignore* and continue through the last hallway.

Within seconds, I'm at the auditorium's entrance, flanked by two gargoyle statues, each balancing a fire-filled urn on its head.

I pause and take a deep, calming breath before opening the heavy carved doors and slipping into the back of the darkened theater.

Once I cross the threshold, I still and allow my eyes to adjust. As I move away from my position, the doors slam behind me, causing several eyes to flick to me, glaring in annoyance at the interruption.

I offer a fake apologetic smile.

My roommate waves her lit-up cell at me from a few rows away, and I quickly move toward her, then dramatically slide into the seat she's saved for me.

"Thanks for joining me." She hisses at me, signing each word with her hands.

"I got caught in the rainstorm," I attempt to whisper.

Mags fixes her annoyed gaze on my shirt.

"Dad sent it," I explain.

She quietly snorts. "Obviously."

"Anyway, that's why I'm late."

"Your shirt?" she asks, confused.

"No. The rain. I had to go back to the suite to shower."

Magali Grayson is petite but very powerful when angered or deceived. She narrows her gray and coffee-flecked stare at me. I can tell she suspects that I'm not being fully truthful about the real reason for my tardiness.

It doesn't help that one of her supernatural abilities is sensing deceit. That, and Mags also knows me better than anyone, and right now, she knows that I'm hiding something. I shift in my seat under her scrutiny.

"I may be unvoiced, but I'm not stupid." Her hands fly wildly as she pins me with a knowing look.

"I never said you were stupid. You are, however, annoyingly persistent," I mumble under my breath.

She snaps her fingers at me, her version of growling.

"There is nothing wrong with my hearing."

Magali was born nonverbal, an uncommon condition for our kind. Gargoyles have finely tuned hearing and heightened sight abilities, which help us demon hunt. In addition to our keen senses, we're also able to heal ourselves, and therefore we don't suffer from diseases or physical ailments, like humans do. Even so, more extensive injuries do require us to stone state sleep in a protected chamber in order for our bodies to fully rejuvenate.

Being nonverbal is extremely rare for a protector, but it doesn't hinder her abilities. If anything, it allows her hearing and sight to be stronger, more acute. Even though she can hear others when they speak, Magali has to communicate through sign language. And angry facial expressions. Similar to the one filled with annoyance she's giving me now.

I sink deeper into the padded auditorium chair and avert my eyes from hers. At this, she lets out an aggravated breath, causing her dark bangs to fly away from her mocha-colored forehead.

My best friend is that girl you love but secretly envy. She's exotically stunning, smart, popular, a perfectionist, and every year is at the top of our training class. She also has a penchant for neatness and is compulsively on time.

Though we're opposites, we've been best friends forever. When she was five, her family moved from South Africa to the States. One day, she strolled into my kindergarten class as if she didn't have a care in the world, plopping down next to me.

As soon as she pulled out her watermelon-scented lip balm, she became my instant favorite among all the girls. We've been tethered to one another since.

My attention returns back to her and I smile, attempting to win her over.

She playfully rolls her eyes in return.

"Your mom texted me earlier."

I grimace. "Why?"

"She needed to talk to you and said you weren't answering your phone. In typical helicopter-mom fashion, Abby threatened to send your aunt to 'hunt you down.'"

Mag's smile turns wicked and I narrow my eyes.

"Which aunt? Eve?" I ask.

"McKenna."

I groan. "You've got to me kidding me!"

"Just text her and let her know you're still breathing."

I pull out my cell and silence it before shooting a quick text off to my mom letting her know that I am in fact, alive, and there is no need to send in the cavalry.

My aunt Kenna can be—well—tough. On a good day.

"Where is everyone?" I ask, slipping my phone back into my pocket and looking for the rest of our group.

"Ethan had some Knox clan business to attend to. Ryker and Ireland are probably *attending* to one another." She attempts to hide her bitterness.

Magali has had a longstanding crush on our friend Ryker Daniels since starting at the Academy. Unfortunately for Mags, Ryker set his sights on Ireland Presley two years ago, during our first day of training. Her pride is still bruised over Ryker's choice in mates.

I offer her an understanding smile.

The low rumble in the auditorium turns silent as the Academy's chancellor, Dr. Henry Davidson, makes his way with a commanding presence to the podium positioned at the center of the stage. We both watch with boredom as a handful of tenured administrators follow the elder gargoyle and dutifully take their seats, while the head of the Academy prepares to address this year's attending protector classes.

I skim the dim room, floating over the profiles of other students. There's no sign of Tristan. My shoulders sag in disappointment. Since he's new, I figured that he would be at the welcome assembly. Wishful thinking, I suppose.

Magali snaps her fingers in my face again and I swing a pointed glare her way so she can sign. "Who are you looking for?"

I falter and cringe. "N-No one."

Her perfectly manicured eyebrow arches.

It really sucks when your best friend is a lie detector. I shrug in response and face forward, pretending to be enthralled with the soon-to-be-given welcome speech.

For some odd reason, I feel protective over Tristan. I don't want to share him with her just yet.

Dr. Davidson clears his throat and leans toward the microphone. "Good afternoon, protectors. Congratulations on earning a coveted spot here at the Academy. Your attendance makes you part of the elite. I'm sure you don't need to be reminded that this institution was founded on three basic principles: duty, honor, and protection. Today, we continue to instill these ideals in each protector class that trains and passes through our doors."

He pauses, making eye contact with the first row. "We graduate the best of the best. Let there be no misconceptions—we are not here to coddle you. We are not here to cater to you. We *are* here to make you better protectors."

"For those who are new, your three years with us will be rigorous. For those who are returning, this year will be your hardest yet. There are no free passes. Here you work and train hard. You show loyalty. You abide by your oaths, and in turn, you graduate with prestigious assignments given by the royal family."

"You get one chance. And only one. Welcome to the Royal Protector Academy."

THREE
DON'T TOUCH MY COOKIES

SERENA

THE ORIENTATION DRAGGED ON FOR HOURS. The entire time, my mind had been elsewhere, worlds away from reality. A glare from the sun hits my eyes, causing me to squint as Magali and I make our way across campus toward the dorms.

An unfamiliar tingling sensation runs through my veins as we approach our suite's door. I attempt to calm myself and control the anxiety that seems to be curdling in my blood, but the feeling just intensifies the closer we get.

On edge, I watch with annoyance as Mags fumbles for her key card before swiping it, and the lock to our place clicks open. Guarded, I follow her in, slamming into her back when she abruptly stops walking.

A surprised yelp escapes me from the sudden collision, and I push away before I can process what has her motionless.

Stunned, I slowly blink at the sight of our friend Ethan sitting on the couch. That's a normal occurrence; it's *whom* he's hanging out with that has me paralyzed.

What the hell is he doing here? In my suite!

I stare at Tristan, watching him laugh casually at something Ethan said. His booted feet rest on my coffee table as he chomps away on my cookies.

My lips part in disbelief.

Perhaps I've entered an altered state of consciousness. One where deliciously hot guys, whom I've been daydreaming about all day, simply appear in my suite, without invitation. Plausible explanation, right?

As if hearing my thoughts, Tristan turns, angles his head, and locks gazes with me. Nervously, my hand wraps around my protector jewelry and my fingertips brush across the stones. I just need to touch something, anything, to help soothe and ground my emotions, which seem to go haywire when I'm in his presence.

Tristan's darkened gaze drops to my bracelet. He watches me fidget with it for a second before the side of his mouth quirks into an almost sad, understanding smile.

I stand there staring at him for a brief moment before bowing my head and, with a sigh, forcing myself to stop. I hate how out of control he makes me feel inside. Especially since I don't even know him.

At my reaction, Tristan bestows another breathtaking smile and turns his attention back to Ethan. The nagging feeling of being dismissed by him hits me. And for some irrational, unknown reason, I don't like it.

I snap my head up in the direction of the good-looking protector and examine him, as he continues to chew on the baked goods my dad sent me in my monthly care package.

Wait—is he eating my cookies? Oh. Hell. No.

Care package baked goods are coveted, and I do *not* share with strangers, especially hot and unnerving ones. Stepping around a still-dazed and unmoving Magali, I storm toward the couch at the two laughing gargoyles.

"Hey Serena," Ethan smiles brightly.

Once I'm standing in front of them, Tristan slowly lifts his gaze, locking it back onto mine. As if goading me, he takes a rather large bite of the chocolate-chunked treat.

For some absurd reason the sight of him eating the cookie my dad made for me—*my* cookie, sets me off.

"What are you doing?" I demand, yanking the half eaten pastry away from his kissable lips. *Gah.* I really need my hormones to stop side-tracking me when I'm around him.

Ethan's eyes widen at my foolish outburst, and Magali remains rooted in her spot. Her expression is now marred by curiosity as she watches the whole scene unfold.

"Do you two know each other?" Ethan asks.

"Yes," I reply, at the same time Tristan says, "No."

"That was clear," Ethan replies under his breath.

"I was eating that!" Tristan points to my hand.

I lift the crumbling dessert. "My dad sent me these."

"Annnd?" He has the audacity to look stupefied.

"And my dad's cookies are off-limits."

Tristan studies me as if I've gone batshit crazy, which, considering my overreaction and outburst—I have. After a brief moment, he slowly stretches, rising to his full height from the couch, then bending his neck from side to side before taking a step toward me.

I notice his warrior frame move with careless grace as he prowls toward me. I scramble back, putting space between us, which just seems to encourage him to continue the advance.

He smiles at me like a predator.

I stare.

God, he smells good. His scent is a combination of spice and citrus. Maybe cigarettes too. I hold in a moan as he moves closer.

"Am I to understand that you don't want me eating Callan's—cookies?" he asks, amused.

At the sound of my dad's name falling from his lips, a coldness settles over me. How does he know my father?

"You know who I am?" I seethe.

At the accusation, Tristan's brows furrow together.

"I told him, Ser," Ethan interjects. "Jeez, calm down."

I give Ethan a pointed glare. He knows I don't like strangers knowing I'm royal blood and the London clan heir. I return my annoyed focus back to Tristan, who is just observing me with an unreadable expression.

I inhale.

By the grace, why does he make me emotionally unstable when he's around?

"Don't touch my cookies, Tristan." Yeah, that just came out of my mouth. In threat form. *Kill. Me. Now.*

He narrows his eyes at the bite in my words and sucks in his lower lip, holding back a laugh. After a moment, he steps closer.

"What are you doing?" I whisper. My voice is so unsteady and rickety that I barely recognize it.

"Approaching you," his tone is low, lulling.

My cockiness has dried up. "I—what?"

"I'm approaching you, slowly," he adds.

"Slowly?" I repeat, barely audible. "Why?"

He dips his head. "If I charge at you, you'll run."

I lift my chin. "You think I'd bolt?"

"I scare you. And when you're scared, you run."

I swallow. "You have me all figured out, do you?"

A triumphant smile falls across his mouth. "I do."

"You don't," I exhale. "And I'm not afraid of you."

Once there's no space left between us, his fingers gently wrap around my wrist. The cool metal of his rings sets off a warm sensation in me.

It's calming.

Safe.

Frightening.

Tristan lifts my hand holding the destroyed cookie to his mouth. He licks his lips and my breath hitches.

It's obvious he knows the effect he has on the opposite sex. Each of his moves is calculated and meant to seduce. Right before he's about to take another bite, his eyes darken and a smugness appears across his face.

"Be afraid. Because it's not your dad's cookies I'm after."

Our gazes tangle, and it's then I realize I'm in way over my head when it comes to him.

And I like it. Too much.

I clear my throat. "What are you doing here?"

His frame straightens, and he releases my wrist, taking a step back. Tristan has about a foot and a half on me in height. Enough to intimidate whomever he wants to.

And right now, he wants to intimidate me.

"I live here," he states casually.

Looking around the suite, I meet Magali's wide-eyed, puzzled expression. She shakes her head back and forth, letting me know she has no clue what he's talking about.

Returning my attention back to Tristan, I point my index finger toward the hardwood floors. "Here. As in—my suite?" The pitch in my voice has kicked up a notch.

Magali nudges me, stepping next to me. "Our suite," my roommate signs, finally regaining her wits. "I'm Magali. Your other roommate."

Tristan watches her hands glide and grins brightly.

"It's nice to meet you, Magali," he replies, both verbally and using sign language.

She blushes and smiles. Not many protectors know how to sign, and I can tell that she's impressed by him. *Traitor.*

"I can hear. Feel free to speak to me without signing."

Tristan nods. "Will do, roomie."

Mags turns to me, smiling. "The new guy's hot."

I glare at her before rubbing my forehead.

"So, you. Are going to live here. With us?"

"Yes. I was assigned this suite as my housing."

I just blink. I'm too shocked to respond.

His tone is casual. "I put my stuff in the empty room," he points to the hallway. "Ethan said that was okay?"

I hear the words coming out of his mouth, but they make no sense. Nothing about this does. There is no coed housing at the Academy. It's why Ireland and Ryker moved off campus. By the grace, even Rulf is required to stay in separate living quarters, across the hall.

"Yeah that's totally fine," Mags steps in. "Ireland was our other roommate, but she moved in with her boyfriend, Ryker, a few weeks ago," she explains, her expression becoming crestfallen.

The three of them stare at me as if waiting for me to say something.

I remain motionless through the awkwardness. I know they expect a response, but I'm too confused and shocked to actually string words together in sentence form.

"That explains the pink walls," Tristan responds without a hint of sarcasm. Instead his tone is almost sympathetic toward Magali and what she's feeling.

A frown distorts her pretty features.

I swivel my attention back to Tristan and unstick my tongue from the roof of my mouth. "So, you're going to live here?" I wave around the space. "With us? Every day?"

Tristan presses his lips together, clearly annoyed at being asked the same thing twice. "Will that be an issue?"

"Not at all," Magali quickly replies, causing Tristan to flash her another smile that could light up the world.

"Wait a minute," I implore. "We don't live with boys."

I'm stretching. I can't live with him when he smells all yummy and looks like he just walked out of Heaven. See? I'm already using cheesy lines.

"It's a good thing I'm all man then," he counters.

Unable to tear my gaze away from him, I swallow.

"I . . . don't . . . do men either." I frown at myself.

The sides of Tristan's lips lift smugly.

"That's your business, raindrop."

Wait, that came out wrong.

"Guess you do now." Ethan's eyes gleam in delight at my obvious verbal misstep. "Live with boys, that is, Serena."

Tristan's smile broadens he tries to hold back a laugh.

Magali appears in my sight line, her eyes narrowing. "Since when have you ever followed rules, Ser?"

Damn, she's right. Even I can't argue that point.

A silence falls over the group as they all watch me.

"Fine." I cross my arms. "You can stay."

Tristan snorts. "I wasn't asking for your permission."

"Well, you have it anyway."

A shadow passes over his face. "Good to know."

My heartbeat stumbles. Why do I get the feeling I've given my blessing for more than just living arrangements?

"Glad that's settled," Ethan mumbles. "Tristan, just a heads-up— Mags is mine, so just keep your hands to yourself."

She playfully pushes at Ethan's shoulder. "Stop being stupid, we all know that you're not my type," Mags teases, and sinks into the couch, with Ethan following her.

Ethan frowns. "It's because I'm Taiwanese, isn't it?"

Mags and I share a glance.

This is an ongoing joke between the three of us.

"Actually, it's because you have a boyfriend," I retort.

"I'm gay?" Ethan feigns surprise.

Ethan loves to do this. He enjoys the shock factor; although, at times, I get the sense that it's more of a test. If you don't flinch at his preference in mates, then you are in.

I study Tristan's response. He looks anything but surprised at Ethan's declaration, which is strange.

Ethan has an easy way about him, but unless you know him personally, you wouldn't know that he's gay. He's very private, therefore it's not common knowledge.

I watch my tall protector friend smirk at Tristan's lack of reaction. Ethan's shoulders visibly relax on his long, muscular body as he rubs his fingers together.

Mags claps, clearly excited that Tristan passed the test.

"Serena, we should celebrate getting a new roomie with pizza and beer," she suggests.

"I like you," Tristan says simply.

She beams under the praise, and a ridiculous pang of jealousy roils through me. I squeeze my eyes closed and attempt to shut Tristan out, trying to regain my wits.

A dark chuckle floats out of him, into me. When I open my eyes, Tristan has moved closer and is leaning toward my ear. His warm breath tickles the outer rim.

"Don't worry, raindrop. I like you too."

"I wasn't," I squeak out. "And stop calling me raindrop."

He contemplates me for a moment. "No."

I straighten my shoulders. "No?"

"If we're going to live together, you should know that I don't like being told what to do. It's a great nickname and I'll be using it. Often. And without warning."

I level him with a look. "Fine. Bring it, protector."

"Oh, I will. Trust me," he whispers, eliciting a shiver down my spine with his proximity.

Damn him.

I inhale.

There is nothing I love more than a challenge.

I've got this.

I can live with Tristan and all his hotness.

Two semesters.

Ten months.

That's it.

I can totally do this.

TRISTAN

I CAN'T DO THIS. I CAN'T live with her. I look back toward the open patio door, into the unlit living area, before taking another long hit off my cigarette.

My eyes close as the nicotine invades my brain. It's been days since I last had one, and the headache I'm enduring makes it seem like the world is constantly yelling at me.

I growl into the inky night before opening my eyes and taking in the darkness. My powers reach out, trying to connect with nature, as I listen for the whistle of the wind across the trees, or the gurgling sound of water a crystal spring makes. Anything to help calm me.

Nothing. Tonight, there is nothing.

My body is still on edge from enduring Serena's intoxicating presence this afternoon. Like a crazy stalker, I watched every motion her perfect mouth made as she chewed on her pizza. I flinched every time she smiled at Ethan instead of me. I studied the way she and Magali finished one another's sentences, wishing for that connection with her.

Every five minutes, I fought the urge to slam her against the wall, push my hands in her hair and force my tongue into her mou—

The soft whistle of the wind pulls my attention to the outline forming out of thin air, of my best friend Zander. At the sight of him, my shoulders relax for the first time today.

As soon as he's in solid form, he scans me from head to toe and narrows his eyes at the cigarette hanging off my lip.

"The Queen would be displeased if she knew you were smoking again," he points out.

I take one last pull before crushing it under my boot.

Zander is the second in command of my mother's royal guard, under his father, Rionach. His dad and my mom married when Zander and I were five, solidifying our best friend status and truly making us brothers. Princes.

"So don't tell her," I counter.

"Ass." He smacks me in the back of the head.

I sigh in relief at his presence.

"You okay, man?" he asks, eyeing me once again.

"'Course. I've just missed your ugly face."

He shakes his head, grinning. Zander's bloodline and playboy personality make him anything but ugly. These days, his bed is like a revolving door.

"What are you doing here, Zan?"

"I'm here to make sure you're . . . adjusting."

Ah. "Tell my mother I'm *adjusting* just fine."

He snorts, tipping his chin to the remains of my crushed cigarette. "I can see that."

I glare at him, annoyed by his judgment.

"It's been a long day," I grumble.

He looks around, taking in the campus, which is now blanketed in total darkness. His face scrunches as he examines our surroundings. "The earth realm is a shithole."

"Not every realm looks the way ours does," I remind him.

"Human souls have no melody. It's why the ocean is so angry all the time. Constantly churning. The energy here is depraved. Even you must feel it?" he prods.

I look around, using my soul sight, a gift from my mother's bloodline. He is wrong. The auras that surround human souls are brilliant and vibrant. Most supernatural beings are envious of the beauty that a free-willed mundane soul possesses.

Myself included.

"There is beauty within the darkness," I mumble.

"Your charge is hot." My friend abruptly changes the subject. "Although your attraction to her seems a bit cliché."

I throw him a pointed look. "How do you figure?"

"A free-spirited female has drawn your attention . . ."

"Fuck off." I roll my eyes at the implication.

My anger causes Zander to grin. He loves goading me.

"I've known you your entire life, Tristan. I can see she's caught your eye. If you wanted a spirited, beautiful girl, there are plenty at home to choose from."

"Serena is simply a charge. One I'm required to protect while Gage clears my name with the royal family," I remind.

Zander frowns at my father's name.

"You sure you're okay, man? You're prissier and more . . . angry than normal."

I give a firm nod.

Even though he's right.

I'm not okay. Not even fucking close.

The lock on the front door of the suite clicks, and I look at my watch. Three in the morning? *What the hell?* I hear huffing right before the door flies open, and Serena staggers in and falls onto the floor in a swearing heap.

Flinching, I resist the urge to run over to her and help her up. I'm not supposed to be her knight in shining armor. I'm only supposed to make sure she stays alive. And by the number of F-bombs she's throwing out, I'd say she's alive.

"What do you see in her?" Zander whispers in my ear.

I sigh. "A means to an end. One that I control."

Zander chuckles. "Control is an illusion, my friend."

"If I don't govern her, we all lose."

"And what if she's a beginning and not an end?" His normally bright eyes take on a dark hue and his raven hair fades to the night's inkiness. "What happens then, Tristan?"

I return my focus to Serena. She's attempting to pick herself up, while laughing at her own predicament. Her drunken state is about to snap that last bit of sanity I was holding onto this evening when it comes to her.

"Then we're all screwed," I snarl out, and continue to watch her fight with gravity for a few more seconds before deciding that I can't take it any longer. Rubbing my hands over my face, I exhale and walk toward her sprawled-out form, cursing under my breath.

"And so it begins," Zander mocks behind me.

I crouch down and brush a silky strand of hair away from her glassy eyes, careful not to touch her skin. If I do, I'm afraid I won't be able to stop. Her flowery spring scent wraps around my head, making it difficult to function.

At my closeness, she rears back in surprise.

"What are you doing?" she asks, quietly.

"Is this a trick question?"

"No."

"I'm helping you up."

"Why?"

"Because you're inebriated."

She gives me a smug look, which almost causes me to reach out, grab her face, and kiss her stupid.

Behind the self-assuredness there's a sadness. It's buried, but I can see it, because I see her. And as beautiful and forlorn as she is now, it's about to get so much worse for her. She has no idea what's at stake or what the future is about to drop into her lap. I do.

"Do I look drunk?" she retorts.

A silent pause beats between us.

"Yeah, raindrop, you do." I use my pacifying tone.

That earns me a half snort, half laugh. Serena leans toward me and hushes her voice, as if we're sharing a secret.

"Well, Tristan," she exhales dramatically. "I'm pretty shit-faced. The sorceresses were hosting a welcome back bonfire. Their brew is—" She hiccups and rubs her nose wildly with the back of her hand, as if it itches.

"Where is Rulf?"

"Rulfff?" she draws out and giggles.

I roll my eyes. "Your guard, Serena. Where is he?"

She shrugs. "Don't know. Don't care."

I'm going to rip his throat out. I've only been around them a day, and I can already see he's doing a shitty job.

Serena's eyes widen and she stops laughing. "Dude," she tries to tap my arm but misses, and her hand ends up flopping around in the air awkwardly. "Dude," she says again, garnering my attention. "I'm like that kid from that sixth sense movie."

"What?" I ask. She's not making sense.

"I see a satyr," she whispers creepily.

Zander appears behind me. "She's plastered."

"You think?" I throw over my shoulder.

"Wait," she hisses. "You see him too?"

"Serena, this is Zander. Zander, the drunk is Serena."

Zander's grin widens. "Nice to meet you, Princess."

Her faces scrunches, like she just sucked on a lemon. "Don't call me that," she mutters. "Don't ever call me that."

He holds up both his hands in surrender. "Apologies."

Serena's unfocused gaze shifts to me. "Why are you hanging out with male nymphs?" she blurts out, then smacks her forehead with her palm. "I can't believe I didn't realize this before. You're—you . . . pre-fer . . . Ethan?" She heaves a heavy sigh. "I knew you were too good-looking. Are you straight? I mean, into me. I mean, into females?"

Zander and I share a look before he chuckles. "She's a handful. You sure you got this, man? I have to get back."

"Yeah, I'm good. Thanks for checking in."

"Anytime." He pats me on the shoulder, before dipping his chin respectfully to Serena. "Good luck with that badass hangover you're gonna be sportin' tomorrow, champ."

She groans at the thought, and he dissolves into thin air.

"Seriously? Nymphs? They're, like, all . . . sex and nakedness. And touching. They like to have lots of sex."

I ignore her ramblings. Most likely she won't even remember Zander in the morning. "Let's get you up."

"Why?" She tilts her chin into the air.

Christ, she's adorably stubborn, even when tanked.

"You can't sleep here, so get up."

That earns me another withering glare.

All right, Serena St. Michael can't be bossed around. New approach. Licking my lips, I extend my hand to her and grit my teeth in anticipation of hers sliding into mine.

She doesn't budge. Instead, she studies my hand like it's a foreign object she's never seen before. Maybe she passed out with her eyes open. I give her a predatory look and lean toward her. *God*, I just want to devour her pouty mouth.

"I normally don't like to repeat myself, Serena. Last time. Get your ass up off the floor and I'll take you to bed."

A light blush crosses over her cheeks and it's then I realize what I just said. I tense at the realization.

"Bed? Really? I don't know," she stumbles.

I push my hand through my hair. "That's not what I meant. I have no desire to actually take you to bed," I lie.

Hurt at my statement, she stills.

"Just leave me alone, Tristan," she whispers.

Her heavy breaths caress my lips.

I lean in a sliver more, taunting her.

"Please," she begs, and blood roars in my ears.

What I wouldn't give to have her underneath me, saying my name and begging me over and over again. My outstretched hand clenches into a fist and I pull it back, while I check my secondary bloodline, which is full of lust.

This isn't a game.

She's not for me.

Frustrated, I stand and walk away from her.

FOUR
WHO ARE YOU

SERENA

M Y INSIDES ACHE AND THE POUNDING in my head won't fade. Damn witch infusions. My fingertips feel around for my blankets, but they're not there. I release a whimper and roll over, smacking my nose against the hard surface below me.

Ouch. "Where is my bed?" I ask in a hoarse voice.

I try swallowing, but my throat and mouth feel like I've eaten a hundred cotton balls. Turning onto my back, I squeeze my shut eyes as unwelcome images of last night flash through my mind.

After spending the afternoon with our new *roommate*, I remember needing space. And air. Lots of air. All day his scent wrapped around me. It invaded every breath I took.

My being around Tristan is like an addict being around drugs. By the end of the day, I was shaking so badly that I needed to either crawl into his lap and latch myself onto his mouth or I needed to escape.

I press my lips together. I still can't figure out my nonsensical reaction to someone I've just met.

In a lame attempt at evasion, I decided to meet up with some sorceress friends at a party. Given my state this morning, that was not one of my more mature decisions.

My stomach roils and I groan, remembering how many drinks I'd downed in an attempt to forget Tristan exists.

The last thing I recall before passing out is fighting with the lock before I fell onto the floor, where I'm currently laying—in last night's clothes.

Awesome.

Then the recollection of Tristan holding out his hand to me—offering to take me to bed—hits me, and my body cringes.

And did I see a satyr? What the hell? Nymphs never appear for protectors unless summoned. Did I demand one? I must have been really out of my mind.

My eyelids slowly flutter open, then instantly squeeze shut again at the morning's light. *Damn*, that was painful.

Hot mess doesn't even begin to properly describe my current state. I wince and grunt as the alarm on my iPhone blares next to my ear, startling me. A text from Mags comes in letting me know she set it. Followed by a second text demanding I get up before I'm late for my first day of classes.

I pout and roll onto my hands and knees, managing to push myself into a standing position. After the room stops spinning, I head into the shower to freshen up and attempt to make myself presentable.

Twenty minutes later, I'm tossing my hair into a loose bun and throwing my messenger bag onto the floor in the kitchen. Desperate for water, I head to the fridge, grab a bottle, and see a note from Magali saying she's left a bowl of cereal, a glass of juice, and two Advil on the counter.

My vision swings to the empty bowl and bare glass.

Scowling, I walk over to them and see a second handwritten message. This one is from Tristan, letting me know that since I was passed out on the floor, he took it upon himself to eat my cereal and drink all my juice.

"Lovely," I whisper to no one.

For a moment, I just stare at his handwriting, fascinated with every loop the pen has made on the paper.

After a few seconds, I snap out of it. "By the grace, Serena, you're bordering on stalker material now."

I swallow the Advil and chase it with water just as the front door swings open, hitting the wall with a loud thud.

"You had me spelled?" Rulf storms in.

Wide-eyed, I take in his completely disheveled appearance. His sable hair is sticking up in all different directions, and there are heavy dark bags under his slate eyes, which are narrowed at me.

He's pissed.

Really pissed.

"Morning, sunshine," I say, smirking.

Rulf's expression turns even more furious. "You had a witch hex me last night so you could run off and what, Serena? Party? UNPROTECTED!" he roars.

A feeling of guilt crawls up my throat; I instantly push it away. "Coffee?" I ask in a light tone.

"One of these days, princess," he purposely uses the nickname that turns my blood cold, "you are going to have to face reality and stop acting like a petulant child."

"Rulf, it's not as if I walked into a demon's den," I grumble. "Don't you think you're overreacting a tad?"

His eyes grow wilder. "I am here to GUARD you!"

I clench my jaw. "I never asked you to."

"You're my assignment. My responsibility, per a royal decree established by your aunt and uncle. Who happen to be the king and queen. Stop being reckless and pretending that your bloodline and oaths mean nothing."

I hold his angry gaze and my shoulders fall. I've never seen Rulf this enraged with me before. Normally he's annoyed, agitated, and sometimes huffy, but not like this.

"They don't!" I shout back.

"Not this again," he rubs his hands over his face.

"What if my fate has a different ending?" I ask.

"There are no alternative endings to your destiny when you are the royal heir. Your fate is inescapable, Serena." His expression and tone soften. "It would do you well to start accepting that." He turns and slams the door behind him.

I stare at the empty space he was standing in for a moment, before collecting myself and heading to my first class. Regardless of my lineage, he is wrong. I know, within the deepest part of me, that my destiny isn't entirely sealed.

The whole way to my lecture, I replay Rulf's words in my head. When I finally get to class, I yank open the theater door, causing it to echo in the silence of the marble hallway. At the disturbance, fifty pairs of eyes swing my way. I ignore their judgmental glares and step into the room, before meeting my friend Ireland's wide-eyed stare.

She flicks her strawberry blonde ponytail over her slender shoulder, and her gray-and-emerald-flecked gaze shifts from me to the front of the room.

Oddly, Ireland's normally pale, freckled complexion appears more ashen than usual. I take a hesitant step toward her and give her a *what's up* look.

Her brows draw together tightly in warning.

"Miss St. Michael." A familiar voice carries across the seminar room. "Nice of you to join us this morning."

At the sound, I freeze. My world tilts a bit and all the air in my lungs disappears. Astounded, I turn and meet the equally familiar face, currently wearing a scowl.

"Um . . . ," I manage. The heat in my cheeks flares.

Ireland coughs loudly, regaining my attention. I glance back to her and she flicks her eyes to the empty seat next to her, imploring me to sit my ass down.

I study the chair for a moment, before awkwardly shifting my attention back to Tristan, standing at the front of the room. He's wearing dark gray jeans, his motorcycle boots, and a black Henley.

Why his attire matters? I don't know. I'm so confused.

What's happening?

"Take a seat, Miss St. Michael," Tristan demands.

Baffled, I drag away my stupefied gawk and stumble toward Ireland, clumsily sliding into the seat next to her.

"I don't like tardiness. If you're late, don't bother coming to class at all. That is your first, and only, warning." Tristan's voice booms throughout the hushed lecture hall.

My gaze darts around, and I watch the other protectors in the room share secret nervous glances with one another.

"What's going on?" I whisper.

Ireland's boyfriend, Ryker, leans down from behind us.

"How excellent of you to piss off Professor Gallagher before we've even started the semester. Way to go, Ser."

Ireland turns and glares at him. "Shut up, Ry."

"Professor Gallagher?" I repeat, confused.

Ireland scoffs at me with a side look. "Didn't you read the syllabus and class description?"

I press my lips into a flat line. "Do I ever?"

"Well, had you, you would have noticed that Gage Gallagher's son, Tristan, is our guest instructor this year."

I sit upright. "Wait, Gage Gallagher has a son?"

She nods and slides her focus down to Tristan.

"Apparently, a sexy, dark, broody one," she purrs.

"I'm sitting right here," Ryker whisper-shouts.

Ireland rolls her eyes, without taking them off of Tristan. "I see you," she huffs.

Gage Gallagher is a longtime acquaintance of my uncle Asher. He owns several architecture firms across the world, including the one that helped build the Academy.

He's well known within the supernatural world for being a nonconformist and ladies' man. When his human mate, Camilla, was murdered, her death completely broke and gutted him. To my knowledge, Gage hasn't had another *serious* relationship.

This doesn't make sense.

I sit pinned to my seat. Tristan is my instructor? I thought he was a student.

"Since Miss St. Michael seems to be carrying on her own private lecture this morning, perhaps she'd like to join me at the podium?"

Tristan barks through my reverie.

"Um—"

"That is your second *um* of the morning, Serena. I do hope you'll be using the rest of your vocabulary this semester," he mocks.

At my expense, a light rumble runs through the class, and I make a mental note to kill him later, in his sleep.

"Wow, he really hates you," Ireland points out.

I tap my finger on the desk. "Are you just here to state the obvious?"

"No," she pouts. "I'm also the fun friend."

"None of this makes sense," I say, flatly.

"I hate repeating myself," Tristan throws a hard glare my way. My mouth falls open at his words, a reminder of last night. "That said, I'll make an exception today. And *only* today. I'm Professor Gallagher. You are in Protector History 302. If you aren't supposed to be here, get out," his tone is cutting. "Come to class, get your shit done, be on time, and we won't have any issues. Questions? No? Good. Let's begin," he speeds through his sermon.

Professional.

Taken aback by the abruptness of his words, I raise my hand. Or maybe it's my constant need to be rebellious.

Tristan's eyes meet mine in an almost curious manner. As if he can't believe I have the balls to ask a question.

"Serena, my questions were rhetorical."

Annoyance grips me at being dismissed by him.

Again.

That is something that my family does often, which has become sort of an anger-management-trigger for me. I arch a challenging brow and stand, crossing my arms.

"Pro-fes-sor," I draw out. "Gallagher is it? You seem young to be a guest lecturer. I was curious as to your age."

Tristan's expression remains blank. "My age won't be on any of the tests that you'll be required to pass this semester. Therefore, it's none of your business."

At his flippant tone, I fight the urge to drop to the floor into a fetal position. Instead, I lift my chin and take my seat, feigning dignity and meeting Ireland's shocked expression.

"Are you insane?" she hisses.

"Tristan is my new roommate," I choke out.

"What?" she whisper-screams. "You're living with him? That's so hot and totally unfair," she sulks. "I move out and all of a sudden the fun starts. This sucks."

"Stop it," I snip loudly, causing the room to swing their attention back to me. Again. "Sorry," I mutter to no one in particular.

"Serena, see me after class," Tristan snaps.

Yeah, that sounds about right.

I nod and take out my iPad, pressing the dragon dictation button so it records the words falling out of my lecturer-slash-roommate's mouth.

My eyes follow his every movement obsessively.

There's something tragic about him.

And lonesome about him.

And so familiar about him.

What in the hell is going on?

TRISTAN

IN A FOUL MOOD, I TWIST toward the window in my temporary administrative office. In order for my presence to appear realistic, I knew I'd have to take on a teaching and training role here at the Academy. What I did not expect was the magnetic pull toward my charge, who is also a student.

Or that I'd be living with her.

I'd woken this morning and walked out of my room to find Serena where I left her. Passed out. On the floor.

It took everything I had in me not to pick her up and put her into her bed. After witnessing Rulf cater to her tantrums on more than one occasion, I've decided to take a different approach with Serena's protection.

He sympathizes with her need for normalcy, and look where it's gotten him. If I want to keep her safe, I have to be the bad guy. This is probably my first mistake.

Thinking I can control Serena.

Images of this morning flood my mind.

Magali walks over to Serena, touches her forehead and places Serena's cell next to her, after setting the alarm.

"You don't cover her?" I ask, concerned that she's cold.

"She'll just kick the blankets off," she signs.

I observe the pretty gargoyle as she makes her way into the kitchen and pours cereal into a bowl, without milk.

My face scrunches at the oaty dryness sitting in the dish.

Magali waves in front of my face to garner my attention.

"Adding milk will just make it soggy," she explains.

"Ah."

She takes out orange juice and pours it into a tall glass, before reaching into a cabinet and grabbing the Advil bottle.

On autopilot, she places two pills next to the juice and writes a note, as if this is a normal daily routine.

"This a common occurrence for her?" I ask.

Magali smiles, but it's forced. "It's complicated."

Right. Complicated. I get complicated.

A few minutes later, I watch the door silently close, before my gaze rests onto Serena's sleeping form. Complicated doesn't even begin to cover it.

In that moment, I decide there aren't going to be any free rides for her while she's under my protection.

It's time for her to become who she is meant to become.

So instead of taking care of her, like an asshole, I ate her breakfast and stepped over her tremoring body.

At some point, I'm not sure I'll be able to continue to fight the urge the bond creates to safeguard and take care of her. Hence my unmerited anger at her when she strolled into class, freshly showered, smelling like spring flowers.

Late.

My heart thuds against my chest and for a second, I regret what I am about to do. Regardless of how I feel about it, or how hypocritical it is, she will fulfill her destiny.

I exhale and enjoy the quiet, pondering how long I'll be stuck in this world—a world I don't belong to, and one in which I didn't grow up. Regardless of who my father is, the Academy isn't my home. A protector isn't really what I am.

I'm someone who safeguards lies. I have the reputation of a sinner. I am unable to escape my past, and evidently, my future.

My focus falls to the door's handle as it jiggles, alerting me to Serena's presence. It flies open and she storms in, slamming it behind her. Dramatically, she huffs and throws her messenger bag on the floor, placing her hands on her hips. I watch her every move and keep my features schooled.

"You're a professor?" she yells out.

"Yes."

"Since when?"

"I accepted the position two months ago."

"Why would the school place an instructor in student housing?" she grits out.

"I assume all the other housing on campus was taken."

She narrows her eyes. "Lecturers live off campus."

"Maybe this one prefers to remain on."

"Why?"

"Because."

She scowls. "Because isn't a reason, Tristan."

"During Academy hours, it's Professor Gallagher."

Serena inhales and takes two steps toward the desk.

"That's another thing. You're Gage Gallagher's son?" her tone is accusing.

My expression remains blank. "Rumor has it."

"Rumor has it?" she repeats on a quiet tone.

"My family ties are none of your concern. Just as I'm sure you'd prefer to keep your family relations private."

She places both her palms on the desk and leans toward me, narrowing her eyes. "Do I come across as one of those giggly school girls who will believe every lie that comes out of your sexy mouth? Because, *Professor*, I assure you that I'm not."

A silence falls between us. I need to change the topic away from my father. With a predatory glare, I stand and walk around the desk, stopping in front of her.

"You think my mouth is sexy?"

She swallows and lifts her chin, earning my respect as she feigns confidence. Her trembling bottom lip gives her away. I scare the crap out of her. That makes two of us.

After a second, she takes a step back, putting space between us. Unable to help myself, I stalk toward her, closing each stretch of space she's grasping for.

I have no idea why I feel the need to constantly dominate her into submission. Maybe it's her strong will. I'm not used to it, and it pushes all my alpha-male buttons.

Eventually our dance lands her body pushed up against the door. I slam my hands on the wood beside her head, trapping her in my arms, and lean in, my lips almost brushing hers.

"Who are you?" she breathes across my mouth.

"No one," I reply in a smooth voice.

Her stare bores into mine, as if she's trying to see inside of me. I flinch with each layer she successfully penetrates.

"I don't believe you," she whispers.

"I didn't ask you to believe me."

Without warning, she lifts her hands and rests them against my chest. The bold move causes me to close my eyes. I ignore the burning sensation and the fact that I like her touch. Way too fucking much. It's all-consuming.

I swallow a groan and open my lids.

"Everyone is someone, Tristan."

"Are you touching me?"

No one touches me, at least not without permission.

In my world, her hands would be removed from her body for this.

Her eyes drop to her hands before she quickly meets my hard stare. "If you're trying to threaten and intimidate me as a form of evasion, it won't work."

"I threaten everyone, Serena."

"How nice for you," she huffs. "I'm not everyone."

My tongue flicks out and slowly runs over my bottom lip. Serena's stare fixates on the movement before she drags her focus back up my face, holding my glower again.

"We're going to be living together. Yet I know nothing about you," she points out with a nervous edge.

"And you won't." My tone is meant to sound cold.

Her teeth clench. I know this because I'm now staring at her pink mouth, wondering just how soft her tongue would be, tangled with mine.

Before I can contemplate the idea further, our lips are touching. *Shit! Did I move forward? Did she?*

What the—

All rational thought escapes me as we stand frozen, with our lips pressed together but unmoving. A warm feeling spreads through my body and within seconds, I jerk away.

Needing an escape, and angry at with myself for my lack of self-control, I reach around her and forcefully jerk the door open, bumping her away from it in the process.

I storm out in an even worse mood than when I started this morning, because that one simple taste of her was enough to torture me for years to come.

FIVE

BLACK STAIN

SERENA

S TUNNED, MY FINGERS GLIDE ALONG MY still tin-
gling lips. One slightest brush of our mouths and I'm officially
addicted.

How is that even possible?

Stupid, illogical crush.

I stand in Tristan's office dazed and confused, taking everything
in, attempting to try to pinpoint something that will give me a hint, a
glimpse into who he is.

There is nothing.

His office is just as unrevealing as his eyes are.

There isn't even a book or piece of paper anywhere.

Dejected, I watch the dust swirl in the rays of sunlight coming
through the window. After a moment, I step toward the empty desk,
turn and lean against it.

I chastise myself for pressing my lips against his.

Brilliant move, Serena.

He was just so *close*. His scent wrapped around me, and when I touched him, it was like I never wanted to stop.

I became overcome with the need to close the gap between us, so I leaned in and pressed my lips to his.

I rub my temples. "What the hell was I thinking?"

"Rough day?" Ryker asks from the open doorway.

I force a lopsided grin. "Try a rough few."

He walks toward me and I study his outrageously good-looking face. As he nears, he runs a hand through his dark hair and pins me with his aquamarine eyes.

I remember the first time we met Ryker. Ireland, Magali, and I were in our first year at the Academy.

From day one, he quickly became a hot commodity on campus. He's the only protector who, during training, was able to take me down in ten seconds flat, earning my respect and friendship.

"This," he motions, indicating my dismal state, "wouldn't have something to do with our new lecturer, would it?"

I lean further into the desk. "Nope."

He lifts both eyebrows at me and stays silent for a moment before speaking. "You're a terrible liar."

"What are you doing here?" I ask, shifting focus.

"Turns out, I'm Gallagher's teaching assistant for the semester. I needed to speak to him about my schedule."

I snort. "Yeah? Good luck with that."

He chuckles, without humor. "Thanks."

An awkward beat passes between us before he speaks.

"All okay with Magali? I haven't seen her lately," he hesitates. "I think she might be avoiding me."

I toe the ground. "She's good. Just busy."

His expression falls. "Busy?" he repeats, unconvinced.

I lift my eyes to his. "Ryker—"

His features turn grim. "I never meant to hurt her."

"But you did."

"I know," he exhales.

I watch Ryker for a few moments. "Mags just needs a little time to process everything. To figure things out. I know it wasn't planned, but you and Ireland upset her."

He sighs. "You can't help who you fall in love with, Serena. It happens when it's meant to."

I stare at the open door where Tristan just stormed out, and let out a rough exhale. "I wouldn't know, Ry."

Ryker steps toward me and pulls me into an embrace before placing a light kiss on my temple. "For a badass gargoyle princess, you're looking pretty pathetic these days, you know that?"

"Hey," I push at him and giggle. "Mean."

He chuckles while I rest my cheek on his heart. "You have a lot to offer someone, Serena, and when the universe is ready, it will present you with an epic love. I promise."

"What the hell is going on?" Tristan growls.

Ryker freezes, and his hands tighten on my waist.

Tristan's words hang in the air before I manage to look around Ryker and meet his seething expression.

Um, what?

I don't bristle. Confused at his reaction and annoyed with his new constant presence in my life, I decide I've had it with Tristan's shit for the day. My temper is rising at the accusation he's making with his irate glare.

Plastering on a fake smile, I use my sickly sweet voice.

"Whatever do you mean, Professor Gallagher?"

"Serena!" He barks out my name.

Ryker moves to the side and opens his mouth to say something, but I step in front of him, interjecting.

"Oh, do you mean, what am I doing with your teaching assistant? I was just offering him sex in exchange for a passing grade this semester. Since—you know—I tend to be tardy a lot and all."

I smirk at him and adjust my protector bracelet.

Ryker's eyes slide closed just as a predatory smile forms across Tristan's lips. He purposely stares me down, while trying to look authoritative.

"Get out!" The demand is directed at my friend.

Ryker's eyes pop open and he watches me.

I nod my approval for him to leave, but he hesitates for a moment, his nostrils flaring. "Are you sure?"

Tristan grins, wickedly. "She doesn't need your security, gargoyle. She already has a protector."

Ryker snaps his gaze to Tristan. "Well, Professor, Rulf isn't here at the moment, and with the way you're seething at her, for no reason, I think she just might need one."

I step in between the two. "I appreciate your concern, Ry, but I can take care of myself. It's best if you just go."

He looks down at me, unconvinced.

"There is no need for you to get involved in this," I add.

After a moment, Ryker nods and heads to leave, but not before bumping Tristan's shoulder on his way out.

Tristan doesn't flinch.

His wild eyes stay fixated on me.

"What was he doing here?" Tristan growls.

"He's your new teaching assistant. He needed his TA schedule," I answer. "Ryker is a friend of mine. You need to show him some respect moving forward."

Tristan tilts his head. "Is that so, raindrop?"

My heart surges with irritation at his tone.

When the protector's gaze settles on me, the look on his face and in his eyes sends shivers across my skin. After a moment, he curses, slamming the door to his office shut and charging toward me in one smooth motion, releasing a roar that causes the walls in my chest to constrict around my heart.

Taken aback by his temperament, I lean back onto his desk as he pushes into my personal space, placing a warm palm to my chest.

"What are you doing?" I whisper, shakily.

"I have the gift of empathy and soul sight," he explains.

"Gargoyles don't have souls," I remind him.

"No, but if I touch you near your heart, it helps me to feel and understand your emotions better," he clarifies.

I try to move away from his hand, but he shakes his head and keeps me firmly planted against the desk.

"And why would you want to do that?" I ask, losing my willpower to move out of his grasp.

"Do what?" he mutters.

"Understand me?"

He smells like cinnamon, cigarettes and all things forbidden and warm. I bite back a moan.

Tristan ignores my question but I can tell the material between his hand and my skin is hindering his reading abilities because he moves his hand upward, until it's at the base of my throat. Then he slides it up even farther, until his fingers and palm are flush against my neck.

An overwhelming need to be closer to him starts to take over, but I curb it, having learned my lesson ten minutes ago.

Tristan runs his fingers over my jaw, slowly slipping his hand behind my neck. His palm conforms perfectly to it, as if it were made to hold me. *But that's silly, right?*

His chest meets mine and it creates a sensation so powerful, I can't help but shiver in response. My hands white-knuckle the edge of the desk when his breath falls in waves across my mouth. Tristan's gaze drops to my lips, which I part slightly.

"Since you're not an empath, Serena, I guess your erratic behavior around me can only mean one thing," he rasps.

I try to swallow. "What's that?"

A cocky smirk crosses his mouth, but it doesn't match the serious tone he's using. "You're attracted to me."

I don't respond, and Tristan's body pushes mine further into the desk. It's like he's trying to mold us into one being so I won't disappear. And *holy crap*, it feels incredible.

His fingers slide into my hair, pulling me closer. The small sound of pleasure I make causes his mouth to immediately connect with mine, and as our lips move across one another's, relief floods me—I can finally breathe.

His kiss is deep and heart-stopping, but with an edge of something that fills me with nervousness and heartache. I sink into his warm lips as he parts mine, allowing our tongues to explore one another. Never in my life has something felt so good, and at the same time ached so badly.

Almost as quickly as it began, it's over.

Without warning he pulls his lips away from mine, causing me to whimper in protest at the loss of contact. The small sliver of space between us is too much, and I move forward to take his mouth again, but he jerks back.

His eyes, clouded with hunger, stay on mine, but the desire in his face clears, and a frown creases his brow. Tristan looks sad, lost, almost broken. My heart skips a beat at the sudden change in him.

The need to soothe his unhappiness overtakes rational thought. Slowly, I lift my hand to his stubble-covered jaw and allow my fingertips to follow the tight line comfortingly.

The shift in his mood triggers a flash of something behind his gaze. Recognition of his actions, maybe. With a sense of urgency, he immediately removes his hand from me and steps back, creating a gap.

Ungracefully, I try to stand on my own. Once I'm steady, Tristan takes another step back, allowing more space to come between us.

After a moment, he leans in, his breath warming my ear.

"The next time you're overcome with the need to kiss me, raindrop, either do it correctly or not at all."

Mortified at my own actions, my eyes squeeze shut.

When they reopen, he's gone.

TRISTAN

THE SUN CRESTS ON THE HORIZON as my bike makes its way over the winding cobblestone roads, passing the rugged coastlines, toward Torc Mountain.

My mind replays what happened this morning between Serena and me, over and fucking over.

I'm an idiot.

All logical thought escaped me the second she first pressed her lips to mine. I returned to my office, with every intention of apologizing and setting her straight, only to walk in and see her in her friend Ryker's arms.

That's when I lost my shit, and apparently, all sense of right and wrong. The need to taste her, to consume every part of her, flared within me. My second lineage pushed to the top of my blood, causing me to act without thought.

I can't control my mind, as more images of Serena pressed against me flash through my head. I really need to get this shit under control. I can't keep letting who I am override why I'm attached to this assignment.

Pressing my lips together in annoyance, I let out a small growl of irritation at my own moment of weakness earlier.

I continue to weave my way through the hidden paths of the Killarney National Park, but the lush green ride through nature, which is usually soothing, isn't calming me today. Once I've climbed to the middle of the mountain, I park my bike behind a large tree and look out over the lake.

"Got your message." Zander appears out of thin air.

"Thanks for coming." I hold out my hand and pull him into a one-armed hug when he takes it.

"Anytime." He claps my shoulder and steps back.

I pull out a cigarette and light it. He'll hate it, but right now, it's the only thing that will calm my jittery nerves.

"What's going on, Trist?" He watches me.

I blow out a long stream of smoke through my lips.

"I need your help."

"What's up?"

"I want you to help me run a hand-to-hand combat training session—at the Academy." I bite my bottom lip.

His eyebrows shoot up. Zander glances at me, then at the ground, like he isn't sure if I'm being serious or not.

"You're not serious?" he asks.

I remain silent, regarding him. After a second, he swears and runs his hands through his hair, watching me closely.

"I'm a satyr, Tristan."

I dip my chin. "I'm well aware of your bloodlines."

He leans against a tree trunk. "In case you've forgotten, the supernatural world tends to view those with my *bloodline* as second-class citizens who are only good for bedding. I'm not sure the Royal Protector Academy would approve of my assisting you in training their elite protectors. Especially in hand-to-hand, which tends to require a hands-on approach."

My eyes turn angry. "I don't care what they think. You're my best friend and brother. You command an entire army that we've trained together—the finest across all the realms. You're smart, strategic and skilled—"

"And full of sexual prowess," he finishes.

"Which can be controlled," I state.

"You and I know that. Do they?" he huffs.

"Twice a week, for two hours, over the next four months," I say slowly. "That's it."

"Why this training session?" I ask.

"You know why," I reply.

I wait for him to say more. Instead, he takes a step back.

"Is there another reason you need my presence?"

Damn. He knows me so fucking well. "No."

He nods in disbelief. "You sure?"

No. Not at all.

"What are you getting at, Zander?" I growl.

"I think you're afraid to be all touchy-feely with the princess you're protecting. You're scared that she'll start seeing you as her prince, instead of the villain," he replies.

I shift on my feet, uncomfortable because he's right, and irritated that he can read me like a book.

"I'm not her Prince Charming," I counter.

"What makes you so certain?" His eyes hold mine.

"I don't love, or get attached to anyone or anything. That includes a charge that I'm blood bonded to. The. End."

"Ringing endorsement for your future bride."

"Zander," I growl out.

"Fine. I'll help," he exhales.

"Thank you."

"For the record, the darkness you carry around with you—it doesn't mean you don't need or deserve love."

I force away the black stain on my heart and vow to take control of my actions moving forward around Serena.

Zander scans the lake. "So can Princess Serena fight? Or are we starting from square one with her?"

"If I had to guess, she doesn't have a right hook."

SIX

VERNAL PURPLE

SERENA

M Y HANDS TIGHTEN INTO FISTS BEFORE I pop off a right hook, landing it solidly into Tristan's left cheek.

A satisfied grin appears on my lips as I watch him blink a few times out of confusion.

His expression registers shock that I wailed on him.

Standing straight, he rubs his cheek, looks down, and sighs. "I guess I deserved that, raindrop."

At the use of the annoying nickname, I wind up to repeat the punch. Catching me off guard, he grabs my wrists and places them above my head, backing me into the wall.

With a moan, he lowers his head to mine. Right before our lips touch, I gasp and yank myself out of my daydream.

God. I need to stop fantasizing about Tristan.

Tired, Magali and I make our way across campus in silence. I'd forgotten how long the Academy's days are.

Continuing on with the rest of my day was cruel after tasting Tristan's lips on mine. Our brief encounter this morning left me feverish, longing, and moody.

And evidently, a bit violent.

I know Mags senses something is off but surprisingly, she isn't pushing me for information.

A flash of Tristan's forlorn expression hits me. The haunted look in his eyes shadowed me throughout the day. I need to guard my reactions and keep it together around him. Cringing, I remember that he lives with us, and I'll have to face him again when we return to the suite.

As darkness falls, a cool breeze plays with my hair, lifting and twirling the strands as it carries a barely audible whisper over me. There's a raw edge to the hum, almost like it's a cry of distress.

I stop walking and my focus shifts to the direction the sound came from. My eyes scan the silhouettes of trees and bushes that line the lush, grassy forest located behind the old gothic stone buildings.

"Did you hear that?" I ask Magali.

"Hear what?" The crease between her brows deepens.

I become silent and wait a moment longer, for the murmur to resonate with me again.

But there is only quiet. Confused, I turn and face my friend before brushing it off.

"Nothing, I guess."

Had I imagined it?

"Are you sure?" she presses.

Another light gust pushes between us, and this time the murmur is hypnotic and woeful.

I study Magali's face for any hint of a sign that she might have heard it too, but she's just looking at me with a concerned expression.

"You're acting weird. What is going on, Ser?"

Another compelling sigh draws near and my head snaps back to the forest. A strange urgency bubbles within me to comfort whatever is hurting.

Without thought, I start to move toward the wooded area. Magali grabs my elbow, stopping my movement, forcing my attention to her before letting go so she can sign.

"Where are you going?" her fingers fly.

My gaze shifts between her and the trees. I don't know for sure what's making the despondent noise, and since she can't hear it, I'm not about to put my friend in danger.

"I . . . um . . . there's somewhere I need to be."

She glances past me to the tree line.

"Are you about to do something insanely stupid?"

"I don't think so."

Mags cocks her head to the side, assessing me. "You don't think so?" she repeats, slowing her hand gestures.

Another whisper emanates out of the woods, beckoning me. "I'll explain later." I rush toward the forest, before Magali can stop me again.

As I draw closer, a flash of purple catches my attention. The logical part of me demands that I turn around and go back to the suite, but my gut is telling me to continue until I find the source of the forlorn cry.

The smell of pine and wet, decaying leaves assaults my nose as I make my way through the overgrown forest.

Darkness has fully descended, and the night air is cool in my lungs. I take in a deep breath and seek out the amethyst hue.

My eyes close and I focus on my heightened hearing, listening for movement. But the only sound that greets me is the soft sound of water babbling in the stream.

Reopening my gaze, I wander toward the creek and take a seat on one of the large river rocks. The shadows crawl in farther, settling deeper around me, blanketing the forest.

The inkiness causes the exposed bark on the trees to appear black as it curls and folds into itself.

A gentle wind sweeps through the trees. In the distance a crow softly caws, and crickets begin their nightly song.

With a quick twist of my wrist, I summon a thin, steady stream of water to flow out of the brook and into my palm.

Like my mother's, my powers thrive in nature, allowing me to control and manipulate earth and weather elements.

Once the cool liquid connects with my skin, the stream begins to glow amethyst. The color is a peace offering for the xana I know is lurking around the inky woods.

Xanas are half nymph and half fairy. They live near fountains, rivers, and waterfalls—anywhere there is pure water. When the female creatures are sad, their aura takes on a mauve hue known throughout the supernatural world as vernal purple. It's when they're at their weakest.

One must be very careful around the nymph fairies. Like sirens, they lure you with their beauty and promises of great treasures. If angered, they can easily become disenchanted and spell you, causing you to rush to your drowning death in a fit of insanity.

A few moments later, I sense her.

"I know you're there. You can come out," I say quietly.

Silence.

Exhaling, I release the torrent of water back into the brook, causing the entire creek to glow purple for a brief moment before, little by little, the color fades away.

"You don't have to be afraid," I state.

"I am not afraid," she replies, with an edge in her angelic voice.

"Then come out."

"I can summon those who live in the shadows," she says.

"I'm not here to harm you. I sensed your unhappiness."

A quiet settles between us again before she speaks.

"Sensing my emotions is not possible. You are a gargoyle, not a nymph or empath," she points out.

I lean back on my hands. The smooth moist stone calms me. "My powers are driven by nature and the elements. Therefore, I am sensitive to fairies and nymphs."

There is a silent pause before she whispers. "Only two elemental gargoyles exist. Both are of royal bloodlines."

"I guess that makes me one of two," I reply haughtily.

Several moments pass, and just when I think she's vanished, a cool breeze begins to circle around me, sending shivers across my skin. I remain quiet and still as the forest becomes sluggish, as if in slow motion. Colors swirl beside me, and finally the young woman appears.

Guarded, I blink several times at her form before relief washes through me. Though her expression is serious, her silver eyes are filled with kindness and warmth.

She smiles tenderly before dipping her head toward me, bowing slightly as a show of respect.

The motion grants me a full view of her headband, which is made of intertwined white branches. Each twig is embellished with shiny flecks that sparkle when the moonlight bounces off the water and hits them.

When she returns to her full height, I notice her skin has the most amazing sheen to it, appearing silvery. Even her lips, nails, and eyelids are gilded with the grayish color.

"Your Highness, it is an honor," she greets.

My eyes roam across her face, taking in the white branches that also frame her slender visage. The adornments begin at her eyebrow area and continue to the bottom of her chin.

She's lovely.

The nymph lifts her overly long, thick lashes and flashes a pretty glance at me, while she fidgets with the stiff skirt of her dress. It reminds me of a ballet costume.

Warily, the Nordic beauty takes a seat next to me, and once comfortable, her slender shoulders visibly relax.

I offer her a kind smile, forgetting just how breathtaking nymphs can be when they show themselves. Their beauty is designed to allure and seduce you. It can cloud your mind with thoughts of want and sexual pleasure.

She glances at me as she takes out a small platinum comb and begins to obsessively brush the long pieces of white-blonde hair falling in large ringlets down her back. Each elegant motion she makes is more fascinating than the last. I've never been this close to a nymph before.

I recall my mother once telling me that a xana's need to brush her hair is not born out of vanity, but is instead a way they comfort themselves when scared, forlorn, or unnerved.

"My pick is spelled with moonbeams. It's why my hair is luminescent." Her voice is musical as she speaks.

"It's very pretty."

"I'm Freya," she replies.

"Serena." I continue to stare at her. It's hard not to.

"Have you not met a nymph before, Serena?"

"I haven't," I admit.

Freya's eyes widen. "Oh my," she exhales.

My gaze shifts to the forest, and then back to her. I motion to her compulsive brushing.

"I didn't mean to make you uncomfortable, Freya."

She falls silent for a second before her comb disappears.

"You summoned me, by turning the stream vernal. It was an invitation, was it not?" Her tone is unsure.

"I noticed your amethyst hue earlier and your sorrowful cries floated to me. Why are you so melancholy?" I ask.

Freya's voice and face are calm, despite the uneasiness that is emanating off of her. "It was not my intent for you to hear me shed tears, Serena. My deepest apologies."

"I'm a good listener, if you'd like to talk," I pose.

"You are most kind to offer, Princess."

I sigh. "I'd prefer not to be called that."

Freya's expression pinches. "You are not kind?"

"No—um . . . Princess. I'm not fond of the title."

She laughs lightly. "Don't be daft. A princess is who and what you are, Serena. You were born of a noble bloodline. As the next in line to the throne, you are a royal protector."

Apparently nymphs are literal. Avoiding her statement, I flick beams of light off the brook. Each gracefully skims the water's line, bouncing and making contact with a few of the dragonflies encircling us. With each strike, the insects begin to glow vernal, reminding me of lightning bugs.

"Bloodlines don't make you regal, Freya."

She regards me, considering my words quietly before she speaks again. "I'm afraid in our world, they do."

"I'm meant to be more than a royal legacy," I counter.

Freya swings her feet in a child-like manner. "Noble birthrights are essential," she shoots me a side glance. "My father, Oren, is the emperor of the water fairies. My mother, Lily, is a simple woodland nymph. One day, she woke up to discover that she was to become the empress consort of the water fairies—an appointment given to her by her best friend, the queen of the woodland nymphs."

I exhale into the night. Freya is royal. "Then you understand the struggle and chains of noble obligations."

Silence falls over us for a while before her gentle voice cuts through it. "Many years ago, the woodland and water realms were on the brink of war. My parents' union was symbolic. A promise, that from that day forth, and forevermore, both realms would live in harmony and peace," she inhales. "But as with most accords, there is a cessation."

"A cessation," I repeat, playing with the word. "If your parents' marriage no longer preserves the suspension of hostilities between the two realms, there must be a new cessation, right?" I ask.

Her head nods. "I've been promised to a very handsome nymph prince. A prize amongst our kind. Sadly, he has a penchant for bedding many of the females within our world."

I flinch. "I'm guessing congratulations aren't in order."

Freya's expression becomes crestfallen. "Regardless of the prince's side interests, the alliance of our kingdoms is important to the survival of our kind, Serena. Our unification will extend the peace treaty, preventing further conflict."

"I'll never understand why a feud between power-hungry realms is cause for an arranged marriage," I muse.

She offers me a hesitant smile. "It would seem you have much to learn with regard to the supernatural world."

"Enlighten me, then," I suggest.

"The forests need water in order to endure. In turn, the water fairies reside within the safety of the thriving woodland walls. We are all connected, Serena. Every realm in existence, including the earth realm, relies on the others for survival. If our two realms were to go to war, everything surrounding us would cease to exist, because everything depends on water and the forest's endurance in order to live and thrive. Especially the human souls you've sworn to protect. The forest is of critical importance to mundane life. The trees produce the very oxygen they breathe. And without water, the earth realm would perish. If there are no human souls to protect, then your race would also cease to exist.

You see, Serena, we all have our parts to play when it comes to royal obligations and maintaining the supernatural balance."

My gaze shifts across the dark forest. "I understand the delicate balance needed across realms. But you don't love him, this . . . nymph you're betrothed to?"

"On the contrary, I love him with every breath I take."

I place my hand over hers. "Then why are you so sad?"

She exhales. "He has only agreed to the marriage because his loyalty to his lineage will not allow him to do otherwise. Even though we've been friends since birth."

Unrequited love is the worst kind.

I squeeze her hand. "I wish I could offer words of encouragement," I pause. "I've never been in love. So, I'm unsure of what to say in order to help ease your sadness."

"Never?" Freya asks, surprised, before turning her hand over and entwining our fingers as if we're two young friends on the playground.

I shake my head slowly. "Never."

"Close your eyes," she demands.

My brows pinch.

"Just trust me," she pushes.

My lids slide closed and suddenly, I feel the warmth of her energy flood through my hand, up my arm, and into my heart. It grows and ebbs like the tide. It's the most beautiful sensation. Encompassing me, it wraps itself around the pulsing organ. Oxygen has lost value as my heartbeat rhythmically begins to throb in a smitten chant.

I smile, allowing the happiness and love she feels for her intended to fill me and make me whole. It's the highest high.

"That is what the feeling of love is," she whispers.

Then, in an instant, as if a thunderstorm has rolled in, I feel scared, alone, and cold. I'm burning with bitterness, foolish optimism, and dangerous confidence.

As the storm carries on, the warm, happy feeling rips itself away, and in its wake is frigid destruction. The agony of her loss is too much, and I'm forced to yank my hand away from her with a pain-filled scream.

TRISTAN

I FELT HER FEAR BEFORE I heard her screams. Serena's anxiety rushes into me through our bond. Attempting to ignore her unease, I move toward where she is. As her terror surges through me, it takes every ounce of my willpower not to just teleport to her, using an unwelcome protector gift from my father.

As I close in, I detect movement in front of me. Quietly, I approach. Then, acting out of instinct, I instantly rush through the last bit of wooded area that separates us.

Startled, Serena leaps off the rock she was seated on and attempts to crouch in an offensive maneuver, but she's not fast enough. I wrap myself around her and teleport her away from whatever it was that had her screaming as though her heart was being torn from her chest.

When I reappear a few feet away with her securely in my arms, she spins and throws me a defiant look, before quickly jerking out of my hold.

The second I let her go, Serena slams her hands into me, sending me backwards. Unable to catch my footing, I land on my ass. Hard. *Fuck, that hurts!*

"Tristan?" she exhales roughly.

I groan and sit up. "Raindrop."

"What the hell are you doing?" she yells, placing herself in a protective stance, bracing for another attack.

Her bright eyes linger over me before meeting mine.

"It's okay," I offer gently. "Everything's okay."

"What?" Serena barks out, confused.

"I'm here to save you," I explain. "You're safe now."

As if I've punched her, she rears back. "Do I give you the impression that I'm a damsel in distress?"

Her words render me speechless for a moment, before I compose myself. "I heard you screaming," I point out.

"Your Highness?" A surprised female voice interrupts from behind the angry gargoyle who is staring me down as if she doesn't know whether to kiss me or punch me.

At first the nymph has no effect on me, but gradually her voice penetrates, gaining my attention. I snap my head up and recognition assaults me, as I meet the silver stare of the panicked female.

Distressed, she takes a step toward us, but Serena spins quickly and steps in, blocking me from her.

I watch, confused. Is she—protecting the xana?

"I'm fine, Freya," Serena assures, placing her palms up.

"But—" the xana begins, and I cut her off, standing.

"Her *Highness* said she was fine, nymph." My tone is final.

Serena's attention shifts back to me, and she takes a step in my direction, lifting her chin. "I don't know who you think you're speaking to, Tristan, but you have no right to use that tone with her. Nymph or not, she deserves respect."

Freya bristles and whispers. "Actually—"

I shoot Serena a haughty look. "That so?"

Serena snorts. "Freya is not subservient simply because she is a nymph and you are a protector."

"I bet her intended feels otherwise," I snap.

Freya frowns, and I suddenly feel like the asshole I am.

Letting out a deep breath, I lean toward Serena. "Interesting stance on nymphs you have, raindrop."

The gargoyle's jaw tightens and for just a second, I think she's actually going to take a swing at me. Some pathetic part of me wishes she would, so I could feel her skin on mine again.

We all stand in silence for several minutes, not saying anything else, until the tension eventually begins to ease.

When I finally feel Serena's emotions calm, I relax.

With a lazy grin, I stretch my arms over my head, causing my shirt to ride up a bit at the bottom. Both ladies flush at the sight, averting their gazes when I catch them.

Serena clears her throat. "Why are you here, Tristan?"

I return her stare with a shrug. "I was walking and heard you scream. I thought perhaps you were in . . . danger."

Her gaze narrows at the lie, as does the nymph's.

"As you can see, I'm not in . . . *danger*," she mocks.

"Why were you screaming then?" I counter.

Serena looks to Freya, who offers a slight shake of her head, before turning her attention back to me. It's obvious they're working together to hide something. Interesting.

"I, um," Serena stretches.

"Yes?" The annoyance in my voice is unmistakable.

"Thought I saw a frog."

"A frog?" I repeat in disbelief.

"Yes."

"You're afraid of amphibians?" I question.

"Terrified."

"Of a toad?"

"Toads, newts, salamanders, all amphibians really."

I try to hold back my smile. "Why is that?"

She swallows, uncomfortable with lying. "Well," her eyes dart around the forest, searching for an answer. "They're tailless and slimy. Unpredictable when they leap," she adds. "Full of warts and stuff," her voice trails off.

I watch her fake a shiver for effect. It's awkward, yet amusing, that she thinks I'm buying her pathetic reasoning.

"They also have that weird sac in their throat that makes that awful croaking sound," Freya adds in a murmur.

Serena nods her head in agreement. "That, too. The," she forces out the words, "weird sound, thingy, they make."

I raise a brow and press my lips, while filling my tone with sarcasm. "I can see how that would be . . . terrifying."

"Petrifying, really," Serena continues.

"Chilling, even," I add.

"Horrifying."

"Frogs!" I announce.

"Crazy."

We hold one another's gaze in a gentle manner. The connection between us is palpable. For one perfect moment, everything around us fades out and it's just me and her. No one else. It's strangely peaceful.

Serena stares at me, unblinking, her lips slightly parted, as her gaze falls to my mouth.

Like a magnet, I'm drawn to her, and take a step in her direction, but stop when Freya throws me a withering glance. The xana flicks her hair and huffs at being ignored, causing Serena to look away, breaking the spell.

"SERENA!" A male voice barks loudly from behind me.

Our moment now gone, Serena studies the ground with great intensity. My jaw clenches at the heated sound of her guard, Rulf. The need to protect her, even from him, boils.

Having two protectors, one who is actually bonded to her and another who is assigned, is going to be an issue.

It's too bad that only one of the three of us knows about the bond, which means I need to keep myself in check and not kick his ass every time he gets near her.

"SERENA!" he repeats in a roar, emerging from the trees and stomping toward us.

"What the hell is going on?" Rulf bites out.

A playful light crosses Serena's features like a mask she's put on. She smiles brightly and uses a lilt in her tone.

"Hey, Rulf. What are you doing out here?" she asks, as if she ran into him at the store.

Rulf's dark gaze falls across the three of us before landing on his charge. "Magali was worried that you might have gone and done something . . . stupid," he states.

She smiles weakly. "I usually do. About once a day."

With a cold glare thrown at Freya and me, he continues. "It's not appropriate for you to be consorting with nymphs."

Serena crosses her arms over her chest and shoots her guard a warning look. "Freya is a new acquaintance, and Tristan is a protector. There is no danger here. And even if there were, I am a gargoyle and can take care of myself."

"Regardless," Rulf exhales. "I'm here to take you back."

Oddly enough, Serena's gaze meets mine, her eyes seeking my permission. My nostrils flare at the thought.

She doesn't want to go with this idiot any more than I want him to be the one to take her. Rules are rules, though. I step forward, giving her my undivided attention.

"Go back with your guard, Serena. I'll see to Freya."

At my words, Freya's expression hardens to stone.

Serena turns to the xana with sympathy in her gaze. "I should go before Rulf's brain explodes. It was really nice to meet you. Thank you for sharing. Your betrothed is very lucky. I hope that one day that he'll realize just how much."

"Thank you," she whispers.

Rulf takes Serena by the elbow, guiding her out of the forest, and it's all I can do not to tear him apart for even touching her.

I watch until she's safely out of Freya's grasp, then turn my attention to the xana with a scowl, which elicits a smirk from her.

"We need to talk about my brother," I state.

SEVEN
WELCOME HOME

TRISTAN

I KICK OFF MY BOOTS AT the door and toss my key card on the counter before running my hands over my face. It's been a long fucking day.

The light stubble I like to keep on my jawline has grown out a bit, and I make a mental note to tighten it up in the morning.

Heading to the fridge, I grab a bottle of beer and a slice of pizza. I don't have the energy to warm it up, so cold it is. As soon as the refrigerator door closes, the light in the apartment fades and I'm left in the darkness.

I take a long pull from the bottle, allowing the alcohol to soothe the turmoil lingering inside me. I wasn't prepared for the side effects my bond with Serena would cause.

Her heightened emotions came slamming into me tonight. An odd combination of fear, hurt and love.

Nothing she was experiencing felt right, and it wracked my body like a tidal wave.

I heave a heavy sigh and ignore the thick layer of cold grease coating the top of my mouth. The moment I felt Freya's presence, fear spread through my body like ice. Mine. Serena's. It all swirled together.

I still have no idea what the hell Serena was thinking. Xanas can be extremely dangerous if angered. After summoning Zander to warn Freya off, I came straight back to the suite.

I'm tired, hungry, and—if I'm being honest—sexually frustrated after being around a female nymph. They tend to have that effect on male supernatural beings.

Startled, my eyes flick to the set of slightly glowing sapphire ones peering at me from across the counter.

As a side effect of a gargoyle's protector bloodline, our irises faintly glow when our emotions are amplified.

"You're seriously our new roommate?" Serena asks.

I tilt my chin toward the counter. "I have the key card and everything," I reply, and give her a sarcastic snort.

She cocks her head and looks at me suspiciously. After a long bout of silence, she sighs. "I can manipulate the air so that everything around me slows down. It's how I approached you without noise, or you realizing I was here."

Her admission is something I already knew, but I still need to act like it's new information. I look down and then back up at her, before nodding that I understand.

Serena's ardent eyes watch me. "Is Freya all right?"

I hold her gaze. "Why wouldn't she be?"

She shrugs. "I was worried about her."

I take another long pull from the beer bottle before setting it on the counter. "Your guard is right. You shouldn't be consorting with nymphs. They're unpredictable and dangerous." My tone is harsh, edgy.

Especially that one, I want to add, but don't.

"You seem to know a lot about them, Tristan."

"Most male protectors do, Serena," I fire back. "Why are you awake? Isn't tomorrow your first day of training?"

She scoffs and her arms cross around her body as if she's bracing herself. "I thought maybe you and I should get to know one another better. I mean, if we're going to be living together, I think I have the right to know who you are, and what you're really doing here at the Academy. Don't you?"

I swallow the disgusting bite of pizza I took, throwing the rest of the slice down on the counter before I answer. Leaning my elbows on the marble countertop, so we're the same height, I push myself into her personal space.

"Fair enough, raindrop."

She continues to stare at me, assessing me, thinking my agreement to this is some sort of game.

It's not.

She's right, she has the right to know the limited amount of information I can share.

Her expression turns mischievous.

"Do you cook?" She nods at the pizza.

"Nope."

Her smile is slight, but it's there.

"Do you clean?" she asks.

"Nope."

Normally, others do these things for me.

"Just a heads-up, Mags will kick your ass for leaving wet towels on the floor, so you're going to want to work on that." She laces her fingers. "Otherwise, I can't be responsible for her actions. She's tiny, but lethal. And a neat freak."

I chuckle. "Noted."

"Favorite color?"

I pause a moment, staring into her eyes. "Sapphire."

My answer causes her to hesitate and stumble. "Um, how did you get the scar on your upper lip?" she points to my mouth, thrown off a bit.

"Battle wound," I answer vaguely.

"Why are you living in student housing?" she asks.

I casually shrug. "Chancellor Davidson assigned me this suite. I'm guessing it's because I was a last-minute staff addition and the professional housing was all spoken for." My answer is truthful. She doesn't need to know it's also because I'm her protector and apparently need to be here.

Serena contemplates my answer for a beat too long as her gaze roams over my features, landing on my brow piercing. "You don't strike me as the *teacher* type, Tristan. What are you really doing here at the Academy?"

I glance at my bottle, then back at her, deciding how much truth I'm actually going to offer up. "I fucked up. I did something I shouldn't have and got caught."

"What did you do?" she asks quietly.

"It doesn't matter. What does is that my actions got me a sentence of stone petrification." Serena inhales a hiss through her teeth, knowing it's the worst possible outcome for gargoyles. "At the last minute, I was offered an instructor position here at the Academy. If I accepted, and fulfilled my duties, it was promised that my record would be wiped clean and my sentence pardoned."

"Just like that?" she inquires, her brow arched.

"Just like that." I pin her with a hard glare.

Her hand reaches out and she snags my bottle, downing half the contents in one swallow. I try not to react at the impressive fact that she can swallow a lot of liquid at once.

I need to stop objectifying her sexually. Or get laid.

"It's obvious that you know people in high places. Severe punishments don't just get overturned willy-nilly."

"Lucky for me then, I do know someone." I bite out.

"Gage?" She asks, with caution lining her tone. "He's your father, right? Did he work out a deal, or something?"

It's my turn to swallow the rest of my beer in one gulp. I turn and grab another one out of the fridge, slamming the door harder than I intended, before sucking down most of the liquid. I fucking hate talking about him.

"Yeah, raindrop. Gage Gallagher is my biological father." I try not to snap at her. None of this is her fault.

"He's a family friend. I never knew he had a son."

"Neither did he," I sigh.

Serena's expression falls. "Did you know about him?"

"Nope."

"Yet, you carry his last name?" she poses.

"It's complicated," I offer.

I watch while she pulls her bottom lip into her mouth. It's taking all my willpower not to lean over the counter and suck it into mine, ending this ridiculous conversation.

"I'm sorry," she mumbles.

"For what?"

She shrugs. "All of it."

"There's no need to be. The situation is convoluted, and honestly, my family drama is not something I want to get into with you. But yeah, Gage stepped in and got my sentence renounced. So here I am." I wave my hand. "He and I don't have a relationship beyond that."

"What about your mom? I mean, I know Gage was married to Camilla before she was killed. After that, I didn't know he was with any-one before he met Nassa."

Nassa is a sorceress who caught my father's eye years ago. They've been on and off for almost two decades. Another thorny relationship involving Gage.

"My mother and Gage had a one-night fling right after Camilla was murdered. He left the next morning, without a word or a backwards glance," I pause. "Mom raised me."

Understanding crosses her face. "Oh."

"My mom never told Gage about me. Or me about him. We both found out about one another two months ago."

"I'm sorry, Tristan," her tone is kind.

"Again, don't be."

"So you're really here to just work off a sentence?"

I hesitate a moment, searching for the right words. There is some-thing deep inside of me that doesn't want to outright lie to her. "My time here at the Academy is just an assignment. A means to an end for me. Nothing more. I have duties and obligations that await me when I'm done."

Her face softens. "Where is home?"

I shake my head slowly. "I think I've done enough sharing for tonight. We're ten seconds away from watching reality television and braiding each other's hair."

She pins me with an amused look. "One more question."

I arch an eyebrow, curious. "One."

"You kissed me earlier." Her tone is low and serious.

My gaze drops to her lips and she licks them. I have a feeling that I'm not the only one who has mentally relived that kiss multiple times today. "That wasn't a question. It was a statement."

She shrugs indifferently. "Semantics, Professor."

At the sound of her calling me Professor, my cock stands straight up, saluting the sound. *Shit.* Something else I need to get under control. I swallow a growl and shift on my feet, trying to readjust myself without her noticing.

"You kissed me first." Yeah, I sound like a toddler.

She grins and releases a light laugh. "By the grace, that was the worst explanation ever. How old are you?"

I lift a shoulder, brushing off her question. "Your kiss was flat. I thought you should experience a real one."

Pink lips thin in a frustrated line. "I'm not some virgin who's never had a boyfriend. Or experienced a kiss."

My heart sinks a little at this bit of information—knowing that someone else was her first.

Fuck, what am I saying? It doesn't matter. I won't—*can't*—be her anything.

I work my jaw back and forth, trying to control my temper, and telling myself it's just the bond.

"We done here?"

Serena shoots me a look with a challenging gleam in her eye. "Normally when two beings are trying to get to know one another, the other tends to ask questions as well."

A moment passes between us as we silently regard each other. This one is hard for me, since I've read her files and know just about all there is to know about her.

Anything I ask will sound superficial.

Instead, I decide I want to know her, really know her.

"What keeps you awake at night, Serena?" I ask quietly.

Nervous, she fidgets with her bracelet. It's something I notice she does when she's uncomfortable, or ready to bolt.

"All my life, I've lived in the shadows of something—" Her words are chosen carefully. "I mean . . . do you ever feel like you're walking around with a mask on? That no one really knows, or sees, the real you? You go through the motions daily of who and what you're supposed to be, but at night, when you're alone in the darkness, you can finally breathe because you don't have to hide behind the mask?"

Her thoughts come out in a jumbled way as she watches me, waiting for an acknowledgment of understanding.

I get it.

I get her.

My bond to her is what now keeps me up.

"I understand obligatory shadows that hang over you, better than you think I do, raindrop."

She nods. "I guess it's silly, really."

"What's that?"

"Trying to escape one's fate. I mean, can you ever really run away from it?" Her tone is wishful, lined with pain.

I roll my neck and internally chastise myself for what I'm about to say to her, because they're just words. A lie. Words that neither of us have the luxury of believing. She's right. Our fates are sealed.

"I believe we can change the outcome of our destiny. History proves that to us, over and over, again, Serena."

Her eyes meet mine, full of hope.

"Spoken like a true history professor," she quips. "I guess you are teacher material after all, Tristan Gallagher."

I snort. "You win. I guess that was a bit cliché."

She regards me for a moment before speaking softly.

"Actually, Tristan, you win."

"What?"

"Since you're a good kisser, I've decided you can stay."

The room falls silent and I can't help but notice everything about her.

I admire her black tank top, which dips in the front just enough for me to appreciate the roundness of her full breasts. Her auburn hair is pulled into a messy bun on top of her head, showing off her long neck.

Her pretty face is free of makeup.

She's breathtaking.

"Stop staring at me," she says in a quiet command.

"You liked me kissing you?" I ask, my own voice low.

"Yes," she whispers into the darkness.

I watch her with one of those expressionless expressions, hesitating a few seconds, which leads into an awkward silence between the two of us that lingers.

I'm unsure why I'm being unresponsive, but as ridiculous as it is, I don't want to make any sudden moves. I'm afraid it will scare her off, and I like looking at her.

Then I come to my senses.

"I was wrong to do that," I state weakly.

"Do what?" she inquires.

"Kiss you."

I tilt my head and look at her. Her expression falls, but she immediately hides the disappointment and puts on the same bright, fake appearance she gave to Rulf earlier.

Her mask.

And I hate it.

I fucking hate that she's being phony with me.

"It's fine. I kiss all my professors," she tries to joke.

Her gaze locks onto mine, waiting for me to laugh.

I don't.

My mind drifts back to Chancellor Davidson and his obvious affection for her. Is she kidding or being serious?

I can't have a jealous reaction, which is why I need to put an end to whatever this is becoming. Now.

"That's just it, Serena. I *am* your instructor during my time here at the Academy. Regardless of our unconventional living arrangements, or our mutual attraction for one another, it's best if we just leave it at that."

My chest tightens with each word. *Why the hell is that?*

"Sometimes, a kiss is just a kiss. It's okay," she replies.

My jaw clenches at her words. Slowly I bring my eyes back to hers. That was not the reaction I was expecting, and it's causing my entire body to have an internal battle.

We both know the kiss we shared wasn't just any kiss, and even though it's wrong, and I just made it clear we can't, I want to kiss her again. Over and fucking over again.

"I have training in the morning," she blurts out, ending my internal fight. Standing, she fixes her tank top. "'Night."

"'Night." I watch as she walks toward the hallway to her room, wearing her short sleep shorts, and somehow force myself to remain in the small kitchen rather than follow after her.

"Oh, and Tristan?" she adds, turning at the doorway.

"Yeah?"

"Welcome home."

My stomach bottoms out. This isn't home. But being near her is sure as hell starting to feel like it.

SERENA

I STOP AT MY BEDROOM DOOR before facing Magali. As planned, she's standing in her doorway, which is across from mine, listening in on my conversation with Tristan.

"Did you get all that?" I sign so he can't hear.

Mags holds a stern expression. "You kissed him?"

I roll my eyes. "I meant the other stuff."

She shrugs and signs back. "There wasn't a hint of deceit in anything he said. Except the fact that he just wants to be friends," she smirks. "He wants to get in your pants."

Sometimes it helps to have a best friend that's a supernatural lie detector. "Thank you for doing that."

I can see the discomfort cross her expression before she exhales. "Tristan is right. Regardless of the reason, or his age, he is your professor. And our roommate. I know you, Ser. I know his gentle rejection was taken as a challenge, but I think you should sit this one out. His dad is tied to your clan. The *royal* family. Nothing good can come of this."

I glance down the hall to where I left Tristan. All my life, I've wanted something more than just to be the next heir to the protector throne. I've wanted to stand on my own. To escape the shadows of the London clan legacy.

Suddenly, Gage Gallagher's son's presence in my life doesn't seem so infuriating, or strange. It feels predestined. Maybe it's fate. Maybe Tristan is the answer to my silent prayers. It's no secret that Gage has a strained relationship with my clan and race. I've seen and felt it for myself. It's a tension that I just might be able to leverage in order to get what I want: freedom.

I bite my lip in contemplation. Whether he knows it or not, Tristan just became my tunnel of light through the darkness. My way out.

Regardless of his words, which say one thing, his eyes say something else. It's a good thing I love a challenge, because Tristan Gallagher just became the ultimate prize.

No doubt, his presence in my life will upset my family. If they assume we're together, they'll stop at nothing to put an end to the relationship, offering me anything. Maybe I can negotiate my way out of this fate they have planned for me. Change it. Rewrite history.

Maybe I can claim my life as my own, in exchange for letting Tristan go. Easily done.

Magali snaps her fingers in front of my face, returning my attention to her. "Whatever it is you are conjuring up in that crazy-ass mind of yours, stop." She throws me a stern look. "It's only going to get both of you into trouble."

I smile and give her an innocent look, because that is exactly what I'm hoping for.

She frowns. "I'm tired. It's late and I'm going to bed. We have training in the morning. Don't be late."

"Am I ever?" I tease, which earns me a door slammed in my face because, yes, I am always late.

Once I'm tucked into my own bed, I strategize. There's nothing that would tarnish the London clan's royal legacy more than one of their own falling for the son of Gage Gallagher. He's considered a traitor among our race.

"Control of my life, in exchange for walking away from him. I've got this," I whisper into the darkness of my room.

I pull the covers up under my chin and close my eyes. Tristan's destiny is about to become one with mine.

EIGHT
FIRST DEFEAT

SERENA

THE SUITE HAS BEEN QUIET SINCE I woke up more than an hour ago. Normally, I don't want to get out of bed or go to class.

Today, though, is different. A game changer.

To my surprise, Tristan had already left this morning before I got up, which forced me to rework my strategy.

After stalking him on the Academy's website, I discovered that not only is he teaching Protector History, but he's also one of the hand-to-hand training instructors.

My instructor.

Ready to put my scheme into action, I'm showered, dressed, and currently trying to figure out the high-tech coffeemaker that Magali brought into our world.

I'm cursing loudly when she comes out, rubbing her sleepy eyes. Mags's hair is a mess, and her pajamas are completely askew. When she sees me, her eyes widen and she looks around the suite in shock that I'm up before her.

"Good morning!" I chirp brightly.

Her eyes narrow. "What's going on?" her fingers fly.

I wave her off and turn back to the spaceship currently holding my caffeine hostage. "How do I use this thing?"

Slowly she walks into our kitchen and presses a few buttons. Like a miracle, it comes to life and the smell of fresh coffee fills the air. I hug her and she tenses under my unexpected affection before pulling away.

"Did I miss training?" She asks with a nervous look.

I shake my head. "No, I was just up early today."

A frown crosses her lips. "Why?" she mouths.

I pull mugs out of the cabinet and fill them, adding a small splash of cream to each, and then hand one to my roommate. "It's training day." I smile brightly.

Her eyes roam over me before she places her cup down, freeing her hands. "Why are you dressed like that?"

I look down at the tight, white tank top and extra-short black spandex shorts I'm wearing. Normally when I train, I wear oversized T-shirts and bulky sweatpants.

Today, I'm looking to throw Tristan off balance, make him uncomfortable. Hence the small, revealing workout outfit. I'm hoping he won't be able to focus . . . except on me.

"It's comfortable," I explain, with a gleam in my eye.

Mags takes in my appearance one more time. She knows the outfit isn't even close to being comfortable and I hate it.

"I'm going to shower. Honestly, Ser, I don't want to know." She gives me an eye-roll before leaving. Magali knows that if she makes Tristan too off-limits, in my eyes it will just make me try that much harder with him.

An hour later, we're dodging the torrential rain as we make our way to one of the training centers. Once in the gym, I take in my appearance in one of the mirrored walls.

By the grace.

I am the complete opposite of attractive at the moment. My white tank is soaked. I sigh at myself and fold my arms over my chest. I'm not shy about my body, but having my nipples stand at attention to salute the entire training class isn't ideal.

Me and my stupid ideas.

Water creeps down my limbs and I try to fight off the goosebumps from the room's chilly air against my skin.

My hair is drenched and dripping with beads of water, causing it to stick to my face in an unattractive way.

To top it all off, my mascara was not waterproof. So now I have dark circles under my eyes and ridiculous black lines running down my face.

Lovely.

I exhale. This isn't how I meant this to work out today. I'm a hot soaking-wet mess.

Upon seeing me, Ethan's eyes widen in surprise before he quickly stands and grabs two towels, coming to our rescue. He hands one to Magali, who, by the way, looks like as if she's just stepped out of a photo shoot where they lightly spritzed her with water so she glistens and glows.

Noticing I'm scowling at her, she holds up her oversized hooded sweatshirt and shakes it at me, as if her *told you so* expression wasn't clear enough, before storming off to stretch next to Ethan's boyfriend.

Sometimes, I hate how perfect she is.

Ethan turns to me and gently attempts to wipe the black marks off my face. It's futile; this stuff is caked on.

"Why do I get the feeling that this is your something stupid for the day, Serena?" He grins.

My chest rises with my deep intake of breath.

"I only get one?" He's right, this was stupid.

After a few wipes, Ethan gives up and hands me the towel, which I use to squeeze the excess water from my hair.

He dips his head, trying to get me to look him in the eye.

"Penny for your thoughts, Princess?" his voice soft.

Ethan is the only breathing creature allowed to call me Princess— and get away with it. For whatever reason, when he says it, it doesn't sound like a sentence, but rather a brotherly term of endearment.

I glance up and open my mouth to spill everything to him about my brilliant-stupid plan, but the doors to the gym open and in walks the reason I look like a drowned raccoon. My friend's eyes follow mine straight to Tristan.

"I'm not sure I should be telling you this," he pauses for a moment, then turns back to face me. "If I wasn't with Lucas, and Tristan was into me, I would jump on him in front of everyone in this room, claiming him as mine."

An awkward tension-relieved laugh falls out of me.

"No seriously, Ser. Instructor or not, he's fucking hot."

I shake my head in amusement and lift my gaze to find Tristan standing in the middle of the gym, watching us. He's flanked by a few other trainers, causing the other protectors in the room to fall silently into submission.

Tristan oozes confidence and self-assuredness. It radiates off of him in waves. He commands the room because he knows whatever he's bringing to the table is a million times better than what anyone else has to offer.

It's sexy. And infuriating. But mostly, sexy.

My skin heats when his eyebrows dip over his cognac-colored gaze. Tristan's lips part as he takes me in.

The thin, wet material of my tank top allows my chest to be on full display for him, and all of a sudden, my plan seems really, really, really stupid. Yet, I don't shy away.

A flash of understanding crosses his features, and a wicked grin turns his mouth up at the corners. He's accepted my challenge and it's *game on*.

Instantly my humiliation is replaced with dread.

"Everyone outside," Tristan shouts.

I frown at his words and look around, confused.

"What?" Lucas speaks up.

"We're training outside today," Tristan replies, bored.

"In the rain?" Ethan interjects before looking at me.

Yeah, this would be my fault.

Tristan pulls his head back, his face morphing into a fierce scowl. That's when I notice his jaw twitching under his scruff. "That a problem?"

Silence.

"Good. Everyone out," he bellows.

I watch everyone get up and make their way to the doors. Magali looks at me sympathetically before handing me her sweatshirt, which I decline.

I don't want her to be wet and cold because of my asinine decisions. She hesitates, but after a brief standoff becomes convinced I won't budge.

Angrily, she storms past me with the rest of the group.

"Serena, you might want to put something on," Tristan suggests in a quiet tone, when it's just him and me left.

"It's just a little rain, Professor," I flirt. "Afraid I'll melt?"

A warm smile crosses his lips as he leans into my personal space. His lips are a breath from mine, taking away all the air around me, so I can't breathe.

God, he smells divine.

"I know how much you like the rain," his tone is low and seductive. "I also know how much I like seeing you wet."

My stomach clenches at his words.

"Then enjoy the eyeful," I reply, throwing the makeup-stained towel down, and with all the self-assurance I can muster, I turn and sway toward the double doors.

Into the rainfall.

With Tristan's voice following me.

"Bring it, raindrop."

TRISTAN

I'M NOT LIKE ANY OF THE training instructors these protectors have ever had before. The others were royal guards, or gargoyles who successfully completed several divine assignments and now prefer to shape the next generation.

I'm not either of those things. I'm here for one reason, and one reason only: to make sure their future queen is prepared.

In her dossier, I read that Serena's father was concerned that her hand-to-hand combat skills were lacking—his specialty. While Serena has been at the top of her training classes, hand-to-hand has always held her back. As I understand it, she prefers to use her powers over her natural strength. This will turn into a serious weakness if she doesn't stop being defiant about using them.

As the other trainers take their places behind me, I look around at the group staring at me. They have no idea what they're in for. I respect them, though. They're warriors waiting to fight, to be called upon. They are without fear.

All except Serena. She's in the back of the group, her eyes closed and her hands out, soaking in the elements, no doubt strategizing how she'll use the weather to her advantage.

This is what I need to put an end to. Through our bond, I sync my breathing and heartbeat with hers. Ignoring her emotions, I focus on her in order to put up a mental barrier, so she can't source and enhance her gifts.

Confusion falls over her face as she looks around, trying to find the reason she can't pull in and absorb the elements. *Good*, she can't sense the bond, or my interference.

"That's right, raindrop, I blocked you." I mumble.

Ethan's head darts up and I scold myself, realizing too late that I was not quiet enough to escape his heightened hearing. I keep forgetting that I'm not among my kind, but instead among those who share the protector blood that runs through my veins. Evading Ethan's questioning glares, I continue on my mission to scare the crap out of the sentinels in front of me.

"How much do you all remember from previous training?" I bark into the downpour.

"Everything," a few students cockily reply in unison.

"I want you to forget it all," I order, and wait as the protectors look around, baffled. "You are here because each of you lacks the ability to properly execute hand-to-hand combat. Over the past two years, your training scores have become low enough that you're all in jeopardy of not being assigned," I state in a military tone. "Or graduating."

My eyes shift over the shocked expressions of the group, landing on Serena, who apparently couldn't care less about my declaration. She continues to stare off into the distance through the black junk around her eyes. Oddly, it makes the blue even more alluring and deep.

Sensing my gaze on her, her focus shifts, meeting mine. I drop my stare, immediately wishing I hadn't.

Her soaked spandex clings to her like a second skin, highlighting every curve of her body. It seems an abnormal fashion choice for her. I'm hoping she lost a bet and this isn't standard training attire for her. Otherwise, I'm screwed.

A flashback of our first encounter hits me—Serena standing in the rain, naked. I squeeze my eyes closed.

"SERENA!" I shout, losing control of my actions.

It's not until I meet her wide-eyed stare that I realize I'd yelled her name out loud, unintentionally.

"Tell me what you know about hand-to-hand fighting," I command, quickly catching my misstep and ignoring the stares of the other beings surrounding us.

"Um . . . it's an offensive drill, using kicking and punching." She replies, confused at having been singled out.

"That's non-lethal. Tell me about lethal," I probe.

"It can encompass striking weapons used for grappling, like knives, sticks, and improvised weapons. Participants engage in combatant behavior. Given a protector's powers, it seems a bit barbaric and old school to me, wouldn't you agree, Professor?" she questions.

I don't miss the taunt in her tone. "It's the most ancient form of fighting known, so yes, it's *old school.*" My eyes leave hers and focus on the rest of the protectors. "The main focus of your training will be KAPAP-based. We'll up your physical endurance, elevate and strengthen your spiritual connection to your supernatural gifts, and develop your defensive and offensive skill sets through cold weapon usage. You will leave here bruised. Battered. Tired. And most of all, with a superior skill set. Any questions?"

The group is quiet as they ponder my words. This isn't going to be an easy class for them. I'm here to make sure they pass. Training them will be as effortless as breathing.

My gaze collides with Zander's. I'm grateful he's agreed to help me. For years, we've been charged with training my mother's army. He's the only other being I trust with my existence, and this assignment. Zander may not be a protector, but in our world, he's a respected general. If anyone can help me shape up these protectors in record time, it's him.

"The instructors before you have been personally hand-picked by me. Only two of us have gargoyle blood running through our veins. In order to properly protect a charge, you'll need to train with other supernatural beings. Acquire a sense of how they fight. Move. Think," I state. "You'll train in rotation, switching every two weeks. In this first cycle, I'll allow you to pick the instructor of your choosing. Decide wisely—you'll be ranked based on this initial round of instruction. Those with the highest scores will remain in class. Those who fall short will be shown the door."

"Wait, you'll kick us out if we rank low?" I'm asked.

"Yes."

"We won't graduate," the same protector points out.

"I suggest you rank high then," I reply, uncaring.

My statement is met with annoyed murmurs.

"Let me introduce you to this semester's trainers," I continue, ignoring their displeasure. "First up is Zander. By now, I'm sure you've sensed he is a satyr."

I watch recognition fall across Serena's expression.

"Zander is second in command of the Woodland Nymph Royal Guard, appointed by Her Majesty, the Queen. He also happens to be royalty, a nymph prince," I announce.

Most supernatural beings tend to look down upon nymphs as pure-ly sexual creatures, using them for their own physical needs and then discarding them when they're done. Regardless of his nymph blood, Zander is a prince in the supernatural world. They're required to respect him.

Zander tips his chin to the class before his eyes land on Serena. "Nice to see you again, champ," he winks.

She offers a shy smirk back.

I motion toward the two vampires beside me. "This is Atieno, prince of the vampire world and Lord Valentin's son. Also, his newly changed mate, Princess Vega." I take another step down the line. "This beautiful lady is Sorceress Eleyna." I smile at her and continue. "Most of you know Gabriel, since he was your instructor last year for weapons training." The gargoyle nods to the group.

Suddenly, the students' eyes widen as they notice the final training instructor in line that I approach.

I turn to face the group. "Demon training is essential when you protect charges against the dark army. We're grateful to have Charles, head of the Cambion Society, to assist us with your instruction this semester."

The energy buzzing around the class drops and feels different; it's full of shadows and quiet.

They're nervous.

"These are your instructors. Regardless of their background, you will show them respect. Take what they have to offer as a gift. Learn. Train. Become better," I bark. "Step forward in front of the trainer you'd like to work with this cycle," I encourage and step aside, waiting.

Whom a protector picks, of their own accord, will show the in-structors what type of warrior they will be.

My gaze slides to Charles. Most of the protectors won't pick the cambion, mainly because he's half demon and half human. It's unfor-tunate, because those who have the balls to work with him will get the most out of their training.

Within seconds, half of the females, and a handful of the males in the class gravitate to my good-looking best friend, including Magali. I smirk. They can't help the pull. He is a male nymph after all, designed to allure and seduce.

It's in his blood.

I know Zander will take good care of Serena's best friend and that's important to me, so I interject and assign Magali and a male student to him. The smile on Zander's face as he takes Magali's hand lets me know he's pleased.

Given his current situation, I throw him a warning look that says she's a student only. Displeased at the reminder, he grunts and then nods in agreement.

As the remainder of the class pairs off with each supernatural be-ing, I notice Serena just sits back, watching.

Catching my gaze, she steps forward. Never breaking her eye con-tact with me, she stands in front of Charles.

Interesting.

"I pick you," she says.

He smirks at her, before extending a cordial hand. She takes it with-out hesitation and I'm hit with an unexpected jolt of pride that she's not afraid of him. A half-demon.

"Your Highness, it's an honor," Charles states.

Serena bristles and pulls her hand back. "It's Serena."

Charles scans her expression with a glint of something, maybe amusement, in his eyes. "Serena," he dips his chin.

"I'm Ethan," her friend says, stepping next to her.

"Nice to have you both on my circuit this week," he responds in a polite tone.

Once everyone is paired, I continue.

"You'll never be able to really protect a charge if you don't hone your skills," I state, cracking my neck. "Isn't that correct, Charles?"

"True. Demons use their strength when they attack, but they can also use elemental magic," he adds. "They can be extremely strong, de-pending on their level of demon blood. There's one thing you should never do," he throws out.

"What's that?" Ethan questions.

"Dismiss a half-blood as a weaker, inferior demon," Charles says, lips twitching before he lunges for the gargoyle, laying a swift kick to his abdomen.

Ethan doubles over, half surprised, half in pain.

"Looks like these pathetic excuses for guardians need a lesson in speed," Charles taunts.

I hold back a laugh. "Protectors, thanks to Ethan, your asses are running today. We'll tell you when to stop."

We're going on ten miles. The soggy air pierces my lungs as I slow my speed to match the gargoyles behind me.

Serena picks up her pace, working her muscles harder than she should be, but keeps doing it so she's beside me.

"What's with all the running? I realize the importance of stamina, but shouldn't we be moving on to something a little more physical?" she wheezes out, in uneven breaths.

"My job is to prepare you to defend and fight the darkest supernatural creatures in existence, right?" I ask.

"Yeah," she exhales.

"So tell me, suppose Rulf isn't around. It's clear that you don't have the gift of teleportation. What if your powers aren't able to be sourced and weapon combat isn't an option? How do you not get yourself killed right away?"

She drags her gaze away, shrugging. "I suppose that it would depend on whom I have to fight off."

I stop running, which causes the rest of the group behind me to stop as well. Most of the students collapse onto the wet grass, happy with finally being able to rest.

"Me," I state.

"Is this a trick question?" she scoffs.

"I'm serious. How would you resist me?"

She looks at me, opening and closing her mouth.

"That's what I thought. How about this," I motion to an open area. "Show me what levels you're fighting at," I suggest. "That will determine your future running time."

"You want me to fight you?" she questions.

I don't answer her. Instead, I take off my soaked shirt, along with my leather rope, which has my insignia dangling from it, tossing both to the ground.

Turning to face her, I wait for her to approach me.

"The guy is a god," I hear Ethan whisper to Lucas.

"Exaggerate much?" Lucas snorts.

"I'm serious. I saw him earlier with a training class. He's all broody and rough, but when he fights . . . holy shit."

Serena stares at me a moment, and then nods. "Okay."

"I look forward to seeing you take a fall, raindrop."

Her lips twitch as she fights a grin.

"That so, Professor?"

"That. Is. So."

"I'll never fall for you, Tristan."

Ignoring the double meaning in her words, my gaze drops, locking onto her wet shirt. Maybe this wasn't the smartest idea I've had all day.

I turn and address the exhausted class.

"The key is to never let another being take you down. If it does happen, you need to fight and get back up, got it?" I state, while the other trainers and class watch, fascinated.

"I know how to take a fall," Serena states, annoyed.

"Do you?" I counter.

An awkward moment passes between us.

"Yes. And I can even pick myself up, too. I'm a big girl."

In an instant, I have her pinned on the wet grass beneath me. I study her expression as she lays there in complete shock. Offering her a lopsided grin, I try to ignore the way her warm, soft body feels under mine.

"I thought you knew how to take a fall, raindrop?"

"Get. Off. Me!" She snaps angrily.

"Make me."

She rolls her hips, keeping her chin down, but it does no good. I'm stronger and have her secured. Ticked off that she can't get out from under me, she scowls and pulls in energy.

"Stop sourcing the elements!" I demand, pushing her body further into the soaked earth. "No gifts. Protect yourself from me," I encourage. "Hand to hand, Serena."

She groans, and I tighten my grip on her wrists.

"Even without a warning, you have a second before you fall. That is enough time to strategize how to get back up and position yourself correctly to do so. Now, get up."

"I can't," she bites out.

"You can," I implore.

Her eyes are heated and her body becomes slack as she swallows hard. "You've officially taken me down, Tristan."

For some odd reason, her words hit me hard, as if there is hidden meaning behind them.

"You let me," I accuse.

My gaze roams across her, and I release the hold I have on her, stand and extend a hand to help her up.

Angrily, she slaps it away and, after a few attempts, manages to stand on her own two feet, holding her side.

I lean into her space. "You knew what to do, Serena."

Aside from Ryker, no other protector at the Academy has ever pinned her. The fact that I did—it was too easy.

Either she truly wasn't prepared, or she allowed it.

"Yeah? Then tell me, Tristan, how should I have protected myself from you?" she asks, in an outraged bark.

I look at her and don't blink. "You run."

NINE
RECKLESS ABANDONMENT

SERENA

FEELING HOSTILE, I REPRESS THE URGE to seek Tristan out and throw something at him. Or punch him in his perfect jaw.

"*You run,*" I mock his words. "Asshat."

Sighing, I take a pull from the beer bottle sweating in my hand. The hops soothe my beat-up pride.

After training, I returned to the suite, forgoing the rest of my classes. I'm exhausted and my side hurts. Carefully, I reposition myself in the empty bathtub.

Having a protector take me down that quickly was a first for me, or second if you count Ryker's previous victory.

Before I could make contact, Tristan had come at me at a ridiculously high speed. In one deft motion, he grabbed me like I weighed nothing and threw me to the ground, pinning me there, and bruising my side in the process.

The sting of defeat claws inside my veins, making its way up my throat. I swallow the bile, and blame Tristan and his beautiful distracting chest.

What business did he have taking off his shirt anyway? Clearly he did it as a distraction. One that worked.

I stare at the faucet, mouth slack. I had every intention of coming home and sinking into a warm bath. Instead, here I sit. The cold, hard ceramic is doing nothing to relieve my bruised ego. Even worse, I'm still in my ridiculous training outfit. The caked-on black makeup is now fading slightly as I sulk in my own self-deprecation.

Closing my eyes, I try to allow my body to relax so it can heal itself. Instead, my relaxation is interrupted by a vision of cognac eyes looking levelly into mine, while strong warm hands hold my wrists down on the wet grass and a hard body covers mine.

Our conversation replays itself over and over. After the fifth time, it occurs to me that Tristan's words carried a deeper meaning than simply an instructional moment.

I groan and shift. My whole body aches. Between the miles of running and the ass-kicking from Tristan, I'm beat. A shiver runs over me, remembering the rough skin of his fingers as he clutched my wrists, his face hovering inches from my own, his lips a breath from mine. I rub one of my eyes to try and pull myself out of the moment, my palm coming away smeared with black eye makeup.

"Fantastic," I pout.

"Rough day?" Tristan asks from the doorway.

I jump, startled at his deep, calm voice.

My eyes seek him out, and his piercing stare renders me speechless. Holding my breath, I study him for a moment.

"I'm in the tub," I state, when I come to my senses.

Little lines appear between his brows. "I can see that."

I narrow my eyes. "Privacy would be appreciated."

A muscle in his jaw twitches. "The door was wide open."

An unhappy sigh escapes me. "An oversight."

Tristan stands there, his gaze lingering on my legs, then slowly moving up before landing on my face.

A look of desire clouds over his eyes.

"There isn't any water."

I pin him with a hard glare.

"And you're dressed," he adds.

"Your penchant for stating the obvious is mind-blowing."

"I think you're also missing bubbles," he goes on.

"I'm not a bubble-bath kind of girl."

Tristan takes a few steps into the bathroom. With a predatory smirk, he crouches by the side of the tub, curling his hands around the sides.

His lips are less than an inch from mine.

"What kind of girl are you, Serena?"

Why does it feel like all our conversations have hidden meanings? He waits me out while I fuss with the label on the bottle, peeling it to reveal the glass underneath.

"The kind who doesn't like getting her ass kicked," I pause, placing the bottle on the tile floor, "by you."

Without another word, Tristan yanks a fluffy hand towel off the rack next to us and turns on the warm water.

Quietly, he wets and soaps it before shutting off the faucet and leaning close to me. With a slow and steady hand, he gently begins to wipe the dark lines off my face.

"What is this shit?" he asks, his voice raspy.

"Mascara," I whisper.

His brow wrinkles.

"Makeup," I add, unsure why he's asking.

He continues to wash it off. "I'm no expert, but I think it's supposed to go on your eyelashes."

"Another excellent observation," I counter.

"Why is it all over your face?"

"The rain." I respond, in a quiet murmur.

"The rain?"

"It's not waterproof," I explain.

"Then why are you wearing it?" Another swipe and he leans back, taking me in, before throwing the wet, stained towel on the floor. "Why, Serena?" he prompts.

I offer a shrug. "I was trying to seduce you."

His eyes travel over my body. "Yeah?"

I stare at him. "Did it work?"

He smirks. "Nope."

My gaze is locked onto him. "Damn."

A dark and burning look crosses his eyes, sending a shiver of fear and anticipation down my back.

"You might want to look into a different hobby."

I swallow. "A different hobby would be a shame."

"Yeah?" he whispers. "Why's that?"

"I thought I was just getting the hang of this one."

Another frown causes me to take in his perplexed face.

His hair is falling into his eyes, begging for me to sweep it to the side. Without thinking, I lift my hand and move the pieces, my fingertips grazing his forehead.

At the contact, Tristan hisses through his teeth, causing me to pull my hand back. But before I can, Tristan's fingers wrap around my wrist, holding me in place.

"Why are you sitting in the tub, Serena?" he asks.

"You bruised my ego. And my side," I admit.

"It's the first defeat, not the second, that cuts a protector to the bone," he says in a gruff voice. "Ryker took you down once before. You're a royal protector, a skilled warrior. Why did you let me knock you down today?"

"I didn't let you," my voice is unsteady.

"You did."

"You took me by surprise," I accuse, "and threw me to the ground. It was a fair hit. And it hurt." I shift painfully.

His focus dips to my side.

"You should focus more on training and less on me."

"You distracted me," I snip.

"Distractions will get you killed, Princess."

I gape at him and release my anger at the use of the royal term I despise. "Then stop being one, Tristan!"

"Today had nothing to do with me." His tone is a warning.

"It had everything to do with you!" I try to pull my wrist out of his grasp, but he tightens his hold.

"Didn't your clan ever teach you that revealing a weakness is a sure way to bring about your death?" he barks.

I stiffen. "You waltzed into my life and turned it upside down. Not the other way around." I release an awkward laugh. "I mean, by the grace, there are days that I don't even think I really like you very much." I exhale a shaky breath.

"But?"

"But, then you kissed me."

"You kissed me first," he counters.

"Yeah. I did. Want to know the sad part? You're the one hiding secrets and a past—I mean, we've lived under the same roof for a whole week and I don't even really know you. Yet, I feel like I can't breathe without you. You're like an addiction, and I'm an addict in need of a fix. So when you go and take off your shirt, and look all . . . Of course I would be distracted. What being with eyes wouldn't?"

Tristan watches my outburst calmly, with no change in his expression. He simply beckons me forward, as if I hadn't said anything at all.

Suddenly, his free hand is at the base of my throat, feeling my pulse. I don't flinch, because now I know he's using his empathy gift, trying to get a handle on my erratic emotions. The hand wrapped around my wrist moves mine to his face, pressing my palm flat against his rough cheek.

Slowly, he leans forward, creating our own personal space, where it's just us. Nothing else.

His breath falls in waves across my lips and weirdly, I can feel our heartbeats sync, becoming as one.

A warmth floats through me, making its way down to my side, healing me.

"You healed me? How did you do that?" I whisper.

"Magic," he replies in a quiet whisper.

The tingling in my side grows. Only bonded protectors can heal one another, and yet, here he is, doing it.

Without thinking, I move forward the slightest bit, so that my lips brush his. That small amount of contact causes a fire to suddenly explode in both of us, and within seconds, our mouths are molded together in an all-consuming manner.

Tristan's hand on my throat wraps around my neck and pulls me closer to him. My fingers slip into his hair and press him to me, hard. In one smooth move, I'm out of the tub and straddling his lap.

The coolness of his rings pressing against my back, underneath the hem of my shirt, is a welcome sensation against my heated skin. Every nerve ending in my body is on fire as his hands glide down to my ass, squeezing and holding me to him, encouraging me to rock against him.

All rational thought escapes me, as one of his hands runs over my body and hooks in the front of my tank top, pushing the material down to expose my breast.

His lips assault my mouth, then move to my neck, sucking and biting their way across my skin as I continue to rock against his denim-covered lap without shame.

The minute his mouth latches on to my nipple, I buck against him, throwing my head back with a load moan. My insides clench and unclench, and my core tightens with need, while he expertly sucks and teases.

I release my grip on his soft strands and wrap my hands around his wrists. The leather of his bracelets is rough and smooth at the same time under my palms, fueling my need.

Tristan's warm, wet tongue slides over the flesh of my breast, which seems to have a direct line to my core. Each stroke is a sweet, painful torture that I never want to end.

"I want you," I moan.

At the release of those three words, Tristan slows down. My insides quiver at the intensity of his gaze when his lust-clouded eyes meet mine. Pushing both hands into my hair, he pulls my forehead to his, just as I bring my fingertips to my lips. I try to swallow my disappointment that he stopped.

"I'm not what you want, Serena. Your emotions are heightened right now. Your judgment is clouded."

"You are," I attempt to convince him.

"The truth is, I'm no good for you."

"You don't know that." I stroke his jawline.

"You deserve better."

"Let me decide what I deserve, Tristan."

"I can't keep you." His voice is raspy and strained.

"I didn't ask you to."

Tristan closes his eyes and runs his nose across my jaw.

"We shouldn't be doing this," he whispers.

"I want to," I counter.

"Tell me to stop," he growls.

I search his eyes. "Don't stop."

In an instant, Tristan grabs the back of my neck and kisses me like he's making love to me with his mouth. His hard length pulsates through his jeans, between my legs.

This is neither sweet nor loving; it's hot and demanding.

Holy hell.

"Yes," I whisper.

I open my mouth to him and he sucks my lower lip into his, Tristan's tongue dancing across my mouth with a slow intensity—the kind that leaves you without air in your lungs and your thighs pressing together in search of more.

We pull away and I stare at his mouth as he speaks.

"Just remember, I'm the unhappy ending."

TRISTAN

I AM A SELFISH ASSHOLE BECAUSE in this moment, I need to be inside Serena more than I need to breathe. Looking at her naked form underneath me, I wait for her to tell me no.

To tell me to stop.

To tell me that letting me inside of her is a mistake.

To tell me that I will only bring her heartache and pain.

The minute she whispered yes, that was it. I'd like to think I'm gentleman enough to stop if she had said no, but the truth is, when it comes to her, I'm not. So here we are.

Between the feel of her soft, pale skin under my fingertips, her silky hair splayed across my pillow, and her flowery spring scent wrapping around me, I'm choking.

What the fuck am I doing?

My body is desperate, in a way I've never been before, as a frenzied sort of madness takes over my senses.

My nostrils flare as she rolls the condom on me. When she's done, she catches me staring at her lips and reaches out, grabbing my face and pulling me to her, so I have no choice but to stop thinking and slam my mouth against hers.

This time, my kiss is harder. Punishing. Because with each touch of her tongue, her lips, my defenses crumble.

I push the anger at my lack of control into every stroke and she meets me, kiss for kiss, moving her lips beneath mine. Not backing down.

A deep moan escapes from the back of my throat. Within seconds, everything else fades away. Powerless, I lose myself in the feel of her lips. It's just her and me. And the hunger and fire burning between us.

Trying to get control, I pull away. She whimpers in protest. Smirking, I kiss the corner of her mouth before trailing my lips over her collarbone, while my thumb rubs circles around her clit and my fingers run through her folds.

Serena releases a soft mewl and the sound becomes my addiction, a very, very bad one. My body hums with the primal urge to claim her, as the tension builds between us.

I move my hands away and without a second thought, push inside her, hard. Fast. Unromantic. Thoughtless.

"Fuck," I pant out.

She feels like heaven.

"Tristan," she gasps, my name a prayer on her lips.

My forehead drops to hers and I still, because my body is throbbing with a need that is unlike anything I've ever felt before. The heat radiating from within her is too much.

After a few trembling moments, I faintly hear her voice.

"Are you okay?" Serena asks, looking right into my eyes.

Her breathing is heavy and the weight of her gaze goes straight through me, penetrating each layer.

It's all too much.

Too personal.

Too emotional.

Which is why it needs to stop. All of it needs to stop.

Needing to break our connection, I pull out of her, flip her over onto her hands and knees, and shove into her from behind. She deserves better, and how I'm treating her kills me, but in the heat of this moment, it's all I can offer.

It's what I am.

"Yes," she moans, arching her back and pushing into me.

Fighting for control, I run my hand up her back, sending shivers across her skin. Squeezing the back of her neck, I force her to lift her head and arch even more as I move behind her. Each pump into her is more mind-numbingly perfect than the last. The need for relief has us both frantic.

The friction between us ignites the sparks in my core.

I lean over her, squeezing her neck harder, and with my other hand, reach down to rub her clit, sending her over the edge with a hard and fast orgasm that produces a scream.

A primal growl escapes my mouth as I grab her hips and slam into her a few more times before one final thrust has me releasing a guttural roar, while I pulsate long and hard.

It wasn't romantic.

It wasn't hearts and flowers.

But it also wasn't promises or lies.

Regardless, she just fucked me in more ways than one.

TEN

IT'S IN MY BLOOD

TRISTAN

T'S SILENT EXCEPT FOR THE CRACKLING and popping of the kindling fueling the roaring fire. I bring the bottle to my lips and tilt it back, swallowing with my eyes trained on the orange flames that climb higher and higher in the hearth.

A sharp hiss passes through my lips, a reaction from the sting of the alcohol as it slides down my throat. I take in a deep breath through the burn—a futile attempt to calm myself down because for some reason, the air won't stay in my lungs. I feel paralyzed, yet, at the same time, I'm coming off an adrenaline high after having slept with Serena.

What the hell was I thinking?

I keep trying to convince myself that it was just one time. That it's not a big deal. They're all lies, because when she looked at me, with her trusting eyes, I wanted to possess her. Own her. Claim her as my own.

The moment realization set in, I got dressed, and without a word or a backwards glance, left her in my bed. As foolish as it sounds, it was the right thing to do.

I sink further into the modern, black, leather sofa that wraps in an

L-shape around a granite coffee table. For a brief moment, I close my eyes and just exist.

The sound of expensive shoes on metal breaks through the silence. My eyelids open and my focus slides to the spiral staircase, leading to the second floor mezzanine.

With a swagger and air of cockiness that matches my own, the gargoyle dressed in all black makes his way down each stair, before coming to a standstill in front of the floor-to-ceiling windows that overlook Paris.

A lit cigarette hangs casually off his bottom lip, while the Eiffel Tower shadows his lean form. He looks me over before running a hand through his golden hair. I push away the idea that watching him is like looking into a mirror. We aren't the same, shared DNA or not.

After a moment of assessing the situation, the protector slides his hands into the front pockets of his dress pants and narrows his sea-green gaze at the bottle in my hand.

"I have crystal tumblers," he states, around his cigarette.

I take another swig directly from the Baccarat decanter.

A challenge.

He releases a disappointed sigh.

"That bottle of Louis XIII de Rémy Martin is meant to be sipped," he adds, as his right hand escapes his pocket, moving to his face and pinching the cigarette between his index finger and thumb. He removes it from his mouth before running his thumb over his bottom lip in contemplation. "What are you doing here, Tristan?"

"Ironically, I didn't have anywhere else to go," I reply.

His face is void of emotion. "What about Ophelia?"

At the sound of my mother's name, my eyes meet his defiantly. "She's busy with my *father*, Rionach."

My words are meant to be cutting. To hurt. But they don't. They don't penetrate his uncaring exterior.

Without flinching, Gage Gallagher saunters over to the bar, flicks his cigarette into the fire, and grabs two glasses.

He walks back and sets them on the table, pouring a small amount of the expensive top-shelf liquor into each.

Gage hands a glass to me and takes a seat in a chair across from me. Studying the amber liquid, he swirls it in his glass a few times before bringing it to his nose and inhaling deeply.

"Christ. This is awkward," he mutters into the drink.

"Yeah?" I ask sarcastically, eyeing him.

"It feels like only a few months ago I was protecting a divine secret. Suddenly, I have a twenty-two-year-old son."

I look around his concrete loft, avoiding his glare. "Nice place." Hematite, my protector stone, is embedded into everything. It must also be Gage's mineral. "It's not really kid-friendly. I could fall down the stairs, or put my fingers in the exposed electrical outlets." I point out.

"Then I suggest you don't do either." He waits me out, tossing the entire contents of his glass back in one swig. "How did you get in?" He places the tumbler on the coffee table, then sinks back into the chair.

"Teleported."

"Interesting," he replies in a murmur.

"A protector gift from you, *Dad*," I draw out the word.

He clears his throat. "I prefer Gage."

I lick my lips and lean my head back against the cushion. I'm not drunk enough for this conversation. Not even close.

The fire snaps and pops through the silence.

"I didn't know," he states in a flat tone, "about you."

"Would it have changed anything?" I ask, my focus trained on the oak beams running across the high ceilings.

"No." *Ouch.* I knew this, but his confession stings.

"Then why mention it?" I counter dryly.

"I owe you an explanation," his tone unremorseful.

My nostrils flare. "I'm too old to care that you used my mother to numb the inner turmoil the death of your true love and mate caused you." I level him with a cold glare.

Gage's eyes become hollow, his gaze distant. "First off, don't ever speak of Camilla. And second, given your *reputation*, I'm sure you can appreciate two beings losing themselves in one another in order to escape reality."

"There is no escaping reality. As queen, my mother knows this all too well. I have a feeling she was at a disadvantage when it came to your advances," I bite out.

"I didn't take advantage of Ophelia. We enjoyed each other's company for a brief moment in time. The End."

I snort, sit up, and place the glass on the table before flashing him a stern expression. His words are a reminder of what I just did. I guess being an asshole is part of the Gage Gallagher DNA strand. Needing to take my frustration out on something, I decide he's as good a punching bag as any.

"Except it wasn't the end, because I'm here." I counter.

"Yeah, well, shit happens, Tristan," he retorts. "As Ophelia explained it to me, you grew up with a mother, father and brother. You were loved and cared for. That's a better life than any I could have possibly offered you."

I refuse to acknowledge the scars and wounds etched deep in my psyche from growing up without him. Yeah, Rionach was always there, but I wasn't his blood.

"You're an asshole." My voice is gruff.

Gage's expression is clear and calm. "Says the protector hiding in my loft to avoid whatever it is that he's running away from. Then again, I'm not sure I care all that much."

"If you don't care, then why did you bother to help me after the royal court sentenced me?" I counter.

"Ophelia asked me to," he replies coolly.

"You expect me to believe the Queen of the Woodland Nymphs asked a traitor for help?" I ask. "As *I* understand it," I throw his words back at him, "you walked away from leading the Paris clan. From your race and friends. You turned your back on your protector oaths and loyalties."

A sour expression crosses his face. "Let's get one thing straight, Tristan. I expect nothing from you. We aren't friends. Hell, we aren't even acquaintances. We don't know one another. Where Ophelia—your mother—is concerned, believe anything you want. As for why I walked away from my clan, I have my reasons. They don't concern you. What should matter to you is your current reality."

"Which is?" I taunt.

"Like it or not, I am your father. Was I there? No. Would I have been? No. Does that make me an asshole? Yeah, I guess it does in your eyes. Maybe with time, we'll get to know one another, but right now, you need to focus on your assignment, which grants you the right to freedom. So, I'll ask you again, all bullshit aside, what are you doing here, Tristan?"

We stare at each other for a long, silent moment.

"I fucked up," I state.

His eyebrows dip low over his eyes in a fierce scowl as his gaze roams over me. After a moment, he pulls out a cigarette and offers a second one to me. I wave it off, watching as he lights his and sucks in the nicotine. I could really use one right now. More than breathing. But I refuse to take anything Gage offers directly to me.

"Lay it all out for me," he exhales the thick smoke.

"I took on this assignment on as a punishment exchange. That was supposed to be all," I begin. "It's becoming . . . more. I think she's becoming . . . more," I admit.

He releases a dark chuckle that feels like it's masking a hidden meaning. "Protector assignments are always more when there is a beautiful woman at the other end."

"I should have just let them sentence me. Though I can't believe the extent to which they decided to discipline me."

"You killed a royal protector. What'd you think would happen when the holier-than-thou London clan found out?"

"I killed an enemy who infiltrated my army. He was working for both the woodland guard and protectors."

"Regardless. You spilt royal protector blood and almost started a war within the supernatural world," his voice firm.

"What would you have suggested I do? Let him kill my mother?" I retort. "Our realm is already on the verge of war with the water dimension. Oren is out for blood this time."

Gage tilts his head to the side and considers me silently for a long moment. "Oren is a power-hungry twat. How he became the emperor of the water fairies is beyond me. That said, things are not always as they seem. You're impulsive and you act without thought. It's why you're in this position in the first place. Not everyone is your enemy."

"Oren is the enemy!" I shout.

"No. The only nemesis you have is yourself," he retorts.

I narrow my gaze. "Is that so, Gage? After two months, you think you know me well enough to know who my adversaries are? You don't come from *my* world. Or understand *my* race. Remember, I only share half my blood with you. You know nothing of our realm, so don't speak of, or take sides in, a war you have no understanding of."

Gage stands, rising to his full height. "I understand the darkness that lingers within the supernatural world better than you think. But my blood running through your veins is even darker. I may not be from your world, but I am a gargoyle, as are you. And right now, I'm the one you are indebted to for your continued existence. Not Ophelia."

I stand, too, and cross my arms.

"You want a thank you?" I snip.

"No. I want you to focus on your assignment. This oncoming war is larger than all of us. It's not just about the water and woodland realms falling. If the Diablo Fairies get hold of Serena, your entire existence as you know it will vanish, and none of the shit you're spewing will matter."

"Why do you care so much about her? You and the St. Michaels aren't exactly . . . close," I ask.

"I don't give a fuck about Serena. Or the gargoyle race."

I just stare, taken aback at his cold expression. "You know, I can't decide if you're the good guy, or the bad."

"I don't take sides, Tristan. My loyalty is to those I love. Dead or alive. You, though, are blood. Whether you live or die happens to matter to me. So for fuck's sake, stop thinking with your mother's lineage when it comes to Serena St. Michael, and start acting like a protector. Or your existence won't be the only one that will cease."

I huff. "You're going to educate me on how to be a protector? When you safeguard no one, or nothing."

"Untrue. I protect what's mine," he replies.

"I hope that includes me, Gallagher." A deep raspy voice infiltrates our conversation, coming from the petite woman descending the staircase and making her way toward us.

At the sound, Gage's body stiffens. She approaches him slowly, almost as if not to spook him, while pinning him in place with her wild emerald gaze.

"I believe we established that last night," Gage replies.

Her deep purple lips morph into a small smile.

An odd feeling floats through me.

I like the way she looks at Gage, like he's not broken.

She turns to me and holds her hand out.

"Nassa, sorceress of prosperity."

"Tristan," I announce, taking her soft hand in mine.

So this is the sorceress that my father has been on and off with for years. Theirs is a sordid, complicated tale. One in which I don't want to get involved. It's not my place.

I study the dark plum highlights strategically placed throughout her shiny raven hair. She's pretty, delicate even.

Not at all what I imagined her looking like.

She curls her black manicured nails around my hand firmly, pulling me closer as she searches my eyes. "Shit, Gallagher. He looks just like you," she exhales in awe.

I quickly yank my hand out of hers, causing her to stumble forward a bit before catching her footing.

Gage takes a slight step between us. If I didn't know any better, I would assume it was almost protective in nature.

His gaze narrows at me. "I suggest you not get emotionally involved with your charge," he warns. "It leaves you vulnerable. She isn't yours to play with, Tristan."

Nassa snorts. "That's the advice you're giving him?"

He looks back at her. "Don't get involved, buttercup."

Thwack.

The hard sound of the back of her hand meeting his ribs echoes around the concrete loft. She's tiny but she can hit.

"Christ! Stop slapping me." Gage rubs his side.

"I keep warning you that if you keep calling me that, I will continue to smack the shit out of you. Don't ever let it be said that I don't keep my word," she growls.

"I've been calling you that for years," he points out.

Nassa throws him an angry glare. I can't tell if it's playful or if she really is going to stab him one of these days.

Gage faces me. "This is what happens when you let your guard down," he motions to Nassa. "She's in love with me."

"You're an idiot," the sorceress snips at him.

I rub my palms over my face. "This has been . . . interesting, but I have somewhere other than here to be. Thanks for the hiding place . . . and unsolicited advice."

"The bad unsolicited advice," Nassa corrects.

"Tristan," Gage's voice deepens before I teleport. "It's not allowed. She isn't yours. Don't start a war over her."

I motion my chin toward Nassa and slide my gaze toward Gage. "Enjoy living in your happily ever after."

Gage scoffs. "I'm not the happily-ever-after guy."

Nassa's expression falls the slightest bit at his words.

In this moment, it truly sinks in.

I really am Gage's son.

In more ways than just a shared bloodline.

SERENA

THE MOON'S SILVER RAYS CUT THROUGH the window, leaving shadows on the walls. I eye the clock, hoping Tristan is enjoying his little outing, because when he walks through the door, I'm going to kill him for running out on me.

Was I expecting flowers and declarations of love? No. However, I certainly wasn't expecting to be left naked in his bed while he ran away to God only knows where.

The door opens, and I watch as Tristan quietly slides back in, placing his keys on the counter before stiffening. Sensing my presence, he slowly turns and faces me.

At the sight of him, my anger-filled rage takes over, and I flick two daggers at him. They embed themselves in the wooden door with a hard thud, one on each side of his head.

"Good to know that you can throw knives with precision and accuracy," he states, unfazed.

I watch as he yanks out the weapons from the wood. "It's a hobby of my Aunt Eve's. She taught me."

The air fills with electricity as Tristan moves around the room. His presence is suffocating, causing me to keep my focus on the two small holes the daggers left.

"I was curious as to how you'd handle this. I see you've decided to go the black widow route. How romantic of you."

I throw him an unfriendly smile.

"Are you implying that one misstep after sleeping with me can lead to a lethal end for you?" I ask in a light tone.

My words cause him to pause and become motionless. A moment later, he composes himself and walks over to me, holding out his hands and handing me back my weapons.

"We need to talk," he states.

My brow arches. "You sure you want to return these?"

"I'll take my chances."

He's silent as he waits for me to take them. I clasp my palms around the weapons, brushing his fingers in the process. Immediately, he jerks away, and in a stupid girlie moment, my feelings are hurt by the action.

While Tristan isn't exactly overflowing with welcome and warmth, he does wince and sigh at his response to me.

"Sorry," he offers.

"For what exactly? Having sex with me? Sneaking out and hiding after? Or flinching at my touch?" I tick off.

He blinks at me and clears his throat.

"All of it."

"You ran," I state.

"I did," he admits.

A silent beat passes between us before I speak.

"Where did you go?"

"Paris."

"Paris?" I repeat.

"I had some business to attend to."

I blow out an annoyed breath. Paris is where Gage lives. Did he see him? Why? Honestly, it's not my place to ask, and I fear if I push him, then I'll just piss him off even more.

"Serena," he begins. "It's not that I didn't enjoy your company, but as you've probably figured out, I don't do—I've never really learned how stay after—"

"Sex?" I cut him off.

He shifts uncomfortably. "Could you stop saying that?"

I huff out a sigh. "We're adults, Tristan. I'm not asking you to mate with me. Or be the love of my life." Every inch of him tenses. "We simply indulged in an impulsive moment, on both our parts. The End," I shrug. "It's done."

His forehead crinkles. "You deserve better than that."

I scoff. "Why? Because I'm royal blood? Would you be apologizing like this if I were a nymph?"

"I wouldn't have come back." Tristan's tone grows cold. "Nymphs are designed to be used for sexual pleasure. You deserve respect. Not to be used for selfish needs."

I ponder his words. "We used one another. There is no harm in that. What isn't okay is that you ran out on me."

Tristan's eyes are hard but soften at my words.

I place my daggers on the end table next to the oversized chair I'm sitting in, before standing and taking a few steps in his direction.

Once I'm directly in front of him, I bend down, and with my arms on either side of his body, cage him in on the couch. Then I lean in near his ear. "Next time, stay."

"There won't be a next time." He looks at my mouth.

"Is that a promise?" I ask.

"All I can promise you is the worst. I'll always let you down; that won't change. I won't change. Don't think you can fix me, or take the darkness away. You can't," he says.

I push away and cock my head to the side. "Okay, then."

"Serena." His tone is firm. "There won't be a next time."

A slight tingling sensation runs up my spine at the roughness in his voice. Unexpectedly, I'm hit with visions of all the dirty, sexy things I want him to do to me.

A smile falls across my lips. "If you say so."

"I do."

My gaze holds his, searching for truth in his words.

"Good night, Serena."

"Good night, Tristan."

ELEVEN
SECRETS REVEALED

SERENA

I TRY TO KEEP MY NERVOUS energy to a minimum. After all, she can smell fear from a mile away. Literally. I clear my throat and square my shoulders as Mags stares me down.

"Morning," I chirp brightly.

"I know." Her expression is flat.

"Know what?" I say dryly.

Her gaze lifts from the pancakes she's making.

She pins me with her *don't be stupid* look. "I warned you about this, Serena. On multiple occasions."

Busted.

I wince. "I can explain."

"I don't want an explanation," she shoots back harshly.

"Why are you so mad?" I ask, confused.

"Because I hate when you do this."

"I don't do *this* that often," I bite out.

Actually, never.

"Yes. You do. All the time," she argues, and steps around me, pulling a water bottle out of the fridge.

I turn slowly and face her. "It was a one-time thing, Magali. A momentary lack of self-discipline," I assure her. "One that I am fully regretting this morning. Trust me."

"What?" Her face scrunches. "Stop being dramatic."

"No really. Regrets all over the place. Not to mention the guilt and shame," I lie, trying to calm her down.

She twists the cap back onto her water bottle and sets it on the counter, furrowing her brows. "Serena—"

"Honestly, it was a huge mistake. Big. The biggest ever."

Magali tilts her head to the side. "What did you do?"

"I'm sorry, what?" I squeak out, not understanding.

"This can't just be about the towel," she signs.

"What towel?" I ask.

"The wet one you threw on the bathroom floor and left overnight. The one with your makeup smeared all over it. You know I hate that," she explains. "It ends up smelling all gross and moldy. How hard is it to hang it up to dry?"

Oh. The towel. Stupid. Stupid. Stupid, Serena.

"Right. Crap. Sorry. Yeah, the towel." I ramble.

Her gaze narrows, but before she can inquire further, the door to our suite opens and in walks Zander with Rulf behind him, pushing him farther into the space forcefully.

"This satyr belong to someone in here?" Rulf asks sternly. With one final push, he thrusts Zander toward me.

Magali smiles brightly. "He's mine."

"What?" Rulf and I say at the same time.

"He's here to see me," she clarifies.

A triumphant smile appears on Zander's face.

"I tried to tell him but he didn't believe me," he explains.

Magali shoots Rulf an annoyed expression.

"I invited him for breakfast."

Rulf raises an eyebrow. "That all you invited him for?"

"Of course," she retorts, with her hands flying wildly.

With a grunt, Rulf grabs a pancake off the plate and throws me an exasperated glare before leaving.

Zander stands in the middle of the room looking sheepish.

"Good morning, ladies," he greets, presenting to Magali a bunch of wild flowers that he was hiding behind his back.

I watch my best friend melt into a huge puddle of goo as she takes and sniffs them, then mouths a *thank you* to him.

She rarely mouths words unless she's extremely comfortable with you, so that in itself is curious.

"I didn't realize it was customary to bring your trainees flowers." I don't try to hide the sarcasm in my voice.

Zander looks at me and winks. "That's because you're training with a demon, and they have no manners," he jests.

"Half-demon." Tristan comes up behind me and I freeze.

Our gazes meet in the reflection off the microwave.

One look and suddenly, he's everywhere, taking up all the accessible air in the room. It's amazing how his mere presence immediately renders me stupid. I really need to learn to get my emotions under control around him.

Last night was no big deal.

I squeeze my eyes closed and remember the look in his, right before he freaked out and pulled out of me.

Like I was his everything.

With effort, I return my attention to Zander, but falter when I notice the playful light in his eyes has disappeared, as he watches Tristan and me closely.

Tristan steps forward to stand next to me, and I concentrate on breathing. Everything inside me tightens in response to his nearness. I look to Mags, who is filling a vase with water, oblivious to all the tension.

The side of Zander's mouth kicks up. "Speaking of instructors and trainees, what have you two been up to since we last saw one another?" His tone is light.

"None of your fucking business," Tristan retorts in a gruff voice, before smacking him on the back of his head.

Magali turns around just in time to see her guest get whacked. "Hey! No hitting at breakfast," she scolds.

I watch quietly as she grabs the plate of pancakes she whipped up and places it down in front of Zander, who's made himself comfortable on a stool at the counter.

Tristan takes the second seat, and I'm left standing while Mags places coffee, fruit, and bacon on the counter.

"How long have you two been friends?" I manage.

Zander's smile drops as he looks, confused, between me and Tristan. "Since childhood. Five or six, I guess?" his answers comes across more like a question than an answer.

"Us too," Magali beams, causing Zander to light up.

I turn my attention to Tristan.

He's watching Zander and Magali, with his lips turned down in an unhappy manner.

"That's a long time to befriend a *dangerous* male nymph," I tease, and instantly regret saying it when I see Tristan's face line with shadows.

"Nymphs are dangerous. Satyrs are not," he states.

"Why is that?" I prod.

"Nymphs have the ability to turn you mad. Satyrs just have the ability to bed you," he replies harshly.

The insinuation of his words causes a silence to fall and hang over all of us. Most beings within the supernatural world use nymphs for their own selfish needs, and then just discard them.

Magali and I were brought up differently. We were taught that every being has value, regardless of bloodlines and supernatural ties. With the exception of goblins; my uncle Asher and aunt Eve have this unnatural hatred of the little green creatures.

Magali knocks on the counter, gaining our attention.

"So you're a prince?" she asks Zander.

"I am," he dips his chin.

"That must be cool," she tries to end the unease.

He lifts a shoulder. "It has its moments. Mostly it's a lot of pomp and circumstance. Right, Tristan?"

We all swing our gazes to Tristan, who has fallen silent, his mind obviously somewhere else.

"How would Tristan know what that's like?" I question.

Once again, Zander throws me a curious glance.

"We're brothers," he replies. "Didn't he tell you that?"

I glance at Tristan and swallow. "Brothers?"

His eyes pierce mine before sliding to Magali.

He flinches, knowing he can't lie.

She'll sense it.

"Your mother is Queen Ophelia? Queen of the woodland nymphs?" My voice cracks, because all of a sudden my unmerited attraction to him makes complete sense.

His secondary bloodline is satyr, meant to seduce.

"Does that change your opinion of me, raindrop?" He waits for my answer. I swear he's holding his breath.

At my silence, Tristan's face falls.

Irritated at my lack of response, he stands, grabs his empty plate and steps around me.

His arm brushes mine ever so featherlightly, and every nerve in my body kick-starts at the brief contact.

I watch him throw the plate in the sink and turn back to me, leveling me with a harsh look.

No, it's not the satyr blood that draws me to him.

There's something else there, something deeper.

A darkness that calls to me.

One I can't shake, and it both excites and terrifies me.

TWELVE
PROMISES

TRISTAN

M Y GAZE STAYS LOCKED ONTO SERENA'S. I'm pissed that she thinks her attraction to me is because I'm half satyr. The fucked-up part of all this is that it's most likely the protector bond, the one she isn't aware of, that is the reason for our unnatural sudden pull and attraction.

I shouldn't have healed her last night, but she looked like she was uncomfortable and I couldn't help myself. The idea of her being in pain—pain that I caused—unsettles me. The shared connection I opened to restore her just sent us both into a clusterfuck of heated need.

Her eyes dart to her bracelet and she begins to run her fingers over the stones. The action causes anger to build in me, at the fact that I make her uneasy.

I'm suddenly seeing visions of Zander's face on the other side of my sword, for opening his big mouth.

Fuck, why do I even care?

"Well, does it?" I ask her again, keeping my voice from sounding angry at her reaction. Even so, my question came out as a hoarse whisper.

I'm finding that when it comes to Serena, I struggle. Her presence makes me both weak and strong. I hate it.

"It just caught me off guard. That's all," she replies.

I nod. "Right," I clip out.

My entire body is tense, and her answer does nothing to calm me. I inwardly groan at my interest.

Commotion outside the doorway pulls all of our attention to the other side of the room, as an uproar of voices become louder the closer they approach.

Without warning, the door swings open, and in walks Serena's dad, Callan, followed by Keegan, his eldest brother, and Asher, the current reigning king of the gargoyle race.

The St. Michael brothers' expressions are intimidating on the dark-haired, blue-eyed royal protectors that lead the London clan of gargoyles.

Within seconds, Rulf joins them, bringing up the rear.

"Dad?" Serena squeals, turning to face her family.

"Hey, pumpkin," Callan responds, approaching her before pulling her into his arms and kissing her on her temple. "You all right?" his eyes narrow at me over her head.

"Yes, of course. Why?" Serena asks.

"Abs has been trying to get a hold of you for a week. We're here to make sure you're still breathing," he gives her a toothy, megawatt smile. "I am begging you, call your mother, Serena. Often. Daily. Just . . . call," he exhales.

"I texted her," she argues.

Callan shakes his head. "Nope. Doesn't work. My girl is convinced that evil knows how to text. She needs to 'hear your voice.'" He rolls his eyes, obviously not agreeing with his mate's helicopter parenting style.

Serena's shoulders sag as she steps away from her dad.

"Do not make that frowny face at me," he warns, placing his hand over his heart, as if in pain.

Callan clearly adores his daughter and is wrapped around her finger. That makes two of us.

"I'll call," she exhales, and nods toward her uncles. "Why is *everyone* here?"

Callan shrugs. "It takes a village to raise a child."

"I'm a grown woman," she counters. "Not a child."

"No you aren't," Keegan states in a rough tone.

Her uncle Asher approaches Serena and drops a kiss to the top of her head. "We're just worried about you. That's all, Serena. We love you and care that you're safe, yeah?"

She nods her head in understanding.

"Who is this?" Callan's focus shifts to Zander.

"That is the breakfast satyr," Rulf interjects.

Callan's gaze roams over Magali and Serena. "Explain."

"I invited him for breakfast," Magali signs.

"What time did he arrive?" Keegan inquires.

"About an hour ago," Rulf replies.

"Is that your way of asking if he spent the night?" Asher asks, turning to his older brother.

Keegan shrugs. "I'm trying to be more . . . polite."

Asher dips his chin. "Polite looks good on you."

"No, it doesn't," Callan responds, looking at Zander. "These girls are not to be played with. One wrong move and I'll slit your throat." He pauses, holding his stern glare on Zander for a beat to make sure his words have sunk in. "Now, what type of hair product do you use? I like that your hair is styled but still appears soft."

Serena and Magali share a glance. I guess they're used to his erratic behavior.

"Aveda Men, the grooming clay. It's also the reason for the extra shine," Zander offers with a relaxed smile.

Callan nods. "I love the glossed look."

"DAD!" Serena pleads.

"What? He has great hair," Callan reasons with a smirk.

Ignoring the ruckus, I turn my attention to Callan's shirt. It reads: *I'm a dad. Mess with me and I'll lick your face.*

My brows pinch.

Callan notices the movement, and offers me a smirk.

"Licking is germy and gross. It's also unexpected," he says. "The element of surprise is a protector's best defense."

"O-Okay," I reply, unconvinced.

Serena looks between us nervously, her fingers toying with her bracelet again. "Tristan, this is my dad and my uncles," her voice is small, unsure. It's not like her. "Everyone, this is Tristan Gallagher— my . . . boyfriend."

Everything around me becomes still, as each one of my muscles tenses at her announcement.

I steal a quick glance at Zander, whose face is draining of all color, before I meet Serena's twinkling gaze.

What the fuck is she doing?

A slow burn makes its way into my chest. I've always been attracted to danger. Serena, though, is an entirely different kind of dangerous, because without her knowing it, what she just declared damned us both to hell.

I chance a look at Callan. He's speechless and pissed.

Again, that makes two of us.

"What?" I croak.

Serena takes a step toward me and I jerk back, crossing my arms. Now I'm giving her my own ticked-off look.

What is she up to?

A bright smile plays across her face, as if I've challenged her. Never in my life has someone dared to turn the odds against me. Until now. All of a sudden, my heart belongs completely to a girl with sapphire eyes and auburn hair.

"Trist," she coos, and I narrow my eyes at her use of the nickname. "I know you want to keep it a secret, but my family will understand. I swear," her voice is sickly sweet.

"Serena—" She stops me, placing her hand on my arm.

Her touch twists me. I feel the turn deep in my gut, like a slow, painful knife wound ready to bleed out. Hell, I feel it in my chest as my heart pounds in an out-of-control rhythm.

"The. Fuck?" I hear Asher roar.

Exactly my point. Well said.

In an instant he's advancing on me, and Zander is on his feet and in between us, protecting both Serena and me.

"Hold up, Your Highness. I'm sure this is just a simple misunderstanding," my best friend says.

"Serena, a moment," I snap, grabbing her by the elbow and dragging her aside in the most platonic way known to civilization. "What the hell are you doing?"

"Telling Dad about us," she beams.

"There is no us!" I all but yell at her.

She arches a brow. "That's not what you said last night."

I blink a few times, then squeeze my eyes shut.

The growl that escapes from Callan is low and deep. I'm certain it could be heard across all the realms in existence.

"Stop this!" I demand, reopening my lids.

"Stop what, schmoopie?" she smirks wickedly.

"I'm not your boyfriend." My tone is unkind.

"You and I are meant to be together. Suck it up."

Asher and Keegan share an irate look, and Callan shifts on his feet while patting himself down dramatically.

"What are you doing, Callan?" Keegan asks.

"Looking for my weapons. That way I can kill him," he answers, pointing at me in a strangely calm manner. "At the same time, I don't really want to get blood on my new shirt. Abs hates doing laundry. I guess I could just kick his ass."

"Serena, I think you should stop, yeah?" Asher suggests. "You're making your father crazy. More so than usual."

Serena whips around and faces her uncle. "I would have thought that you most of all would recognize true love when you see it. I'm disappointed in you, Uncle Asher."

Asher mopes in almost a pout, wounded by her words.

Callan's expression turns perplexed as he studies his daughter's face. "Do you have Stockholm syndrome?"

She sighs. "Dad, Tristan would have to be my captor."

"Are you saying the words coming out of your mouth are of your own accord?" Callan frowns. "You're not being coerced in some weird form or another? Enthralled?"

"Nope. I have freely given my heart to him."

"Fuck it! I can do my own laundry," Callan states, and Keegan quickly grabs his upper arms, holding him back.

"Serena, this behavior is . . . sudden," Asher scolds.

"Dude, let me take care of this," Callan implores.

"Why you?" Asher shoots back, annoyed.

"I'm her Dad." He points to his shirt. "It's my job."

Asher snorts. "I'm the king. My word can be final without her rolling her eyes at me. Or getting whiny."

"Now you want to be the king?" Keegan mocks.

Asher throws a hard glare his way.

"Callan's a wimp when it comes to the pouty face she always makes," Asher continues. "One tear and she's at an all-you-can-eat candy buffet. Then puking all night."

"That's true," Keegan agrees.

Callan grimaces. "Dude, one time—when she was two."

Magali steps between us, facing Serena, her hands flying quickly through the air as she signs with annoyance.

"What are you doing, Ser?"

"I chose him," Serena's voice is void of emotion.

Believable? No.

Totally convincing? No.

I'm going to kill her.

I rub my hands over my face with Serena watching.

Magali picks up on her lie and shakes her head no.

Letting her friend see that that she knows better.

"You can't help whom you fall in love with." Her mouth keeps moving but the words coming out aren't registering as making sense. "Or so I've been told, recently."

Callan stands frozen, speechless.

Asher approaches Serena's back and Magali moves to her friend's side so her uncle can get closer to her.

Serena's eyes follow my uneasy movements as I brace myself, preparing for what I know he's about to tell her.

"Tristan is your protector," Asher states in a firm tone.

Blood in my ears is the only sound I hear as I watch Serena's playful expression become crestfallen, almost broken.

"My what?" Her whisper is far too loud in the silence.

"I assigned him to watch over you while you finish your time here at the Academy. With Callan and Abby's approval," he continues. "He's here for your protection, meaning he's under oath and blood bonded to you."

Serena's features become unreadable. But I know that the hurt and betrayal is only hidden behind her eyes as she studies me.

"Is that true?" She directs the question to me.

The despair lining her voice startles me, and I flinch before wiping my forehead with the back of my hand.

I need a solid minute—or ten—in order to answer her, because the devastation bleeding out of her gaze is starting to become my undoing.

My nostrils flare as I take a few deep breaths.

"Yes," I answer in a clipped tone.

Her gaze is furious and wild, as an awkward beat passes between us. Then, without warning, she schools her features, placing her mask back on as she stands straighter.

"Good. That's good. We're already bonded then." The sound of fake happiness cuts me deeper than even I knew was possible. "It means that we are meant to be after all."

"Serena—," I attempt but she turns away.

"Suck it up, Tristan. Mags and I have class," she lies.

My jaw clenches.

She's running.

"Rulf will go with you two," Asher states firmly.

"Fine." She grabs Magali and storms out of the suite without another word or backwards glance.

Fantastic.

Once they're gone, Callan comes toward me.

I lift my palms, surrendering. "Let me be clear, Callan, what Serena said is not true. I'm unsure of her motives, but she's goading you and using me to do so."

"Which part is untrue? That she loves you, or that you are meant to be?" Callan counters, with a clenched jaw.

"I'm not her boyfriend," I state, which just pisses him off even more for whatever reason.

He growls and steps into my space before taking in a deep breath. "Then why do I smell my daughter on you?"

Ah, fuck.

I slept with her last night.

I lift my chin.

"You injected him with her blood for the protector bond." Zander answers in a calm tone, stepping between us.

"Some protectors would take advantage of the situation. Are you one of those assholes, Tristan?" Asher asks.

Yes. "No," I bite out.

A ghost of a smile crosses Asher's face as he studies me.

It's like he knows—understands, sees past my armor.

"Let's all take a breath and discuss why we're really here," Keegan steps in, trying to defuse the situation.

"You mean this isn't a social call?" I snort.

"The Diablo Fairies have been making some bold choices lately. We believe they're getting ready to attack," Asher explains, and stretches his neck from side to side.

"As Michael predicted," Keegan says slowly.

The *Michael* he's referencing is the archangel Michael, warrior of Heaven and Serena's aunt Eve's father. Years ago he made a deal with Heaven and Hell in order to protect Eve, one that unknowingly placed Serena in danger now.

My heart stops and my fists clench at the thought of Serena being hurt. *Why do I care so much?*

Callan senses my rage and his expression hardens.

"We're assuming you're prepared?" Keegan asks.

"And focused on her protection?" Callan adds, harshly.

I suck my bottom lip into my mouth a few times trying to curb my desire to kill her father for his rudeness. I, too, happen to be royalty, and the way he's speaking to me would get him killed in my realm. Protector or not.

"Isn't that why you chose me? Let's be honest here, it had nothing to do with Gage's request to spare me, and everything to do with the cessation," I state.

Callan steps into my space. "Just protect her, Tristan."

I square my shoulders. "On my honor and with my last breath, if necessary," I vow truthfully.

SERENA

A FAINT THROBBING MAKES ITS PRESENCE known in my heart. It's the barest of aches, but somehow it hurts as if I've been stabbed in the heart. I stumble and falter in my steps.

Magali grabs me by the shoulder, yanking me around. "Serena, stop!" she demands. "Or I will restrain you."

I shrug out of her grip, watching her as I back up. "No."

As soon as I turn around, my face is pushed against a rock wall that protects the coastline from the harsh Atlantic sea water below, churning in angry motions.

"It wasn't an empty threat," she manages to croak out. Her voice is a choppy, barely there whisper from non-use.

Any other time, I would have admired Mags for her quick moves, but right now, it just pisses me off even more. I keep still until she loosens her grip, and then spin out of her grasp, kicking her in the stomach.

She gasps, and her fingers fly angrily. "Wanna fight?"

My shoulders sag. "No! Of course not. I'm sorry."

Taking two deep breaths, Mags straightens before lifting her fingers to sign. "What is going on, Serena?"

I pinch my expression. "I don't know."

"What do you mean, you don't know? You just announced that Tristan was your boyfriend and then completely freaked out when you found out he is your secondary protection," she reminds me.

I exhale and jerk back. "I know!" I shout.

Magali just waits for me to pull myself together.

"I'm sorry for yelling. I just . . . can't explain it."

"Try me," she counters.

"He's Ophelia's son," I start. "A nymph prince."

"So is Zander. Big deal."

"He's my protector, Mags. Unlike Rulf, they've injected him with my blood. Without me knowing. It's kind of a bit of a personal violation. Don't you think?" I rant.

She pauses and takes a step in my direction. "It's how our world works. You know this. So, stop lying and tell me why you're really upset. It's not that he's a satyr prince, or that he's your protector, Serena. Why are you really hurt?"

My eyes lock onto her soft gaze. "It's—"

"SERENA!" Rulf shouts, and my head turns to him.

Within seconds, I'm pushed onto my back, with Magali covering my body. She reaches for the knife in her boot, and offers me a pleading look to stay put as she pushes up and turns. I watch her pinch the weapon, ready to release it.

Immediately, I stand and face a tribe of warriors approaching us. There must be hundreds of them watching us with a fierce display of pride, strength, and unity.

Magali shoots me an angry look for being upright and not listening to her, before she turns back to face the army.

As the warriors approach they violently stomp their feet with their tongues protruding. While performing a rhythmic body slapping, they chant in a loud battle cry, charging at us.

Each movement is a terrifying challenge.

In an instant, Rulf steps in front of Mags and me.

"What are they?" I exhale.

"Diablo Fairies," he answers in a hard tone.

My focus remains on the woman leading the well-choreographed dance. Her skin is a dark chocolate color, with white paint drawn in tribal patterns all over her muscular, unclothed legs, stomach, and arms.

Her exposed feet are adorned with gold gladiator sandals. Leather straps snake up her calves with rubies studding the fronts, all along the middle of the crossed bands.

Gold jewelry adorns her upper thighs and arms, and a skull with three white feathers hangs from her waist, scarcely covering the lower part of her body.

A small red cloth conceals her breasts from sight, held up with a turquoise and gold necklace that looks more like a piece of armor. Another skull decorates the front of the heavy necklace. Bronze rings crawl up her neck, and large hoop earrings fall from her ears.

She's wearing a wooden warrior mask, with a deep pink diamond gem set in the forehead and matching gems in the eye area. Four horns protrude out of the top and sides, and it's decorated with more white feathers.

The sudden appearance of Tristan, Zander, my father, and my uncles shifts my focus from the army to them.

"Kupuva!" Tristan barks out.

"What?" I ask, as he steps to my side.

"Kupuva, she's their leader." Rulf motions to the dark-skinned woman, shaking a wooden staff—with another skull sitting at the top of it—at me violently. This skull has two horns that match her mask and red feathers hanging where its neck should be.

"We'll hold them. Tristan, take Serena to your realm," Uncle Keegan commands. "We need asylum for her."

"Not a chance." I prepare to fight off the army.

"You don't have a choice," my dad informs me.

"I'm a protector. I fight," I argue.

"Serena, don't squabble," Rulf interjects.

"I'm not leaving Magali here," I fight back.

"I'll protect her." Zander promises.

Uncle Asher steps in front of me. "We don't have time for you to argue with us, Serena. Tristan's realm will offer you safe haven. As your king—" he swallows, the pain of what he's about to say causing a dark shadow to cross his expression. "As your king, I order you to go with your protector without another word."

I jerk back as if slapped.

It's rare Uncle Asher uses his royal status on another clan member. Especially me.

If my aunt Eve were here, she'd kick the crap out of him.

Tristan steps in front of me with an apologetic look on his face. His hands grip my upper arms, pulling me to him.

Leaning in, his lips brush my ear.

"Sorry, raindrop."

THIRTEEN
SAY SOMETHING

SERENA

WITHIN SECONDS, TRISTAN AND I DISAPPEAR. A few moments later, my eyes open and I'm fighting for balance on the hard ground. Red deer scatter around us at our sudden appearance.

The sound of their hooves breaks through the quiet of the wooded area we've teleported into. Once I'm steady, I push Tristan away and step back, taking in where we are.

"You teleport?" I snap.

"A protector gift," Tristan explains in a calm way.

"Where are we?" My angry voice screeches.

"The base of Torc Mountain," he replies.

"In the Killarney National Park?" I pose, hoping we're still in County Kerry, Ireland, so I can go back.

"Yes. But don't even think about it," he says.

"They're in danger, Tristan. We can't just leave them. What if they get hurt, or worse?" I swallow the worry.

"They're skilled warriors, Serena. There is no need to be concerned for your family's safety," he replies. "Or Magali's."

I pause to get my bearings.

"Why am I the one that needed to be shoved aside?"

"Your king gave the order," is all he says.

"How did you know I was in danger?"

His face is rigid.

"The bond," he answers, gripping my elbow and pulling me forward. "For safety reasons, we need to keep moving."

I try to squirm out of his grip, but he's too strong.

Instead, I focus on not stumbling as he drags me through the forest, moving uphill at a quick pace.

"Why did you listen to my uncle Asher?"

"Because, believe it or not, I respect royal decrees."

We're quiet as we make the short climb to near the view of Middle Lake, before continuing toward the cave located at the top of the waterfall, hidden behind draping, thick strands of weeping willow tree limbs.

Tristan stops, and we stand in front of the dryad as he asks its spirit to grant us access in his native tongue.

"Eímai Tristan, gios tou Ofilía. Evlogíes sti gi, to neró kai ton ouranó pnévmata. Tha akoúso, odigós mou. Anoíxte ta chéria sas kai na kalosoríso mou spíti." His voice is deep and hypnotic.

Enthralling.

At the release of his words, the tree branches part like a curtain opening in a theater, revealing a portal to his realm. The air ripples in entrancing, clear waves.

Tristan puts his hand on my lower back as we step through. The entry closes once we're safely inside.

Once in the realm, we're greeted by two large sequoias.

"They guard my mother's land," Tristan explains.

Two nymphs shimmy and twist out of the bark, the outline of their lower bodies embedded into the trunk.

"Their soul spirit is one with the tree. If the nymph dies, so does the tree," he says.

"Okay." I curb my shock at the sight.

"Phoebe. Atlanteia," Tristan acknowledges.

"Your Highness," they respond, in unison.

"This is Princess Serena of the London clan. She has sanctuary while in our land. She is to be protected as if she were one of us," he commands in an authoritative tone.

The sentinels share a quick, surprised glance before bowing and again speaking at the same time. "As you wish."

Phoebe tilts her head to me, dipping her chin.

"Welcome. It is a great honor, Princess."

I try not to flinch at the royal term. "Thank you."

"We grant you entrance," Atlanteia announces.

Tristan's hand pushes lightly on my lower back, encouraging me to walk between the two trees.

I do so and remain silent, waiting until we're within the forest before I stop, turn, and cross my arms in defiance.

"If you ever introduce me as a princess again, I will stab you in the heart and end your existence," I spit out.

His voice drops an octave. "You are one."

I lower my voice. "Not everyone needs to be made aware of it. Given this morning's revelations, I would think you would understand and respect the need for privacy."

Tristan lets out a harsh breath and takes an intimidating step toward me.

"You're fucking beautiful."

I still, unsure how to reply to the sudden change in conversation. *What is he doing?*

He stops in front of me and runs his fingertips over my cheek before taking my chin between his fingers and lifting my face so I'm forced to look at him.

"When you're mad your aura takes on this amazing red color. It's intoxicating."

"My aura?" I swallow.

"I have soul sight, remember? One of my satyr gifts."

"But I don't have a soul," I counter.

"You have an energy field."

"Oh," I respond, trying not to quiver under his touch.

"We should go."

"Go where?" I whisper.

"My home."

"Why not just teleport us there?" I ask.

"I'd prefer not to. My protector gifts draw attention in this realm," he explains, staring at my mouth.

"My dad and Magali—," I begin.

"Will be okay. Trust me," he finishes and assures me.

Trust him? After he's lied to me. *Amazing.*

He removes his hand from my face, offering it to me. After a moment of contemplation, I place mine in his. Our rings clink as he tightens his grip and pulls me toward a stone pathway that winds through the woods.

We walk in quiet as I take in the peaceful lush forest. Clear blue ponds with bright-green, larger-than-life lily pads and white floating flowers are interspersed through the dense trees.

It's like a fairytale land.

The sun's rays hit each leaf surrounding us, beaming a buttery light and warmth in every direction. Everything here, even the air, feels cleaner, more striking, and tranquil.

"You speak ancient Greek." I observe, tired of the silence.

"All nymphs and satyrs do. Our kind has been tied to the ancient Greek gods since creation," he responds.

I let my hands caress the sunflowers as we pass.

"Why did you tell your father I was your boyfriend?" Tristan asks without looking back.

"Um," I search for the right way to explain.

"My favorite word of yours," he jokes.

"Whatever," I roll my eyes at his back.

"Just tell me the truth," he encourages.

"Do you promise not to get mad?"

"Pretty sure I already did," he reiterates.

"I know how my family feels about Gage. I thought if my dad and uncles heard you and I were together, they'd offer me anything to not be with you," I divulge.

I cringe inside at the way the words sound.

Asinine.

"You wanted to use me as a bargaining chip for your freedom?" he restates. "You saw me as a way out?"

"Yes," I admit.

"How's it working out for you?" His tone is emotionless.

"Not well. Turns out you're my bonded protector."

I stop walking, yanking his hand so he turns.

He puckers his brows. "I was under oath not to tell you."

"That doesn't sound like an apology for lying."

"It's not. You know how this works, Serena."

I bite my bottom lip. "Unfortunately, I do."

"Then you know why I couldn't tell you."

I try to release the hold he has on my hand, but his grip tightens and he tugs me closer to him.

"That's why you were placed at the Academy?" I glare.

He dips his head so he can look me in the eyes.

"The truth is that I was in trouble. In order to have my sentence revoked, I agreed to protect you. Your clan placed me at the Academy as an instructor and trainer."

I hold his gaze. "I should've known. Who else knows?"

"Chancellor Davidson," he replies.

"Is becoming my friend—kissing me—sleeping with me—part of the plan too?" I ask, not wanting to know the answer.

"It wasn't my intent to get this close to you, ever. I intended to protect you from afar, but—" he swallows.

Feeling brave, I take a step toward him. "But what?"

He looks away, then meets my eyes again. "I couldn't."

"Why?" I breathe out.

"I'm inexplicably drawn to you," he admits.

"My point exactly." I search his face. "Is the draw the protector bond? Or is it the satyr in you enchanting me?"

His Adam's apple slides up and down his throat while he works through his thoughts. "I've never used magical enthralls on you. Not once. Even you should feel that. As for the protector bond, I think we've been connected to one another for longer than just the last few weeks."

I become still. "What do you mean?"

"When I was two years old, I was at your uncle's coronation. Your mother asked mine to decorate the wooded area for the gala, as a favor. My mother obliged and brought me with her. I remember thinking how magical everything looked," he pauses. "Your mom approached me, saving me from your aunt Kenna who was hounding me about something. Abby bent down, tapped my nose and tickled me. I remember noticing how beautiful she was. Without thinking, I placed a hand on her stomach and—" he stops.

"And what?"

"She was pregnant with you. I could feel your emotions—read your aura—experience how happy you were to be coming into this world. A vision of you hit me. Your sapphire gaze," his focus slides over my hair, "your long auburn locks. I remember knowing how breathtaking you were going to be. How lucky someone would be to get to love you," he murmurs. "I think that possibly, I connected with you before you were even brought into this world."

I exhale slowly, taking in each word he's offering me.

After a moment he squeezes my hand. "Say something."

My throat is dry. "I'm torn. On the one hand, I want to slap the shit out of you for bonding with me without my permission. On the other," I lift my gaze, "if you keep saying things like that, I'm going to want to have your babies."

He freezes and I laugh. "I'm kidding. Settle down, protector," I inhale. "I like you, Tristan. So much more than I ever want to admit out loud. I'm drawn to you and I know in my heart it has nothing to do with either of your bloodlines. It's you. Plain and simple."

Tristan's eyes are wild with emotion as he takes me in and yanks me so our chests touch. "I like you too, raindrop."

The wind shifts, and the trees begin to bend and twist, almost as if they're bowing. The air around us becomes electric, and I watch as Tristan's expression contorts.

Without hesitation he drops my hands and takes a step away from me with an apologetic look before he speaks.

"Hello, mother."

FOURTEEN
THE WOODLAND REALM

SERENA

MOTHER—JUST WHAT EVERY GIRL WANTS TO hear after she admits to liking someone who confessed to bonding with her in the womb. *And why did he jump away from me so fast?*

The air whistles around me, and I turn in a composed manner and come face-to-face with Queen Ophelia.

I've heard rumors throughout the supernatural world about her insane beauty. They say it brings mere mortals to their knees, and haunts the demigods in their dreams.

Standing in front of her, I can say it's all true. She's beyond stunning. My lips part in awe. It's like seeing a rare flower that you've only heard exists until it's in front of you.

The sun beams off her golden-blonde hair, highlighting the long strands. She has it braided on one side, entwined with lime leaves. The scent is citrusy, crisp, invigorating.

Cognac irises that mirror Tristan's meet my awed gaze, and a kind smile crosses her cherry lips as she curtsies. The long, flowing forest-green dress she's wearing cascades across the grass in a dream-like fashion. A chiffon olive cape drapes over her slender figure as she returns to her full height and her gaze meets mine.

"Princess Serena, it is a great honor to welcome you into the wood-land realm." Her voice is sweet. Angelic.

After a moment, I come to my senses and curtsy. "Your Majesty, it's I who am honored." I find my voice.

Queen Ophelia dips her chin, pleased with my manners, and holds out an olive branch, which I take with a smile.

"The twig is a friendship token among the woodland nymphs. It is a symbol of peace and love," she explains.

"It is a most treasured gesture, Your Majesty," I reply, recalling my training in formalities of state. "Thank you."

"Mother," Tristan steps toward her, taking her hands and kissing each cheek lightly. "You look beautiful, as always."

At the sight of him, her eyes light up, filling with adoration. Her palm lifts and rests on his cheek. "It's good to see you, Tristan. Are you well, my dear boy?"

"I am, though I won't be if you keep referring to Serena as Princess. She's not fond of the title," he informs her. "It angers her. To no end. Like, death-threat-inducing rage."

The queen's brows pinch before she slides her concerned gaze to me. "Apologies, Serena. I meant no disrespect."

I force a smile and vow to kill Tristan in his sleep—with a pillow. Suffocation is definitely the way to end him.

"It's fine, Your Majesty," I reply. "Truly, you're welcome to use the title. Or call me whatever you'd like."

Tristan throws me a victorious smirk before turning back to his mom. "She prefers to be called raindrop."

"Raindrop?" his mother repeats, bemused.

"Actually, I don—," I start, but he cuts me off.

"Have you received word from Zander?" he asks her.

She nods. "The Diablo Fairies have been held off, for now. Serena's family has returned to London." Her gaze slides to mine. "Your guard was badly injured, but is being cared for. Zander has placed your friend,

Magali, under the safekeeping of a young protector named Ethan," she explains, and turns to Tristan. "Your brother will be returning this evening, once Magali is settled, per a promise he made."

I exhale, grateful for the news, yet worried about Rulf.

"Good," Tristan replies.

Queen Ophelia shifts her focus between Tristan and me.

"Raindrop," she stumbles at the name. "Your uncle Asher has requested that you remain in our realm, under our protection, of course, until he releases the order."

"Serena," I interject, and Tristan chuckles. "I'd prefer to be called Serena, Your Majesty."

Ophelia shoots an annoyed glare at Tristan. "Of course," she sighs. "I should have known better. I do hope, despite my son's tongue-in-cheek behavior, you will do me the honor of being our dinner guest at the castle this evening."

"I would be happy to, despite Tristan's attendance," I respond, and an amused expression crosses Ophelia's face.

"I do believe you've met a worthy verbal opponent, son," she says and turns on her heel—a signal for us to follow.

We make our way through the woodland realm, and I can't help but notice how lush and picturesque it is.

It's almost as if the land was hand-painted, each stroke as lovely and vivid as the next one.

Queen Ophelia runs her fingertips over a tree's leaves as we pass by. In an instant, it brightens, as if waking. The jade color deepens, like she breathed life into it.

"Our realm is ancient, despite its youthful beauty. We owe much of its health to the water realm," she explains.

Tristan grunts next to her.

"We owe nothing to Oren," he retorts.

Ophelia presses her lips together. "Ignore him. When the prince is hungry he becomes disenchanting."

Tristan throws an annoyed glance her way, causing me to smile. I like that they have a normalish relationship.

"He must be hungry a lot, then," I banter.

Queen Ophelia releases a hearty laugh at my jab.

When we reach the end of the path, it forks off, and I wait to see which direction we're heading in.

Ophelia takes my hands and offers a gentle squeeze.

"Rionach and I look forward to hosting you this evening. Until then, I do hope my son will mind his manners and be respectful of the fact that you are a guest in our realm."

I sense her statement is a warning for Tristan, not me.

"We aren't going to the castle now?" I ask, confused.

"I have some realm business to attend to. Since Tristan is your protector, you should accompany him to his home, where he will allow you to rest and freshen up. We'll see one another shortly," she says warmly, and gives me a small hug.

The queen turns to her son. "You may be a protector in the outside world, but in this realm, you are a prince. Remember your duties and oaths. The forest has eyes, son."

His jaw tightens. "Of course, mother."

She places a chaste kiss on his cheek. "Off you go, then."

Tristan and I stand in silence as his mother takes her leave, before he runs his hand through his hair, aggravated.

"Shall we?" he asks, and motions to the other path.

"Sure," I follow him. "What was it like growing up here?"

His steps become measured. "It was . . . wholesome."

I laugh. "Interesting word choice."

We walk next to one another for a while in silence before his voice startles me. "Until Zander came along, it was . . . lonely. My mother was always busy with her royal obligations. My father didn't exist. I had hired nannies, guards, and playmates. At home I was schooled, trained, and taught as much as I could absorb about the supernatural worlds in preparation to one day become king."

I wrap my arms around myself, because it sounds a lot like my childhood. Sheltered and lonely.

"I was under constant protection and watchful eyes for security reasons. Each day was the same. Then one day, my mother hired Rionach to oversee her security detail and army. With Rionach came Zander.

With Zander came entertainment. For the first time in my life, I had a partner in crime. Someone to experience life with. To have fun and get in trouble with. Zander's friendship allowed me to take off the mask I had to always hide behind. You know?"

I meet his gaze. "Actually, I don't. I've never had that."

He stops and wraps his fingers around one of my wrists. "What about Magali, Ethan, Ireland, and Ryker?"

My toe kicks some dirt and rocks. "Their friendships mean the world to me. At the end of the day, though, they know who I am and where I come from. They may have lowered their expectations of me over the years, but they still see me as their future queen. My actions disappoint them in the same way they do my family. They just hide it better. I keep some form of my mask on to please them."

A dark smile curls at his lips. "What about me?"

I avert my gaze from his. "What about you?"

"Don't do that," he orders, placing his palm on my cheek, forcing me to look at him. "Where's the mask for me?"

"I don't need it with you," I reply, barely audible.

"Why is that, raindrop?"

"You break the rules with me. Let me breathe. You see past the façade and embrace the realness. I can just be me."

Tristan swallows. "Though I have the title of Prince, I'm not one, Serena. I can't be anyone's Prince Charming.

"Well then, you're in luck. I hate fairy tales."

TRISTAN

YEAH, WE'RE NOT FOOLING ANYONE. THE tension between us mounts as I stand here with her cheek in my palm. Even though I know I shouldn't, I can't help but touch her.

My skin comes alive with each moment that passes, and I feel like we're becoming something else. Something bigger than either of us are prepared for. The fingertips of my other hand run over the soft skin of her other cheek.

"That's good to know."

"What is?" she exhales on a shaky breath.

"That you can breathe around me," I reply. "Since I'm your pretend boyfriend, I feel like it would suck if you died from lack of oxygen while under my protection."

Her grin appears. "Well, don't get used to it."

"Being your boyfriend? Or your ability to breathe around me?" My voice is raspy.

She steps closer. "Either."

"Wouldn't dream of it," I whisper, my eyes trained on her mouth. And as the guarded walls I put up around my heart come tumbling down, I become addicted to her smile.

In this moment, even gravity can't pull me back to the ground. I lean in first and she meets me halfway.

Our lips are a breath away.

"I was hoping you wouldn't fall for him," a deep voice says, and both Serena and I freeze. With a muttered curse, I release her face and step back.

My heart is in my throat.

"Pardon?" Serena turns and asks Zander.

"It makes it much easier on my conscience to steal you away if you aren't in love with him. Being his—it complicates things between us," he winks.

I curb my desire to strangle my brother.

"It's probably better for your ego this way," Serena replies haughtily, and I hide my pride at her sass.

Zander's grin grows wider. "I do bruise like a peach."

I exhale a harsh breath.

All of a sudden I'm exhausted.

"Is Magali okay?" Serena inquires.

"She is. I left her a little while ago with Ethan and Lucas. They're going to have her stay over for a few nights. Your dad and uncles are okay too. Rulf took a pretty big machete to the gut. He's in a stone state sleep, healing. It might be a few days until he's recovered, so Asher would like you to remain here in the woodland realm until things calm down and Rulf can return to his guard duties. Since my brother is your *boyfriend*, I'm guessing you'll be okay with that," he teases.

Serena rolls her eyes and pierces me with a hard look.

"Why do I have such a giant target on my back where the Diablo Fairies are concerned?"

I tip my head in the direction of my house.

"I'll tell you all about it, but not out in the open."

She nods her agreement and begins to walk forward, when I feel Zander's hand grab at my elbow, halting me.

"What's up, man?" I ask.

"Don't fuck around and get attached to her." His voice is low. He forgets Serena's gargoyle ears can still hear him.

"I appreciate your concern, but I've got this," I reply, and he yanks on my elbow harder, forcing my full attention.

"I mean it, Tristan. I'm not sure what kind of game you two are playing with one another, but you and she have taken oaths that are larger than both of you," he reminds, and hands me a duffel bag. "Magali packed a few things she thought Serena would need while she stays here. I added the condoms just in case. You are both adults. My warning was about feelings only. There is no reason not to have fun while waiting for fate to take over," he adds, his tone lighter.

"See you at dinner," I dismiss him, and catch up with her.

"The woodland realm is beautiful," she blurts out.

"Don't be fooled, darkness lurks," I warn.

She points to the bag. "Weapons?"

"Clothes. Magali packed some stuff for you."

I relax with the direction of the conversation. If she'd heard Zander, she isn't going to bring up what he said. Relief hits me.

Serena stops walking and lifts her head. "Is this yours?"

I take in my house and smile. "It is."

"It's beautiful." Her voice is quiet. "You must hate living at the Academy in that tiny room, when you have all this waiting for you here," she says in awe.

I squint at the well-lit, wood, glass, and stone modern cabin. I'd never admit this to Serena, but this place isn't really home.

It's always empty.

Given the choice, I'd choose the small suite with her.

We walk up the cobblestone pathway, passing the fire pit and Adirondack chairs on the left. We climb the stone stairs, continue to the deck, and make our way to the front door.

I push it open and step aside so she can enter. Hesitantly she does, taking everything in with each step.

"The siding is made from poplar and the trim is made out of black locust log," I explain, needing noise in the silence.

The house is meant to impress.

"It's amazing," Serena responds, turning back to the front wall, lined with large windows looking out into the woods.

I hold my hand out to her without thinking.

"Want a tour?"

She stares at my fingers for a moment before placing her soft palm in mine. Automatically, my thumb rubs over her rings before I guide her around, showing her the living room with high wooden ceilings and a floor-to-ceiling fireplace. The cozy couches and leather chairs add comfort.

'This is the kitchen." I point to the wooden cabinets and counter-top with several chairs lining the outside. "Help yourself to anything while you're here."

She runs her hand over the pool table as we pass it, and I take her down the window-lined long hallway to the stairs.

Serena follows me up the two floors, where I continue to show her the bathrooms and guest rooms, before we stand in front of the master suite.

I push open the doors and reveal the expansive room lined on one side with open French doors that lead to a stone balcony, which overlooks a large lake.

Her eyes widen and she releases my hand, walking toward the two chairs and fireplace that face outside.

"This is . . . beyond breathtaking, Tristan."

"Thank you."

"It's like a log-cabin castle," she continues.

"Well, I am a prince in the woodland realm," I joke.

Serena looks at me. "So you are."

I lift my chin to the chairs. "Why don't you relax a little? I'll put your bag in the guest room across the hall and then we can talk."

She nods her agreement and fatigue falls across her face.

"Be back," I mutter, leaving.

After making sure the guest room is set, I pad down to the kitchen and grab two bottles of water before heading back to the master suite.

I stop in my tracks when I get to the doors.

The fire is lit, all the doors are open to the outside and Serena is curled up under a blanket on one of the chairs, staring out over the lake, wearing one of my T-shirts.

No one except Zander, the housekeeper, and my mother comes into my home. Her presence here is unnerving.

Sensing me, she turns and offers me a shy smile.

"Sorry, I just wanted some fresh air. But then I got a little chilly," she motions to the fireplace and looks down at herself. "I also wanted to get comfortable, so I stole one of your T-shirts. Hope that was okay?"

"You lit the fireplace on your own?" I question, and place the waters on the table between the two chairs.

Her brows pinch before she starts laughing. "It wasn't that hard, Tristan. You just flip the switch on the wall."

I raise my eyebrows and give her a confused look.

"Really?" I question.

"It's gas," she smirks.

"Oh." I sit in the empty chair next to her.

"You've never turned it on?" she asks, snatching a water.

"I can't say that I have," I reply.

"Sad," she exhales, and rests her head on the back of the chair. "If I lived here, I would have it on every night."

My chest tightens at the idea of her living here—forever.

All of a sudden, this house feels like home.

FIFTEEN
DRAGON SPIRIT

TRISTAN

EVERY TIME MY CELL GOES OFF, Serena's focus shifts to the lake. Even though the late afternoon breeze is passing through the open doors, the air in the room is emotionally overcharged and stifling.

She's nervous. She should be. Hell, I'm nervous.

I look down at Callan's text—it's two words. Two simple words that will change her fate: *tell her.*

"It's okay, Tristan," her voice is tired—insecure—and I hate it. "I know how this all works. I know my dad gave you permission to explain it to me, so just—," she exhales. "Why are the Diablo Fairies targeting me? Who are they?"

The silence that falls around us is deafening. I know I need to speak, but I'm unsure where to begin. I lean back and cross my arms before meeting her squinting gaze.

"Have you heard the name Asmodeus before?" I begin.

Serena leans forward, wiggling her brows, and drops her tone seductively. "Do you mean, the demon of lust?"

"The very one," I answer. "Though he's better known through-out the supernatural community as the king of the Nine Hells," I pause. "He also happens to be the uncle to the sorceress of prosperity, Llughnassad."

I watch her closely, waiting for recognition to hit.

"Nassa? Gage's Nassa?" her voice trails off.

I focus back on the lake and inhale, pushing my craving for a cigarette away. I've gotten better about not needing them.

"Nassa's dad is Mammon. Though she's turned her back on him in favor of her mother's sorceress lineage," I add.

Serena slumps back into the chair and fiddles with a string on the blanket covering her lap. "What does this have to do with the angry fairy warriors? Or me for that matter?"

"It's a little bit of history." I grant her an amused look.

Her eyes meet mine teasingly. "Okay, Professor."

"Asmodeus once had a mate, one that he loved very much. No one really knew about her," I continue slowly, so as not overwhelm her with information.

"Who was she?" Serena inquires.

I wince.

"You can't say." It wasn't a question.

She knows the restriction on information protectors are allowed to impart when on assignment, thank God.

"His mate betrayed the archangel Michael. When the warrior of Heaven discovered her treachery, his brother, Uriel, ended her life. Asmodeus never recovered from her death. Though he's promiscuous, he loved her, deeply."

A comfortable quiet settles between us before I dare a glance at her. Serena is chewing on her lip in contemplation.

"Love is unconditional, right? Regardless of her betrayal, it makes sense that her death broke him," she whispers, holding her heart, as if re-calling something painful. "I'm sure her absence has left him outraged."

"He's vowed revenge. At your uncle's coronation, Michael an-nounced that the Angelic Council had reached a second treaty between the divine and demonic realms, preventing the war your family was meant to fight. Peace was decreed for hundred years if each side kept their word."

She bristles. "Why do I get the feeling one side didn't?"

I glower. "Asmodeus breached the treaty when he created the Diablo Fairies, or devil fairies. They're his army, designed for revenge. Kupuva, the leader, is his new mate."

"If he's upset with Michael, why target me?" she asks.

"Your clan is directly tied to the death of Asmodeus's executed mate," I proceed with caution. There's only so much I'm permitted to share about her clan's involvement.

"You're saying my family is the reason she's dead?"

"I'm saying, the gargoyle king is married to the daughter of Heaven. Michael's daughter. Uriel's niece. Asher and Eve's mate bond protects Heaven's gates," I explain. "In order for the dark army to attack the gates, and declare war, Asher and Eve must both cease to exist. Asmodeus has vowed to extinguish the gargoyle race, including your aunt and uncle. Once he does, he will grant the dark army access to the divine realm. At which time, he intends to fulfill his revenge against Michael and Uriel."

"Even if Asmodeus succeeds, I still exist. If my uncle were to cease to be, I would be the next ruler," she says.

I nod. "Asmodeus knows this. It's why he's focusing on the only other being in existence who stands in his way. He figures that by targeting you first, he will weaken your clan—hitting them emotionally. An eye for an eye." I try to sound gentle. "A fragile royal clan allows for an easy race demise. He's a demon. It's simply a game of chess to him."

I'm impressed with Serena's calm demeanor.

"That's why my family created the Academy? To build an army to battle Asmodeus's?" she mutters.

"Michael became aware of the Diablo Fairy army years ago and alerted the London clan. Nassa and Gage have been infiltrating various demon dens, gaining intel. Everyone is working hard to stop this from happening," I assure her.

"Why am I attending the Academy then? Doesn't that make me an easy target?" she inquires.

"It's the safest place for you. An entire school made up of the best of the best within the protector race. Ready to give their lives for their future queen if need be," I retort.

"Do the students there know?" Her tone concerned.

"No."

Her face falls. "None of them?"

"Not one. The lecturers and instructors do."

"Why did they attack this morning? They've never been that bold before, so why today?" Her brows pull together.

"My guess is that Kupuva became aware that both you and your uncle were in the same place at the same time. It was sloppy. Probably something she did without approval."

"They didn't have weapons, except for machetes."

"Diablo Fairies have been created to mirror an ancient tribe of warriors. They're not like Lucifer's dark army, who serve the demonic realm. The fairy army was made for one purpose only: to do Asmodeus's bidding. That means they don't have the same supernatural gifts most demons do. Each one is born of black magic and can cast away a protector's powers using dark spells," I point out. "Don't be misled just because they don't use modern weapons—they are still extremely dangerous, Serena."

She sucks in a breath. "That's why you're so concerned with the protectors' hand-to-hand skills at the Academy."

"Yes." It's true. They'll crush her if she can't fight.

I watch her readjust on the chair to face me. "Someone recently told me that, as with most accords, there is a cessation. Isn't there one in this instance?"

"Who told you that?" I try to sound calm.

Her gaze bores into me. "No one of concern to you."

My eyes roam over her face, hating that I'm about to lie.

"No. There is not."

SERENA

NO. THE WORD ROLLS AROUND MY head like a bullet, cutting through every single hope and dream I've ever had. I shift my focus to the water to help ground me, praying that I don't look like someone just kicked me in the stomach.

I'm a royal protector.

That means we take in information in a calm and thoughtful manner. We consider all angles and strategic possibilities and outcomes before showing emotion.

No outbursts. No freak-outs. It doesn't accomplish anything. It's what I've been taught from birth.

A warm hand covers mine. I look up at Tristan. My fate is written all over his face. There's no way out of this.

Gently, he closes his hand around my fingers, preventing them from brushing over the stones on my bracelet. He squeezes them, gaining my attention.

"Hey."

I just stare at him. *Why can't he be my saving grace?*

"Serena?" His voice sounds miles away, even though he's sitting right next to me. *Why is that?* I must be in shock.

The darkness behind his eyes calls to me. As the air around me becomes unnaturally still, I feel my spirit break.

Outside, the gray clouds roll in quickly, lightning illuminating the sky, followed by the rainstorm.

I know my protector gifts are causing the storm.

The sound of falling rain should soothe me, but instead I feel nothing at all. Numb. Anesthetized.

"Get up," Tristan barks, grabbing my elbow and yanking me in a controlling manner off the chair. He pulls me toward the open doors and out onto the balcony into the storm. For a moment, we just stand there while the heavy rain pounds the forest area around us.

My eyes are trained on him, and it only takes a second to register that we're both getting completely soaked. I watch the beads of water drip from his hair, down his cheekbones, and across his lips. My eyes narrow in on the scar on his upper lip. The one that constantly taunts me.

Tristan cups my chin firmly between his fingers.

"Look at me," he demands, using an arrogant voice.

My eyes blaze with fury at his tone. "I am."

He smiles. "There you are. There's the spark of life."

His fingers on my face relax my core, bringing me back to myself. I try to pull away, but he wraps his free arm around my waist and wrenches my body against his, locking me to him. Tristan's lips graze my ear as he speaks through the thunder. "Trust me. To protect you. To protect us."

I stiffen and try to push away, but he holds me tighter.

His lips brush across my neck in the barest of touches before he pulls back and cups my face with shaky hands.

Only a sliver of air exists between our lips as his hooded gaze meets mine. He brushes a thumb over the pulse at the base of my neck, as if he's trying to push life into it to keep my heart beating.

I tremble beneath his touch.

"I've got you. You. Are. Safe." He doesn't release me. He simply waits until I get myself under control and give in.

"I believe you," I concede breathlessly.

We stand there, trapped by the magnetic pull between us.

The smell of wet earth lines the warm spring breeze, as we regard one another, each waiting for the other to move. To breathe.

A small bead of water collects on my bottom lip and before I can wipe it away, Tristan moves my face closer to his, bends down, and leans in.

In one achingly slow movement, he runs his warm tongue across my bottom lip. When he's done, he pulls his head back a sliver and a shadow passes over his face.

I don't even have a moment to blink before he presses his mouth against mine in the slowest, most sensual kiss.

He takes his time, tasting me like a fine liquor.

A low groan rumbles in his throat, as I twist my fingers in the front of his soaked shirt, trying to get closer.

Unhurriedly he tugs my lower lip into his mouth with his teeth and then sucks it, all while his hands never leave my face. Our tongues lightly taste one another—a potent combination of rain water and cotton candy.

At the same time, he backs us up, pressing me against the outside wall of the cabin.

With each kiss, he claims little parts of me.

I allow myself to get lost in his kiss, in the dizzying sensation of his mouth as it languidly moves across mine.

Tristan pulls away, breathless, his eyes still closed. He drops his forehead to mine, and his hands leave my face to rest on my hips.

"My mother is expecting us," he says, unmoving.

"Do you think she'd be insulted if we postpone?"

Tristan looks at me, and with both hands pushes the wet strands of hair off my face. "Why do you want to?"

"I don't think I'd be good company tonight."

After a moment of studying me, he nods. "We'll reschedule, since we're going to be here for a few days."

"Thank you," my voice is thin and needy.

We stand like this for a moment longer before I muster up the courage to take his face in my palms, looking him directly in the eyes. I need assurance he'll keep his promise to keep me safe. In turn, I'll protect him with my life.

"Thank you for protecting me," I whisper.

He grants me a beautiful smile, one that could light up the world.

"I'm your fake boyfriend. I live to protect you."

My top teeth rake across my bottom lip as I smile.

His hands come up and guide mine off his face before linking one of ours together and tugging me toward the house. "Come on," he utters. "Now that the shock has worn off, let's get you dried off and fed. Then you can sleep."

Breathing a sigh of relief, I tilt my head and throw him a curious look. "You're taking care of me?"

His eyes are mocking as they crinkle at the edges with smugness.

"Apparently, it's a new hobby of mine."

My heart stutters at his words and all of a sudden awareness takes over. There will nothing left in the wreckage of my heart when he's done.

SIXTEEN
MEANT TO BE

SERENA

SIGHING IMPATIENTLY, I CRACK OPEN THE door, letting all the steam out of the bathroom. It's been an hour since Tristan offered to snag some fresh towels for me while I showered.

He still hasn't returned.

I look back at the countertop. The wet T-shirt I was wearing earlier is balled up next to the sink. I can't really put it back on. It's soaked, and smells like rainwater.

What the hell had I been thinking not grabbing dry clothes before I came in here? *Stupid, Serena.*

My gaze slides down the hallway, landing on the guest room door. I can probably make it there in seconds. Enough time to slip in without being noticed. I've so got this.

I push open the door and step into the empty hallway. With quick steps I rush to the door and just as my hand grips the knob, Tristan steps out of a room to my left, holding a towel. He looks up, directly at me, and stills.

The look on his face is something I'll never forget. It's not lust, or love, but torture that crosses his expression. All signs of his earlier care-free demeanor are gone as he lowers his hands so the towel is below his waist. Squaring my shoulders, I turn and fully face him.

"Hi."

"Hi," he rasps.

"Is that for me?" I point to the fluffy, white towel hiding the very prominent bulge in the front of his jeans.

"Is what for you?" his voice is unsteady.

I clear my throat, swallowing the snide remark I was going to make about his erection. "The. Towel."

As color returns to his face, he looks down and then quickly shoves his hands at me. "Yes."

"It's been an hour and I didn't want to wait," I explain, taking it and wrapping it around my body, covering up.

Tristan squeezes his eyes shut and shakes his head, emptying it of whatever notions he was having. His eyes zero in on my face.

"I figured you'd want some time to—relax and stuff."

I smirk, letting myself into the guest room.

"And stuff?"

"You know, girlie stuff," he fires back.

"Oh, I know. I'm familiar with all my . . . girlie stuff." I lick my lips and close the door behind me.

Once in the safety of the room, I lean against the door and inhale deeply, trying to stop my body from shaking.

I wish he didn't unnerve me so much.

Stepping farther into the room, I collect myself and go about the business of getting dressed, blow-drying my hair, and applying some light makeup.

Once ready, I reopen the door, relieved to see the hallway empty. The smell of garlic and tomato hits me, and my stomach rumbles, re-minding me that I'm starving.

I follow the delicious aroma down the hall, taking in the night sky through the large glass window panes lining each side, and make my way back downstairs toward the kitchen.

"I thought you didn't cook," I quip, just as my feet hit the bottom step and I round the corner, coming to a standstill.

"I never said that, champ," Zander replies cockily.

I look around. "What are you doing here?"

"I'm here by means of a royal decree. Queen Ophelia was concerned when you postponed dinner. She seems to think you won't receive 'proper nourishment' while under Tristan's roof. I can't say that I blame her. His cupboards are full of sugary cereal, and his fridge only has expired milk." He winks and points to a stool by the counter, where a glass of lemon water and a plate of garlic bread are waiting for me.

"Sit. I normally cook when Tristan's housekeeper, Maria, isn't here. She does everything for the big baby."

I take a seat, and roll my eyes at the first taste of the buttery, fluffy bread. It's incredible.

"Where is he?"

Zander wiggles his brows. "Why? Nervous to be alone with me?" he smirks wickedly, and slides his hands into oven mitts before taking a lasagna out of the double wall oven and setting it on the stove.

I snort around a mouthful. "Um. No."

He regards me for a moment, before standing in front of me, on the other side of the counter, and leans his elbows on the granite. "He's in his office," his head tilts to the left.

"Doing what?" I ask.

"He's on a call," he replies.

I hold up the half eaten bread. "This is good."

"Thanks. So you're, like, in love with my brother?"

I choke. Literally.

The bite I was chewing catches in my throat, and I have to cough several times to dislodge it. After a moment of allowing air into my lungs, I take a big sip of water. All while he watches me with an amused expression.

"No," I respond.

"Ah, yeah, you are."

"Stop being stupid," I bite out.

"Your eyes get all sparkly and crazy whenever he's around," his own gaze twinkles.

"They do not," I counter, like a child. *Wow.*

Knowing he has me riled, he chuckles.

"I thought he was your boyfriend?"

"Pretend boyfriend," I correct.

"So you're saying it's not the crazy, obsessive, *I will die for you* love?" he responds, pinning me with a look.

"Nope."

"I thought girls wanted the knight in shining armor?"

"Most girls just want to be treated with respect," I reply.

"What about spanking?" he quips.

"Who's getting spanked?" Tristan asks without looking up from his cell phone, as he approaches us and takes a seat.

"Your brother, if he doesn't shut up," I mumble.

Tristan places his phone down with a chuckle, while Zander begins to plate the dinner he made. It all seems so normal. *We* seem normal. But we're so far from it.

"Zander could use a good spanking," Tristan continues.

I throw a victory smirk at his brother, and he rolls his eyes in response before placing plates in front of us.

We dig in and a loud, unladylike moan escapes me the minute the warm sauce hits my tongue. *Heaven.*

At the sound, both brothers freeze and stare at me.

"What?" I ask, with my mouth full.

Zander throws me a disgusted look. "Sexy."

Tristan growls, and Zander's wide-eyed gaze shoots to his brother in surprise and amusement. "Seriously, Trist?"

I watch the two, fascinated. They argue like my uncles.

"Did I miss something?" I inquire.

"Your *pretend* boyfriend doesn't like me saying you're sexy." Zander points his fork at me. "He went all caveman."

"Speaking of which, you are mine," Tristan states flatly.

Zander's eyes widen again and then narrow into slits at his brother's declaration. His fork clanks down on his plate.

"Tristan—" Zander begins, but is cut off by my squeal.

"E-Excuse me?"

"Mine. You're mine." Tristan says simply. Slowly, to be sure that I comprehend what he's trying to say. I don't.

I release a bitter laugh, and watch him to see if he's serious. A muscle flexes across his jaw as his cognac eyes bore into me. "That funny, raindrop?" His expression is hard.

My mouth hangs open, unable to form words. "Um . . ."

"Tristan, I think you need to think this through, man."

Tristan ignores his brother, his focus solely on me.

"Under my protection, nobody lays a hand on you. Until this whole fiasco is over, it's you and me, raindrop. I'll destroy anyone who touches you, or tries to. If another being so much as looks at you disrespectfully, I will end their existence, on the spot and without warning. Your blood runs through my veins, however temporarily. It makes you mine for the time being. Understand?" He stares at me, waiting for a response.

I search for the ability to breathe and find my voice.

"You do know that I am a royal protector? I can defend my own honor and fight for my own life?" I challenge.

"When you declared me as your boyfriend earlier, you handed over your trust to me and officially became mine. Your existence is now tied to me, until it's not."

My eyes dart to the front door and then back to him, as he leans into my personal space.

"If you run, I will chase."

"What makes you think I'm going to run?" I ask.

He lowers his voice. "It's all over your face. I'm not Rulf, Serena. I won't accept rebelliousness or defiance when it comes to your safety. I've explained to you just how serious a situation you are in. As your guard, I can't be worried about you running when I'm supposed to protect you."

I bristle and watch Zander stand taller, folding his arms uncomfortably across his chest. His expression is stupefied.

I turn back to Tristan. "I may be in your realm and under your protection, but I am not one of your cronies or associates. Nobility or not, your word is not law—or final—when it comes to my protection, Tristan."

Tristan tenses before his hand reaches toward my face. I jerk back, but he continues to advance, and runs his thumb over my bottom lip. At his touch, I instantly calm.

"Stop talking, Serena," he uses a quiet tone.

I have no idea why, but I do. *Damn him.*

A knowing smiles crosses his face. "You see that? In the short time I've known you, I've managed on numerous occasions to get you to submit to me with a simple touch. In our world, that makes you mine. Only one of us can be in charge here. Moving forward, it's me. Stop being defiant."

"Ask me—nicely," I demand, trying to take control.

"Raindrop, *please* don't do anything stupid that requires me to rescue you—at least until after breakfast," he replies.

Kind of backhanded for a polite request.

I smile at him and dip my chin submissively.

"I understand," I bat my eyes and, without warning, jab my fork into his upper thigh.

Tristan doesn't flinch, but holding my gaze, he curls his hand around the cutlery and yanks it out, before throwing the bloody tableware onto the granite counter.

"It's evening, so technically, she listened," Zander taunts.

TRISTAN

FUCK, THAT HURT. I WATCH SERENA'S retreating form as she storms up the stairs toward the guest room. Now that she's out of ear-shot, I grunt in pain. Zander chuckles as he takes the first-aid kit out from under the sink.

"I like her," he says, pushing the kit toward me.

"I bet you do." I take out the antibacterial lotion and bandages to clean up the wound so it can begin to heal itself.

"You battle-worn yet?" he inquires.

"It takes more than a pretty, smart-mouthed gargoyle to wear me out," I reply, hoping I sound convincing, because—truth be told—I'm exhausted.

"I hate to state the obvious here, but you do know that you have no right to claim her. Protector bond or not."

"I know," I growl.

"So then why do it? If the queen finds out—" he adds.

"She won't," I bark. "Listen, it's just until I'm done with the assign-ment. Serena is a . . . handful. She needs authority or she'll run all over me as her protector, like she does with Rulf. The only way she'll respect me is by being mine."

"Even if it's not real?" he poses.

"Even if I can't keep her at the end of all this," I confirm.

"You really going to be able to walk away from her?"

I snap my gaze to his and glower. "I have no choice."

Zander exhales and throws me a sympathetic look.

"You're my brother. I know you better than I know myself. Don't lie to yourself about your feelings for her. It's written all over your face. Any fool can see it when you look at her. This plan, it's bad. And it will backfire on your ass."

"I've got it under control," I assure him.

He releases a bark-laugh. "You keep telling yourself that. Maybe after the millionth time it'll actually be true."

I watch him toss his plate in the sink and motion to the lasagna and salad. "Put these in the fridge so the poor girl has something to eat until Maria comes."

"Where are you going?" I ask.

He throws a pointed look my way. "You're not the only one with a stubborn female protection detail. There is a betrothed nymph princess who could use some company."

I give him an appreciative nod and watch as he makes his way to the front door. Without turning, he yanks it open.

"She isn't yours and you aren't hers," he says, his tone final as he leaves me in silence to ponder his words.

Zander is wrong. Serena was mine the minute we met.

I look up the stairs after her. She's so damn stubborn. It's time to draw a firm line in the sand with her. I stand and take the stairs two at a time.

Given Zander's reminders, I need to do this. He's right.

When I approach the guest room door, I still before lightly knocking, hoping she won't stab me in the other leg. Serena doesn't answer. Worried, I push open the door and look around the empty room. Stepping in, I take everything in. Nothing looks out of place. Yet, she isn't here.

I close my eyes and reach out through the bond, sensing she's still in the house. Through her emotions I feel she's calm and rejuvenating, which means she must be outside.

Within seconds, I cross the hall to the master and make my way toward the open balcony, where she's standing.

Naked. *Fuck.*

Her arms are out and her head is tilted toward the sky. The rain has turned into a light drizzle. The dampness on her pale skin is causing it to glisten.

Serena's long silky ringlets move the slightest amount across her back when the wind shifts.

The breeze brings me her scent—spring flowers. I inhale deeply. I love her scent.

My eyes follow the length of her spine, stopping on her lower back. For a moment, I appreciate all her curves.

Recognizing she isn't alone, she looks over her bare shoulder at me, and suddenly I can't breathe. She's so fucking beautiful.

Tonight her eyes are so blue, they almost hurt to look at. They're enchanting. I swallow and lift my hand to run it through my hair, and realize I'm shaking. My heartbeat picks up. Without even knowing it, she's woken up my heart.

This is what happens when you live in darkness. You want what you can never have—a small piece of light.

I look away, breaking our contact.

My hands continue to tremble, as I reach behind my neck and aggressively yank my T-shirt off my body. I need to take control.

Serena spins to face me. My hand snaps out, throwing the shirt at her.

"We should establish some rules," I snarl.

Huffing, she puts the shirt on and stomps into the room before standing by the lit fireplace. "I don't really do rules."

"You do now," I state.

"Like, never go to bed angry?" she throws out.

I glare at her. "That isn't what I mean."

"What do you mean? Be nice? Always wear clothes?"

"Wearing clothes is a good start," I sigh. "Another is not stabbing me with dinner cutlery."

Regret falls across her features. "Does it hurt?"

"I'll live," I scowl.

She has the audacity to look offended at my response.

I stand there just staring at her, because she's so damn pretty, and no matter how much I try to put emotional distance between us, she closes it.

"Now that you know I am your protector we—," I start.

"It's striking," she whispers under her breath.

I look around in confusion. "What is?"

"Your protector tattoo. The one that carries my blood."

I stare blankly at her face. This is a dangerous game that she's playing. If she were to touch it—touch me—game over.

The lump in my throat is getting heavier with the weight of her look. We hold one another's eyes for a long moment before she slowly takes a step toward me.

I lift a hand to stop her. "I don't think it's a good idea."

"Why?"

"It just isn't," I say defensively.

She ignores me and keeps advancing. The mark draws her to me, and for the first time ever in my life, I'm nervous.

Holding my gaze, her fingertips hover over my chest.

"Serena," I warn.

Her hesitation is fleeting. She slowly reaches out, and lightly her fingertips trace the mark covering my heart.

The two lions are designed in a black barbed-wire pattern and make a yin-yang symbol.

The mark pulsates with every touch, and the blood it's infused with—her blood—rises in recognition of her.

I grit my teeth. "Every assigned protector has one."

"You carry the lion spirit," she states.

"The Paris clan does. Gage is my father," I heave out.

She continues to run her fingers over the maze pattern and my world tilts. My heart lifts to greet her touch.

I shiver.

"Are you cold?" she asks, in barely a whisper.

"Irritated," I respond through a clenched jaw, because her touch is causing my body to hum with the primal urge to claim her. A side effect of the bond we now share. *That's all it is, right?*

The palm of her other hand flattens on my lower stomach, and every muscle under her warmth jumps to life.

Her eyes snap to mine. "What does it feel like?"

I swallow. "What does what feel like?"

"Our bond?"

I lick my lips. "It's suffocating—until I see you and can breathe. It's darkness—until your light breaks through. It's the lowest low—until you make me feel the highest high. It makes me want to walk through fire and fight for you. Save you and protect you. It allows me to feel you in my bones, in every crevice of my heart, and in every breath I take."

Without awareness of what I'm doing, my hands find their way to either side of her head, entangling and burying my fingers within the damp strands.

"Stop," I beg.

Her eyes slide closed. "I break rules, Tristan; I don't follow them. So don't bother imposing any on me. As for the bond, I can handle myself. I'll listen to you. Respect you. I'll allow for your protection, but I won't let you treat me like just another assignment. You carry my blood with you—in you—and that makes you both weak and strong. You need me to protect you as much as I need you." She presents me with a sad smile. "See, you and I are meant to be together. Suck it up."

SEVENTEEN
SUN OF VERGINA

TRISTAN

I STUDY HER MOUTH AS THE words glide out. *Are we? Meant to be?* Perhaps in another lifetime she'd be right, but in this one, it's simply not possible. I remind myself it's just the bond talking. Nothing more.

Serena directs her glare at me and I realize I still have her head between my hands. I release her and try to take a step back. I need space to clear the fog her presence always seems to conjure up.

By the look on her face, I can tell she's having none of it. Her hand flattens over the protector mark, bringing it completely to life and causing a fire to roar through my veins. In an instant, I pull her against my body and crash my mouth onto hers, all before she can even blink an eye.

She breathes in every exhale I release. My mouth works against hers. Hard. Demanding. My hands fist into her hair, tugging dominantly so that she'll comply with my need to tilt her head upward as I nip at her lips.

Her hands slide up, snaking around my neck.

"Serena—" I growl.

"Don't speak," she demands, finding my mouth again.

"Serena—" I attempt again.

"Don't think. Just . . . feel," she orders between kisses.

I mutter a few choice words as I taste the mint on her tongue. *God, she's going to be my undoing.* With a grunt, I throw my head back and lift her legs around my waist.

"Fuck. I need you," I rasp, not knowing what I'm saying.

"I need you too." Her mouth moves down my neck, teeth nipping before her tongue swirls and soothes each bite mark.

Walking backwards, I turn and place her down on my bed before attacking her lips again. She moans into my mouth and it urges me to kiss her harder. More demanding, if that is even possible.

Serena's hands slide into my hair and tug lightly, encouraging me. As if I need it. Her taste alone is addictive. Her hands claw at the belt on my jeans, and suddenly nothing else in the world matters.

Just her.

I tear away from her, trying to catch my breath. Serena's blue eyes are dilated, and I watch her chest rise and fall with each pant. *Shit, what am I doing?*

Her right hand wraps around the leather necklace that hangs from my neck, pulling me back to her. I go without a fight, and her eyes search mine. As if she understands my indecision, she inhales one final time.

"What is this?" Her thumb runs across the steel-colored crest that hangs off the strap.

"A Vergina Sun symbol," I pant.

"What does it mean?" her voice is low.

"It identifies me as satyr royalty. Ophelia's son."

"And the hematite?"

"My protector stone. Like yours is the emerald."

She studies the insignia. Keeping her eyes trained on it, she whispers, "Tell me the truth, Tristan. Is this," she motions between us, "because of your satyr blood? Are you enthralling me?" Her gaze snaps to mine.

I look her in the eyes and deepen my tone so she knows I'm serious.

"No. Never would I, without your permission."

Some satyrs charm other supernatural beings to fulfill their own wanton needs. Not me. I regard it as a violation.

She swallows. "And our protector bond?"

I offer a small unconvincing smile. "I don't think so."

Her chin dips in the slightest motion in acceptance. The grip she has on my necklace tightens almost as if she's grounding herself with it. Guessing she needs some form of assurance, I cup her face with one of my palms.

"I can tell you this—I would die you for. Without thought. The bond requires me to protect you."

"Requires?" Her voice is dejected.

"Hey," I force her to look at me. "The bond isn't why I want to constantly kiss you. Touch you. Feel you."

Her eyes widen. "It isn't?"

"No."

"Then, why?" her voice is breathy.

I stare at her. Am I really going to do this? Lay it all out for her, knowing there is no future for us? Yeah. I am. *Shit.*

"The way you taste is my addiction. When I'm near you, I can breathe. And even though at times, I want to strangle you for your fierce independence, I love it. I like that you can defend yourself. That you aren't afraid to say whatever is on your mind. You're beautiful, Serena. Inside and out. You're intelligent, strong, and witty. You are everything in this life that I never knew I wanted—needed to feel complete. I'm attracted to you simply because you're you."

"Wow," she breathes out.

"But, I've said it before, I can't keep you. Regardless of what we feel toward one another, we aren't meant for each other. I need you to really understand that before we take this any further. We're destined to fail before we begin."

She rears back. "Your version of the truth sucks."

I huff. "The truth is, I'm no good for you. You probably already know this by now. I'll let you down and break you."

"What if I don't allow you to?" she challenges.

I release a chuckle. "You're tenacious."

"I know what I want, Tristan. That's all," she retorts.

I exhale. "You deserve somebody to love you, fully. Someone to adore you. I'm not him. All I can promise is the worst. We'd only be lying to ourselves if we continue this."

Her body shifts as she guides me down onto the bed.

We're slipping near the edge, and I'm starting to lose my control to stop this before it starts. The delusional thoughts in my head are taking over; maybe I could wake up to her.

Within seconds she's straddling me. Her fingertips run over my jawline. "I can feel it, Tristan. We're becoming something else. Something bigger than we even know."

"Maybe it's time to walk away, then," I mutter.

"Let me in." She whispers the plea.

I wince. "Why? You'll leave me. Hurt me."

Her eyes water with unshed tears as she shakes her head back and forth. "I won't."

"Everyone else has, Serena."

"I'll fight for you in a way that no one else ever has."

At her words, I break. She brings me to my knees. There is no force, across any realm, that makes me feel the way she does. *Fuck.* I think I'm falling for her.

"Come on, let go," she says, brushing my lips with hers.

"I can't." I squeeze her waist in silent plea for her to stop.

"Can't, or won't?" she counters.

"Just let it be," I state flatly.

I used to recognize myself, but peering up at Serena and seeing myself through her eyes, the reflection has changed. And it scares the crap out of me.

In silence, she considers me. Then, cautiously, she places her hand over my heart. Over the protector mark.

"I'll wait for you," she vows, with a hidden meaning.

"You'll be waiting a long time." *Forever, actually.*

Her grin is wide. "It's a good that I'm patient then."

All around us the air is charged with electric currents. Like the universe is jump-starting our hearts.

I study her. She's serious. Whatever false thoughts are running around her head, she's made her mind up, and I fear that there is no changing it. The protector watches me like she's discovered her new favorite brand of ice cream. It's time for damage control.

But then she sits up, offering me a gentle smile before she lifts my T-shirt over her body, revealing herself to me.

And my fight is gone. All I see, all I want, is her. Forever.

SERENA

THE SILENCE BETWEEN US IS DEAFENING. Tristan's hungry gaze roams my naked body with appreciation. His heart beats hard against the palm of my hand. When he licks his gorgeous lips, it's my undoing.

I lean down and loom over him, teasing.

"Right now, Tristan. You and me," I state.

"I don't think that is a good idea," he shoots back.

"Just once more." My voice is low and smooth, lulling him into compliance. "Just one more taste."

My mouth hovers above his, and I know he won't stop me. Not even a little. I inch closer and his brows draw together.

My lips brush over his in the lightest of touches, before I run my tongue over his mouth and chin, down his neck, and across all the hard planes of his chest and taut stomach.

With each lick, his muscles spasm under my touch, and I grin. At the same time, I manage to finish unbuckling his pants and open the button before sliding down the zipper.

I glance down and smile before crawling up his body to meet his lust-filled gaze. "You aren't wearing underwear," I say, sliding my hand into the front of his pants.

"I know—oh shit." His eyes roll back as I stroke the hard length of his silky erection.

The tip of my tongue darts out and I run it over his upper lip and then his lower one. My mouth presses over his in the barest of touches as I speak across his lips. "I'm going to taste you now," I warn, and slide back down his body.

His gaze follows me and his hands find their way into my hair, fisting it at the top, guiding my head down.

Tristan bites his lip as I take him out. The heaviness fills my hand. Holding his eyes, I lick the entire length and he growls like an animal, which just turns me on more.

My tongue swirls around the tip and his head falls back to the bed.

"Oh, fuck," he moans.

I close my mouth around the top and take him in as far as I can. After the second time, Tristan yanks my head up to his face, hard. The sting tingles around my skull.

With heavy breaths, he stares at me, as if deciding what to do next. I like the way he's looking at me, and my heart suddenly aches with the realization that I am attached to him. He makes life better just by being around me.

"Are you sure?" he pants out.

I swallow. "Yes."

He holds me still. "One more time, Serena. That's it."

"Understood," I whisper.

His lips rise, pressing against mine. When I gasp, he pushes his tongue into my mouth, kissing me senseless.

My head begins to spin, and my heart pounds with every stroke. My core shatters, and everything in my stomach and lower body tightens with need and want. I'm done for.

My control slips and Tristan takes advantage. Dominating me, he flips me onto my back and covers my body with his. His hands slide out of my hair and grip the sides of my face tightly, almost painfully. His rings press into my cheeks. Like he's begging me to stop this.

To stop him.

I won't.

I want him more than I want air right now.

He continues to assault my mouth and with one hand, finishes pushing his jeans off so he's completely naked.

After my lips are bruised and swollen, he sucks a pathway down my throat, leaving bite marks and bruising the skin. It's a slow, sensual, maddening type of torture.

Without any warning, Tristan presses down on my clit and begins to relentlessly circle the bundle of nerves.

I writhe and he holds my head still with the other hand that's still pressed against it.

Within seconds, I cry out, almost blacking out with shock at how quickly my orgasm hit me.

"Good girl," he murmurs, and looks at me.

His praise has me shaking again, as he slides two fingers through my wet folds and brings them to his mouth.

"Fuck, I like the way you taste," he growls, and I pant watching him suck them.

"Don't move," he orders, and I nod, complying.

Seconds later he's standing over me, rolling on a condom as I swallow wantonly at the sight of Tristan looking down at me, sprawled out on his bed.

His face hardens, his mouth drawing tight.

Every nerve in my body is alive and in need of his touch. I reach my hand out for him to take, and wait.

For a moment, he just stares at me, before some of the tension in his face eases and his eyes become hazy.

At the sight, my body begins to ache with need.

Tristan ignores my outstretched hand and instead climbs up over my body, covering mine with his. Once again, his hands cradle my head as he looks deeply into my gaze. My fingers wrap themselves around the leather bands on his wrists, holding on to him.

The tip of his erection presses against my entrance, and I release a needy mewl and begin to tremble under his stare.

"I like you, raindrop," he whispers. "More than I should."

I can't help but smile. "I like you too."

In one slow, torturous thrust, he pushes into me, filling me completely, all the while staring into my eyes.

"Oh, shit, Tristan," I exhale in pleasure. "I—"

"I know what you need. I've got you." He circles his hips at the same time he grinds himself against me. "Trust me."

The movement causes me to inhale through my nose and grip his wrists tighter, as my blood boils in my veins.

"I trust you," I whisper.

Ever so slowly, he begins to slide in and out of me in a measured rhythm. He takes his time, watching my every reaction to his skilled movements, memorizing my responses to him.

As my body climbs higher toward release, his thumbs trace my trembling lower lip.

"Scream my name when you come," he demands.

All I can do is pant in response to the request and nod.

He releases one side of my face and his hand runs along my body, leaving goosebumps in its wake, before his fingers rub over me, sending me over the edge screaming his name.

My orgasm is hard and long, as I pulse around him without shame, gasping roughly for air.

He places a gentle kiss to the hollow at the base of my throat while I continue to writhe underneath him.

His hands slip under my ass and without pulling out of me, he moves us into a sitting position.

I grip his shoulders for support. He slides one hand up my body, stopping with it wrapped around my neck in a gentle hold.

His other hand presses my lower back, guiding my rocking movements, as he takes control of my lips with a slow, sensual kiss.

"God, you feel so fucking good," he rumbles, holding me to him as I move up and down at a slow, controlled pace.

My eyelids flutter a little and I bite my lower lip as my body begins to shake again. He leans down, scraping the edge of his teeth over my nipple, and I release a loud scream.

Tristan moves his mouth to the other breast, and my hands fall from his shoulders to the tops of his arms. My fingernails dig into his skin as I become breathless.

"Tristan," I gasp.

"Fuck me," he groans, and with his hand pushes my lower back, encouraging me to speed up my pace.

My forehead falls to his and I come again with a cry.

He blows out a long breath and with both hands under my ass, guides me up and down so he can thrust in and out of me. With a final grunt, Tristan pushes deep inside me as far as he can go and says my name in a broken sound as he pulses against my trembling inner walls with his release.

Moments later, we're both panting, sweaty, and stuck together. Tristan's hand glides down my back before he pulls me against him in a tight embrace.

When I tilt my head back to look at him, he leans forward and takes my mouth with a soft kiss before pulling away. I run my hands over his face and see the transition behind his eyes almost immediately. He's overthinking again.

Carefully, I climb off of him and stand on shaky legs, his eyes following every one of my movements.

"I'm going to shower," I speak softly, and he nods.

I pick up his shirt off the floor and toss it over my head, covering myself while he stands and pulls off the condom.

I throw him a small smile and walk toward the door, but he grabs my hand, forcing me to turn around and face him.

"In here," he states.

Taken aback, I frown. "What?"

He swallows hard as his eyes dart around the room.

"Shower in here and stay the night in my bed."

I sigh. "Tristan, I'm a big girl. We don't have to do this."

He growls at me. "I want you in my bed tonight."

I take in his demeanor and concede. "Okay."

Leaning down, he places a light kiss on my lips and tilts his head toward the en-suite. "I'll be right behind you."

He's everywhere, taking up all the air. All I can do is agree to his every request and melt with each touch. I nod, trying to recall a single moment in my life when I have been more submissive than I am with him.

Nope. None. I've got nothing. I pout, angry at myself for allowing him to take over my mind and body the way he has. He makes me forget to be strong and fierce, yet allows me to be vulnerable and open.

Releasing his hand, I step around him and step into the bathroom, closing the door behind me so I can breathe.

I hate feeling this way—so out of control.

EIGHTEEN
BAITED BREATH

SERENA

I TOSSED AND TURNED ALL NIGHT. Sleeping next to Tristan made me achy and needy. His heat swirled over me, invading every section of my body. It felt itchy, suffocating.

The smell of bacon hits me as I pad down the stairs. Figuring Zander must be here cooking again, I groan inwardly and plaster a stiff smile on my face before taking the corner into the kitchen.

Once I step inside the room, I immediately freeze at the sight of the pretty, young Hispanic woman chatting with Tristan.

I watch their interaction with curiosity. He says something that makes her giggle, and my heart sinks at the easy, familiar way they're interacting.

Her shiny, straight, black hair sways as her petite shoulders shake with laughter. He's relaxed in her presence. Calm. I immediately hate her. Yeah. I'm jealous.

When she sees me, her eyes widen in surprise.

Tristan turns, and upon seeing me, his entire face lights up, causing my insides to knot. *What is that? Shit. More feelings.*

"Morning." His voice is deep.

"I didn't mean to interrupt." I motion to the girl whose eyes are on me, boring holes into my skull.

Tristan's grin widens as he steps over to me and leans down, placing a long, sensual kiss across my swollen lips.

After what feels like forever, he leans back and smiles.

"Jealous, raindrop?"

"What? No," I state a little too loudly.

"Serena, this is Maria, my housekeeper," he introduces, and she manages to collect herself long enough to come over and greet me. "Maria, this is my guest and charge, Serena."

"Nice to meet you," she says politely, and takes my hand.

"You too," I reply, not buying her nice-girl act.

"I'm making Spanish omelets. Do you like?" Maria asks.

"Sí," I answer, and everyone falls silent. Making this even weirder than it already is. "I mean, yes. I do. Thank you."

She nods her head and makes her way back to the stove.

Tristan smirks and hands me a cup of coffee.

I take a sip and narrow my eyes at him.

"You know how I take my coffee?"

The back of his hand runs down my cheek.

"I know everything there is to know about you, Serena."

I blush. It's unlike me. I hate myself right now.

He pushes the hair away from my face with both his hands, leans in, and presses another gentle kiss to my lips.

"I like that you're shy with me now," he whispers.

"You just like me submissive," I counter.

"Yes. I do. It makes my job easier," he replies.

I try not to let his words affect me.

"Is that all I am? A job?"

"Nope," he winks, and takes a sip of his own coffee. "You're also my fake girlfriend," he teases.

I like this side of him. I didn't expect Tristan to be so casual this morning. I expected him to be cold and distant. Not attentive and kind.

"Well, I can honestly say that you're the best fake boyfriend I've ever had." I sit at the counter and he joins me.

"Yeah? How many have you had?" he asks.

"Fake boyfriends? Including you? One."

"How about real?" his tone is serious.

I shrug. "Um, relationships aren't really my forte."

I'm saved by Maria, as she places our plates in front of us. I salivate at the omelet, potatoes, and bacon before digging in.

"Thank you, Maria," Tristan says.

"Why don't you have the lion crest on your back?" I ask around a piece of thick, hickory-smoked bacon.

Gargoyles are usually branded with their family crest—males from their shoulders to their lower back, and females just on their lower back, and only when they mate with a particular clan. With the exception of me, my entire family is adorned with the dragon.

I know Gage has a lion on his, since he's from the Paris clan. It's interesting that Tristan doesn't bear the crest.

"Gage didn't mark me at birth, because he wasn't there for my birth," his tone is off. "He never knew I existed."

"Right. Sorry." I continue to scarf down the bacon, and chastise myself for my stupid inquisitive nature.

"Why don't you want to be princess?" he fires back.

I pick at the omelet. "I've always just thought I was meant for something . . . different. Expectations are higher when you're the only heir. As protectors, we're bound by laws to safeguard others not of our own choosing. I guess I've just always wanted the freedom to decide my own fate. To be bound to someone of my own choice. To shine my own light instead of living in others' shadows."

"Is that why you're defiant with Rulf?" he questions.

"Rulf isn't blood bonded to me. Still, he was chosen to watch over me my entire life. His presence is a constant reminder of my aunt Eve and uncle Asher's epic love, and my lack of free will."

Tristan tilts his head in my direction. "Given the opportunity, Serena, what would you do with your life if you weren't slated to be the next leader of the gargoyle race?"

I study his mouth. I've never really thought about it.

"I'm unsure what an alternative destiny looks like."

He nods. "When you figure it out, let me know."

I lift my gaze and meet his. "I will."

"We have dinner plans with my mother and Rionach this evening. Today, I thought I'd show you around the realm. Maybe we'll work on your hand-to-hand a bit," he suggests.

"Will Chancellor Davidson be upset that we're gone?"

He shakes his head. "He's aware of the reason behind our absence," he explains. "Asher let him know."

Of course he did.

After last night, I almost forgot why I'm here.

"Can the Diablo Fairies cross into your realm?" I ask.

"No," he shakes his head, wiping his mouth with a napkin. "Our army is on alert. Asmodeus doesn't know that I exist. Or that I am protecting you. The clans are watching him closely and will inform us of any change in his status."

I slide my focus to my breakfast plate, before looking up to see Maria watching me curiously.

Once she notices me looking at her, she averts her gaze.

"Hey," Tristan says, placing his hand over mine. I meet his guarded eyes before focusing on the vein popping out of his neck. "You're safe with me."

The truth is, I'm not safe with Tristan Gallagher.

Safe in the sense of protection from Asmodeus? Yes.

Safe in the sense of my heart? Not even close.

TRISTAN

SERENA LOOKS LIKE SHE'S READY TO vomit. That makes two of us. All morning I've been faking being calm, struggling through presenting her with an easygoing manner.

It didn't go unnoticed by me that when Serena stepped into the kitchen and saw Maria, a murderous rage crossed her features. She was jealous, which means she's developing feelings for me, and that just can't happen. Ever.

Last night, I should have let her go back to her own room to shower and sleep. When she got up to leave, though, I panicked. Something inside of me snapped, and the thought of turning her away after what we had experienced slayed me.

I stare at the tomatoes in my breakfast. I'm confused by my reactions to her, and even more confused by the way my heart is beating uncontrollably around her this morning. As she walked into the kitchen earlier, I was immediately consumed with anger at my own lack of self-control.

Yet, when I turned and saw her, standing in my T-shirt, with bed head and swollen lips, I couldn't help but beam with pride that I was the reason she looked like that.

Last night was amazing. So. Fucking. Amazing. I don't even know how to feel right now. I'm really trying my best this morning not to appear as disoriented as I'm feeling inside. We need to get out of the house and get some fresh air so I don't grab her every five minutes and ravage her, because being inside of her is the most incredible feeling in the world.

Serena clears her throat, and my eyes turn to her.

She's waiting, expecting me to respond to what she just said. I can't. Her eyes search mine and my heart goes all haywire, and for the life of me, I can't figure out how something as good as last night wasn't meant to be.

"What do you think?" she asks.

I stare.

"Tristan?" she prompts.

I keep staring.

She smiles and puts her hand over mine, and that little bit of contact is my undoing.

I stand abruptly, knocking over my stool in the process, and grip my plate tightly before meeting Maria's wide-eyed stare. I all but run to the sink in order to get away.

"Yeah. Good. Whatever you want, Serena," I ramble.

Maria glares at me oddly and gently takes the plate out of my hands. "I'll take care of this, Your Highness."

"Thank you," I choke out, and chance a look at Serena, but she isn't there anymore.

My shoulders relax. I'm glad that she's giving me time to pull my shit together. Exhaling, I head into my office to check emails and voice messages. An hour later, I step into the hallway and am greeted by a pair of dazzling blue eyes.

"Ready?" she asks.

"For what?"

Serena frowns. "I suggested we take a swim earlier."

I stand there, mouth agape.

"In the lake. At breakfast? You said, 'Yeah. Good. Whatever you want, Serena,'" she mimics me.

My eyes drop and take in the tiny black bikini she's wearing. *Ah, shit.* I stare like an absolute idiot.

"Tristan?" she blinks at me, worried.

I clear my throat. "I'll just go change."

"Okay," she beams. "I'll meet you outside."

"Sounds like a plan. I mean, yeah, it sounds like a solid plan. To swim. Together." *Stop talking, Tristan. Just stop.*

She watches me, amused. "I'll just be outside then," Serena turns and walks to the front door.

My eyes roam over her backside and I inwardly groan. That bathing suit is going to be the death of me today. I can't help but stare at her lower back. If we were mated, it's where a matching protector mark would appear. My mark.

The idea of my lions branding her, marking her as mine, has my heart slamming against my rib cage. My chest heaves as I remember my actions last night. I need to rein it in. I head upstairs to change. It's going to be a long-ass day.

I walk outside and take in a deep cleansing breath. The sun is shining and the breeze is warm. It's perfect weather.

"I was beginning to think you bailed on me." Serena looks up at me from her position, sprawled out on a rock. She's soaking in the sun without a care in the world, as if the king of the Nine Hells isn't out to kill her.

My smile grows as I approach her. I hope it hides the fact that I want to jump her bones right here out in the open.

Her eyes greedily take me in, and she swallows.

"You okay?" I ask, with a smug look.

"Yeah, why?"

"You're completely flushed," I point out.

"It's the sun. It's . . . hot."

"Hot?" I repeat.

"So . . . very . . . hot," she draws out.

I lay out a towel and take a seat next to her.

"So listen," I begin. "I have to be completely honest with you. I wasn't really listening to you this morning."

She feigns surprise. "No. Really? I'm guessing you were imagining me naked." She bumps my shoulder and I fall silent. "Holy shit. Were you?"

I count to five so I can sound in control, my hand slowly rubbing the back of my neck. "That's not the point. The point is, I think we should train today. We could do it in the water instead of swimming. Kill two birds with one stone."

A mischievous glare crosses her face.

"You want to *do it* in the water?" she giggles.

I sigh. "How old are you? Train. Train in the water."

Her bottom lip jets out. "Really."

"You do comprehend just how serious this situation is, Serena? I can't protect you all the time. I need you to be able to defend yourself and, to be honest, you have no idea what the Diablo Fairies can do to you."

I can actually feel the wind charge with her frustration as she releases some of her powers into the air.

"Fine," she says, as she stands and dives into the water.

I watch her, thanking God that most of her uncovered body will be concealed by the cobalt water.

Seconds later she pops up. Her hands wipe the water off her face and smooth her hair back.

I just sit here, watching her, like a horny teenager.

Her gaze focuses expectantly on mine.

"Are we doing this or what?" she calls out.

Or what. Say, or what. I stand and readjust myself.

I'm so hard right now, I hope I remember how to fight.

"I'm coming," I shout.

She giggles, again. "Are you?"

I throw an annoyed glare at her before diving into the water. At the same time, I teleport behind her, so I'm completely silent under the water and she can't detect me.

Treading, she flattens her palms. I watch as the wind rushes the water, her attempt to move it and find me. I back away, slowly.

A few minutes pass, and her face becomes distorted with worry. I can feel her concern for me start to take over her abilities. I need to put an end to it, so she can focus.

I sneak up on her and grab her ankles, pulling her under the water. Her legs scissor as she fights my hold, but I continue to drag her down, deeper and deeper.

Her eyes latch onto mine and narrow at me as she fights for control. A murderous look crosses her face, and I snicker. My hands slide up her long legs and wrap around her waist.

We have maybe another two minutes before she runs out of air and I have to teleport us back to land. I needed to pull her under so she can't use the pull of the energy to jump-start her powers. This is me forcing her to use her physical strength.

A wicked expression crosses her face and I purse my lips. This should be interesting.

Her long legs wrap around me in a tight hold, pressing her body against mine. For one brief moment, my heart stops beating. Her hands run over my shoulders, cupping my cheeks and slipping down my throat, curving against the base with a light press. I try to swallow, but can't.

Her head dips in and her mouth closes over mine before she inhales whatever air I have left in my lungs. At first, I think she's kissing me, but after a few seconds, my lungs empty and I realize she's trying to asphyxiate me.

My hands ball into fists before tightening around her waist, and with the small amount of energy I have left, I teleport us out of the water.

The warmth of the sun blankets me. I inhale several deep breaths and blink my eyes open several times before Serena comes into view. Her breath fans my face as she leans in closer to me. I shrink back as my heart rate picks up.

"See, I can win without using my gifts," she smirks.

I'm silent for a moment, impressed with her approach.

"Are you dying?" she holds back a laugh.

"No." I continue to suck in air.

"How do you know?"

"I'd never let that happen. To you, or me."

The grass is prickly against my bare back as she straddles me. I flip her onto her back, hovering above her, and grant her a twisted smile.

"Well played, raindrop," I compliment.

"Still like being my protector?" she whispers.

I stiffen, and my eyes roam the length of her wet body under me, before I catch her gaze and my lips twitch.

"I think I like being your pretend boyfriend more."

A smile crosses her face as she traces my lips with her thumb and cups my cheek. "Yeah?"

"Either way. You leave me breathless."

NINETEEN
TRACES IN THE NIGHT

TRISTAN

TRAINING IN THE WATER ACCOMPLISHED NOTH-ING, and while I'm impressed with the way Serena was able to take me down, it's not a realistic approach against the devil fairies.

My wary gaze settles on Serena as I watch her push to her feet, slower this time.

She's exhausted, and so am I.

We've been practicing all day.

I extend my hand to her, which she takes with a grunt.

"Every muscle in me aches, and my thighs officially feel like someone has lit them on fire," she pouts.

"It will get easier." I look at her as she limps to me. "Your blocking techniques have already improved tenfold."

Her smile is forced, as she twists her hair around her hand and then throws it into a loose bun. I stare at her neck and notice when she winces in discomfort.

"You okay?" I ask, stepping closer.

She nods. "Yeah. Just sore."

My fingers lift of their own accord to massage the muscle in the back of her neck. The touch elicits a shiver from her.

"How'd you get that scar on your lip?" she asks quietly.

"I was running through the woods at your uncle Asher's coronation, and a tree branch caught me," I answer.

"Why were you running?"

I hate what I'm about to admit. "I was worried about Abby when Asher's father and his minions attacked."

"You were upset about my mom?" she confirms.

"She was pregnant with you. I was concerned for *your* safety. I was two, Serena. I didn't understand. Yours was the first aura I read. And it was in utero. My mother's guards found me before I could go back," I point out.

Serena falls quiet for a long time, before her fingertips rise to graze the scar. "Scars are badges of honor. It shows how brave and strong a protector is. If you're ashamed—"

"I'm not," I snap. It's simply a reminder of how long we've been connected. "We should get cleaned up and head to the castle. We're expected for dinner this evening."

"Okay," she responds in a quiet murmur.

I take her hand. "I didn't mean to snap."

"I understand," she squeezes my hand.

No, she really doesn't.

"I'll teleport us. It will be faster."

"Thank goodness," she smiles, and we're gone.

After a long soak in the Jacuzzi tub and a nap, we've freshened up and are making our way to my mother's castle, which is located on the other side of the realm.

Serena wanted to walk so she could see more of the kingdom. As we approach the Victorian log-cabin fortress, an uneasy feeling settles in the pit of my stomach. To be honest, it's been with me all day. Like we're being watched.

I take one last look around the wooded area before opening the double doors of the palace and placing my hand on Serena's lower back.

The action is meant to both guide her and help ground my erratic emotions. But the minute my hand touches her I'm reminded of the way her body feels against mine. The way her mouth tastes.

"Shit," I bark out, just as my mother rounds the corner.

Her eyes widen as she looks back at Rionach, who is following closely behind her. His normally easygoing demeanor falls flat at the sound of my foul mouth.

"Prince Tristan, watch your language in the queen's presence," he barks, like the good general he is.

"Apologies," I offer, half sincere.

A polite smile crosses mom's lips. "I'll overlook it once this evening, Tristan. Let this be the only warning."

"Of course, mother," I dip my head respectfully.

She smiles at Serena and holds her hands out for her guest to take. I watch Serena slide her hands into my mother's, and an indescribable feeling spreads in my chest at the sight of the two of them. I push it away, instead focusing on the regal grace with which my mother guides Serena to the tall man standing to her left—his designated position.

For whatever reason, my stepfather looks older than when I last I saw him. The realm's troubles with the water fairies must be wearing on him.

His golden hair has turned more gray than yellow, and his deep forehead is creased with new lines. His wide nose and large chin make him seem intimidating this evening.

As usual, he's wearing his general's uniform. It's green and gold— regal. A long, sleeveless, leather vest sits over it, presenting a less militia feel, as do his fingerless gloves.

A true legionnaire, he always wears his sword on his waist, like an old friend. Rionach's look is a combination of ancient Greek warrior and Irish guerilla. It made for an interesting combination, growing up under his protection.

"Serena, I'd like to introduce you to my husband, Rionach. Rionach, may I present Princess Serena of the London clan of gargoyles," her tone is formal, noble.

Rionach offers Serena a warm Irish smile, and his blue eyes twinkle at her. "It's an honor, Your Highness." He takes a knee, and Serena dips her head like she's been taught to do.

He stands, and she stares at him a moment longer. "I hope this doesn't come out wrong, but you look like Ronin from that kids' movie, *Epic*," she says, and he smiles warmly.

"I'll take it. He's young and quite handsome," he winks.

Serena laughs, and my breath hitches at the sound. *I need to get my shit together tonight.*

"That he is. As are you," she flirts, and does it well.

I don't like it. I bristle and step to her side, taking her hand out of my stepfather's before standing slightly in front of her in a protective manner.

My action doesn't go unnoticed by mother. Her gaze latches on to Serena's hand in mine, and I release it. *So much for keeping myself under control.*

"Tristan mentioned that you were tired after your day yesterday. I do hope you've been able to rest, and that he has been most hospitable while you've stayed in our realm?"

"He has. Thank you for your kindness and safe haven."

"It is our pleasure," Queen Ophelia responds politely.

"It's about time you two showed your ugly faces," Zander taunts, making his way down the hallway.

I clear my throat. "Why? What's wrong?"

He juts out his chin, motioning between my mother and Rionach. "These two have been all *kissy hand-holding eye-ogling* at one another all night. Like teenagers."

I smile. "That's nothing new."

They've been in love with each other since they first laid eyes on each other. It was love at first sight. It's beautiful in a *he'd die for her and she for him* kind of way. At the thought, I'm hit with an unexpected pang of jealousy.

My eyes slide to Serena, who is watching them with interest. "My dad always told me stories about hidden worlds, where brave warriors watch over and protect beautiful queens," Serena says, and my mother blushes. "It's nice to see there is some truth to the fairy tales."

"What a lovely thing to share," the queen responds.

"Shall we?" My mother motions toward the dining room.

"After you, darling," Rionach allows her to lead us in.

I lean toward Serena's ear. "I thought you didn't believe in fairy tales?" I ask quietly.

She shrugs. "I don't. I believe in love, though."

I stand motionless as Serena follows my mother and Rionach into the opulent room for dinner.

Zander claps me on the shoulder. "It's nice to see you've got things under control," he teases, and we both walk in.

Rionach holds out my mother's chair as she takes the head seat and then moves to her right, pulling out Serena's chair in a gentlemanly fashion.

Zander immediately slips into the seat next to Serena, throwing me a victorious look and leaving me to sit across from her, in between my mother and stepfather.

"This is a beautiful room," Serena compliments, taking in the large ornate gold chandeliers and dark wood-paneled walls. The fireplace has been lit for ambience, as have the candles in gold candelabras strewn about the room.

"It's actually my favorite room in the castle," my mother replies. "Aside from the library, of course."

"Do you read a lot, Your Majesty?" Serena inquires.

"As much as I can." The two of them lose themselves in talk of historical romance novels and alpha males.

I watch their easy chatter and can't help but smile.

Rionach passes the rolls to me with a curious glare, forcing me to look away and focus on buttering my roll.

"Tristan, how is the assignment going?" he asks.

The hurt is still evident in his Irish brogue that I didn't allow him to help me out of my protector sentencing.

Rionach has been a father to me since I was a child. I respect and look up to him. He, in turn, treats me as if I am his own son. The fact that he isn't blood, or a gargoyle, meant that he had no authority to stop my sentencing.

Only Gage was able to do that, and I know it hurt Rionach.

"As well as can be expected, sir," I respond formally.

"I see," he glances at Serena, then back to me.

Zander cuts in, saving me from further questioning. "Tristan is smoking again," he waggles his eyebrows at me.

All conversation halts, and my mother's angry glare makes its way over to me.

"Tristan," she exhales.

"I haven't had a cigarette in over a month," I assure her.

"Still. I thought you'd released the habit. As you know, you can't—" I stop her.

"I know. I've quit. It was a small misstep." I glare at Zander, watching him laugh in amusement.

The staff enter with silver-covered platters, and present our first course. The smell of butternut squash and sage assaults my nose, and I can't help but groan.

"This looks amazing," Serena compliments.

"Thank goodness you had me feed Serena last night," Zander announces. "Poor girl was starving. Tristan only had Fruity Pebbles and expired milk to give her."

I meet my mother's horrified expression.

"Maria came earlier and stocked the kitchen," I reassure her.

"I should hope so," she says, as she sips her soup.

"Tristan has been a gracious host, Your Majesty," Serena defends me, and my eyes glide over her in appreciation.

She's wearing an off-the-shoulder shirt, and her bare shoulder is on full display. I stare at her silky skin, remembering how soft and delicate it felt under my palm.

Coming to my senses, I groan at myself. Apparently I have the attention span of a pubescent middle-school boy. I take a sip of water and pray for the second course to arrive quickly, as Zander chuckles at me.

We make it through dinner and dessert without the world or realm blowing up. My earlier unease is now gone, and I exhale a small sigh of relief that it was in my mind. The conversation flows, and Serena seems at ease with my family. I smile at her unexpected comfort here as we make our way to the library for after-dinner drinks.

The staff bring in six glasses and a selection of liquors to choose from. I notice the extra glass and turn to my mother, ready to ask whom it's for, but the words die on my lips as the doors to the library reopen, and in walks in the bane of my existence, like she owns the place.

"Ah, here's our special guest now," my mother coos.

I swallow the bile in my throat and turn to Zander, who's gone completely pale. He looks like he wants to disappear.

Yeah, I know the feeling. This is going to end badly.

Serena extends her gaze across the room, meeting angry gray eyes, dripping with nothing but hatred.

I fight to control my temper as I take a restrained step toward Serena. My blood turns cold, thinking she might be in danger. At the same time, Zander takes a measured step in the nymph's direction.

"Freya," his voice is low, a warning, or an attempt to calm her down. I'm unsure, since she looks ready to attack.

Freya's gray eyes snap to Zander. "Your Highness?"

"Lets go take a walk, shall we? The gardens are lovely at this time of night," he suggests in a lulling tone.

Freya's face softens, but only slightly.

"I've only just arrived," she replies. "As an invited guest, it would be rude of me to simply leave without being dismissed by Her Majesty," she continues.

"I agree," my mother interjects.

Rionach steps to her side, bends down, and whispers something in her ear. A disappointed expression falls across my mother's face as she meets my eyes with sympathy. A moment later, her regal mask falls back into place and she squares her shoulders, not meeting my eyes.

"Am I missing something?" Serena looks around.

"Well, son," Rionach pauses before continuing. "Aren't you going to introduce Serena to your betrothed?"

Serena's eyes widen before they land on Zander and narrow like she might kill him if he speaks again.

My brother shifts on his feet and takes an unhurried breath. Unrushed, he takes another step toward his childhood friend, but

Serena's faster. She steps between them, I think protecting Freya, while glaring at Zander.

"You're the prince Freya told me about?" she seethes.

Confusion falls across Zander's expression.

Everyone watches Serena with interest. "Freya speaks very highly of her feelings for you, Zander. You would do well to remember that she is a lady, with feelings."

Zander's face pinches. "What?"

"Serena," my mother interjects. "I think you are quite confused, dear. Freya is betrothed to Tristan. Not Zander."

The room falls eerily silent.

Serena hisses in a breath, and hurt eyes meet mine.

If it's possible to hear a heart break, I just heard Serena's shatter into a million pieces.

SERENA

MY WORLD TILTS AND SUDDENLY I can't breathe. The air around me slows down, and all I can hear is the blood pounding in my ears. I see Tristan move toward me, and I put my hand up to stop him. If he speaks in this moment, I will kill him.

Right here in front of his mother and—fiancée.

My hand automatically covers my heart. Holy shit.

I look over to Queen Ophelia, and she looks worried. I need to compose myself before someone gets the wrong idea. Or the right one. I swallow my pride and place the mask back on my face that I'm so good at hiding behind.

"Serena, are you all right, dear?" the queen asks, approaching me and touching my forearm.

I hope she can't feel how badly I'm shaking.

Standing taller, I force a quick bright smile.

"Yes of course. Apologies," I swallow the pain. "Such surprising and happy news." I meet Tristan's steely gaze. "I had no idea. Tristan, you never mentioned your fiancée to me." With every word I'm saying the knife in my heart twists a little more. I turn to Freya. "Congratulations. I wish you both all the happiness." It comes out rushed.

I'm numb as I offer her the unfeeling words.

Freya throws me a withering glare, and it's then I realize her angry demeanor has been directed at me this evening.

Of course it has. And rightfully so.

I watch as she moves to Tristan's side and he takes a step away from her, with annoyance crossing his features. She falters for a moment before returning to glaring at me.

"Serena, perhaps *you*," Zander emphasizes, "would care to see the gardens?" His voice cuts through the echoing sound of my heart banging against my rib cage.

All of a sudden, I can't find my voice.

Zander's hand intertwines with mine, and he squeezes to get my attention. He nods in encouragement. "Say yes."

"I would love to," I whisper.

"Wonderful," Queen Ophelia claps. "Tristan, this will give us a few moments to discuss the ceremony with Freya."

My knees weaken, and Zander wraps his arm around my shoulders, supporting my weight so I don't collapse.

"Now is not a good time, mother," Tristan bites out. "I need to speak with Serena, as her protector."

"Nonsense," Ophelia says. "She's safe with Zander. He's second in command of my army, and quite capable of keeping her safe for twenty minutes. Aren't you?"

"That's me, the twenty-minute protector." Zander turns to Tristan. "I'll take care of her. I promise."

Zander waits for a moment before Tristan nods his head.

"Great. We'll see everyone later. Let's do this, champ," Zander states cheerfully, leading me out of the room.

Within seconds, he has me outside and is dragging me through the private grounds, which are made up of a maze of green bushes and vines. I barely notice the cultivated gardens as we move at a quick pace through each turn.

When we finally get far enough from the house, Zander pulls me toward a bench and sits me down, pacing in front of me and swearing under his breath. In shock, I sit on the bench and just focus on breathing. It sounds easy, but in this instance, not so much.

"I warned him it would blow up in his face," Zander says, more to himself than to me.

I snort. "Good advice."

He stops in front of me, crossing his arms and tucking his hands under his armpits. "He should have told you."

"It would have been useful information," I reply numbly.

"Are you okay?" he asks awkwardly. "You're not going to . . . cry, or anything, are you?" he waits for a response.

"No," I respond.

"I'm not good with tears," he bites his lip in worry.

"I'm not going to cry." My tone is clipped.

"You sure?" He pats himself down. "I don't have tissues."

I drop my head into my hands. "I'm ninety-eight percent sure that no tears will escape my eyes over this, Zander."

"It's the two percent that has me nervous."

"I'll be fine. I just need to breathe, or something," I exhale.

He nods and takes a seat next to me. "Breathing works. In and out. Slowly. If you pass out, I will feel you up."

"Noted."

We sit in silence while he bounces his knee up and down nervously. The motion is making me queasy.

Or maybe it's the fact that Tristan is engaged to someone else. I swallow the bile crawling up my throat.

"Why didn't he tell me?" I ask.

"You'd have to ask him that," he replies quietly.

"Before or after I kill him?"

"Before. Otherwise you won't get an answer."

I slide a narrowed glare his way. "Again, good advice."

"Just call me Doctor Ruth," he counters.

"Wasn't she a sex therapist?" I point out.

"Weren't you and Tristan only supposed to be having sex? With no feelings?" he shoots back. "Sorry, that was rude. I'm not really good at girlie feelings and shit."

"You're doing well," I state.

The satyr sits straighter and smiles. "Really?"

"No." I shake my head. The motion causes me to become queasy again, and I stand and throw up all over the roses.

"Shit!" Zander screeches like a girl and grabs my hair, holding it back while I empty my stomach of the amazing dinner we just finished.

After a moment I wave him off and sit back on the bench, covering my face with my hands as I breathe in.

"He doesn't love her, you know. The three of us were childhood friends. Freya is the daughter of Oren. Our realms are on the brink of war, Serena, and their marriage will prevent a lot of death and violence." His tone is mechanical as he explains, still holding my hair.

My fists clench. "Well, that makes it all okay then."

"Really? That was easy." Zander looks surprised.

"I was being sarcastic," I exhale.

"Hey, what's this mark behind your ear?" He moves closer to inspect it and I grab my hair, letting it fall around my ear to hide the small black symbol.

"Just a freckle." I shoot him an irritated look.

His eyes roam over my face and his tone drops. "Serena, that freckle is in the shape of—"

"It's a freckle. I was born with it. Now back up," I demand through a clenched jaw. "Personal space is a good thing."

I hold his gaze in challenge.

After a brief moment, Zander dips his chin in acquiescence and stops the inquisition.

My stomach roils again and I grimace.

"What can I do?" Zander's tone is sincere.

"Can you take me home?" I ask.

"Sure, we can wait for Tristan at his house." He stands.

"No. Back to the Academy." I lift my gaze.

He winces. "No can do, champ. You're supposed to stay under the protection of our realm. Rulf still isn't out of stone state, which means you wouldn't have protection."

I hate that he's right. "You could stay," I plead.

He regards me for a moment. "I'm not a gargoyle."

I shrug. "No. Everyone at the Academy is, though, and you are second in command to Her Majesty's army. A skilled warrior and—" I stop.

"And?"

I stand and look him in the eyes. "Someone I trust."

Zander clears his throat. "You shouldn't. I'm a satyr. I could bed you within ten seconds of getting you alone."

"You won't," I fire back.

He releases a dark laugh. "Why is that?"

"You have too much respect for your brother. Plus, you like Magali," I reach, though, he did bring her wildflowers.

He grunts. "I don't like Magali."

I arch a brow in disbelief. I've seen him with her. It's why I was so pissed when I thought he was Freya's prince.

"I mean, she does have nice hair and pretty eyes," he adds.

We stand off in silence. He's not budging. Time for the big guns.

"I'll cry." I force my lower lip to tremble.

He shivers. "Let's go."

TWENTY
YOU AREN'T MINE

SERENA

M Y TREMBLING HANDS REACH FOR MY key card, sliding it through the lock before I push open the door to my suite at the Academy. In an instant, Ireland and Magali come at me.

Ireland pulls me into a tight embrace. "Are you all right?" she whispers in my ear, and I nod.

I lean back and throw a questioning glare at Zander.

"You told everyone?" I accuse.

"I told Magali," he winks at her, and she blushes on cue.

"Why?" I scold.

"They're your friends. And protectors," he responds, and steps into the suite, making himself at home.

"Where is Tristan?" Magali signs.

"I didn't go into details," Zander calls out from the couch.

"With his fiancée, planning his wedding," I state.

Magali's eyes widen and her mouth falls open.

"This requires alcohol. Lots of it," Ireland announces, and heads toward the kitchen to raid our stash.

Tiredly, I nod and move toward the couch, sitting next to Zander, while Ireland ransacks the kitchen.

Magali grabs my hand to get my attention. "Are you sure it's safe for you? You're in a lot of danger. I don't think it was good idea to come home without royal protection."

"I'm fine. Let the Diablo Fairies come. I'm not hiding from them," I sigh, and lean back into the couch.

"Well, if they do, we've got your back." Zander states, and Magali throws a withering warning look at him.

"What?" he asks her.

"You are not a protector," she signs.

"Nope. I am a damn good army commander," he retorts.

"It feels so good to be home," I moan.

Ireland steps back into the living room, her arms filled with bottles of booze, and her hands carrying red Solo cups.

"Where are Ethan and Ryker?" I ask.

"Rounds," she shrugs.

"Rounds?" I question.

"Given the attack by the devil fairies, we're all doing nightly campus surveillance, in two-hour shifts. They should be done shortly," Ireland explains without worry.

I frown.

"It's necessary," Magali states, with a firm look.

Ireland lines up the bottles and cups as she and Mags launch into all the things I missed during my absence.

I listen to them here and there.

From what I gather, not much has changed in two days.

Where the hell is Tristan? Why do I care? Doesn't he know I'm gone? Why do I care? Or is he too busy with his fiancée to notice? Ugh.

I let out an exhausted and guilty sigh, releasing all the resentment I have toward Tristan and his part in all of this.

Ireland and Magali share a look.

"Ready to talk about the girlfriend yet?" Mags asks.

"Fiancée," I correct.

Ireland grabs the glass bottle of vodka and unscrews the top, then tilts her head back, taking a long swig.

I watch her in awe, half expecting her to cough, or pinch her face at the taste, but she just places it down on the coffee table and pushes it toward me.

"Your turn." She motions toward the bottle.

I grab it and take a long sip that matches hers. The second the alcohol touches my lips, my eyes water.

"It tastes like ass," I whine.

"Take another, it makes it better," she suggests.

An hour later, I feel numb and the icky gasoline taste is completely gone from each swig I swallow.

Zander watches us, half amused, half worried. He's refused all sips we've impolitely tried to force upon him. He keeps saying he's guarding us and needs to keep alert. *Whatever.*

Ireland slaps her hand on the table dramatically.

"So that's it? You're just going to give up? Walk away from true love. Not look back?" she slurs her words.

"What do you mean?" I giggle, because she fell over and is trying to pick herself back up, but can't. It's funny. *Right?*

Magali steps in and pulls her up, before they each take another long sip. She's such an amazing friend. I sigh.

"Professor Gallagher? You're done?" Ireland confirms.

"Yessss," I draw out the *s* in dramatic form.

Ireland and Magali clap at how long I can do it, and Zander runs his hands over his face. He starts to pick up the bottles, ignoring our protests at their disappearance.

"I think you ladies have had more than enough," he says.

I pout. "He's Tristan's brother."

Magali nods. "He has a nice ass."

Ireland nods. "I second that."

Magali takes another sip of vodka and signs sloppily, "You can't have him. You already stole Ryker."

Ireland leans backwards. "What?" *Oh, shit.*

I take the bottle from Magali's outstretched hand and Zander leans over the couch, plucking it from mine.

This is about to get ugly. I need to do something. I stand and clear my throat.

"Tristan," I pause, probably for dramatic effect but I'm too drunk to really know why, "is dead to me," I announce. "It is my first royal decree." I raise my plastic cup to cheer.

"That so?" a deep voice says from the doorway.

I blink a few times. I'm seeing everything in double.

"Do you see him too?" Ireland whisper-shouts. "Because I thought he was dead to us? O-M-G!" she squeals. "We see dead people," she snorts, and collapses in a laughing fit.

I smile down at her before locking gazes with Tristan.

I try to look nonchalant, but something in me twitches with fear, or anticipation, or something I can't make out, partially due to being inebriated.

All I know is my heart hurts.

"Hey, man," Zander sighs, sounding relieved.

Tristan walks toward him. "Speaking of dead, you're damn lucky you're my brother," he barks.

Zander puts his palms out, but Magali jumps in front of him. Her face contorts awkwardly, and I let out a chuckle.

Tristan tilts back before looking at Zander, confused.

"Is she protecting you?" he asks his brother.

"I think so," Zander exhales, and gently moves Mags to the side. "They've been drinking. Heavily."

"I can smell it down the hall," Tristan scowls.

The door to our suite opens again and Ryker walks in.

He looks around at all of us with a curious caution.

"Why the hell does it smell like a distillery in here?"

"We hate Tristan," Ireland says from the floor.

Ryker looks down at her. "What is going on?"

"I'm an asshole and they're all drunk," Tristan explains.

"Typical." Ryker walks over to Ireland and picks her limp form up in his arms. "I'll take this one. Can you guys cover these two?"

"We've got it handled," Zander replies, and Tristan nods.

Ryker carries Ireland out the door while she waves and giggles. When they pass Tristan, she scowls and points two fingers at her eyes and angrily flicks them back to him, letting him know she's watching him.

He rolls his eyes, and I sway a little on my feet. My head is buzzing from the alcohol. Tristan notices the movement and takes a step in my direction but I quickly move away, causing him to stop in his tracks.

"Well, I can see you two have a lot to discuss. I'm going to go hold Magali's hair while she pukes, and then put her to bed. If you need me, I'll just be in the other room not feeling her up," he announces, and takes her hand.

Speechless, I stare at Tristan, hoping my emotions aren't written all over my face. They're part relief, part shock, and part pure murderous rage.

"Tell me," I say, my tongue heavy and fuzzy.

"Tell you what?" Tristan asks.

"Fine, I'll go first." I know I'm not making sense. "How is your fiancée? Was she pissed off that you slept with me?" My words are horrible and rude, but to be fair, I'm not really thinking clearly. A liter of vodka does that.

Tristan stands taller, and his expression morphs into one of rage. The protector's entire demeanor is intimidating, like he could snap me in two if he wanted.

He tries to rein in his temper. "This isn't a conversation that I am going to have with you while you're trashed. I know you're pissed, and for that, I'm truly sorry. But for you to leave the protection of my realm, and me, there is no excuse. You put yourself in danger, Serena."

"I'm fine," I wave him off.

"YOU ARE UNPROTECTED!" he screams, and his voice bounces off the walls.

I shudder, slightly afraid. "Screw you," I bark.

"Excuse me?"

"You heard me," I point to him. "You should have told me, Tristan.

I was blindsided and humiliated."

"Why? We were just fucking, Serena, nothing more."

I rear back like he slapped me and without warning him, I pop off a right hook, making contact with his cheek.

He rubs the spot. "I guess I deserve that."

"You deserve so much more," I seethe.

"For not telling you that my mother has a business contract with the emperor of the water fairies in order to prevent our realm from going to war?" his tone is cold.

"You are engaged, Tristan," I remind him.

"To someone that I don't love. Someone Zander and I grew up with. She's like a sister to me, Serena," he spits out. "It's not a marriage of love. It's a contract of convenience. One that I'm not currently bound to. As you know, in our world, you are free to be with whomever you'd like before you are formally mated. There has been no vow broken."

"You don't love her?" I ask, needing to hear it from him.

"No," he exhales.

"Yet you're still going to marry her?" My voice cracks.

"Yes."

"Why?" I hold back my tears.

"It's how it works, Serena. You are of royal blood; you know this. Sometimes we put ourselves last in order to protect and keep the peace so that each realm can thrive."

"Oh, I understand birthrights." My tone is lined with venom. My body is shaking and I need him to leave. I lift my gaze and deadpan him. "I could have loved you, you know. I could have been your forever. I would have fought."

"Serena, I never promised—"

My stare is vacant. "You don't feel remorse, do you?"

At my words, Tristan presents me with a cruel look.

"How can I feel remorse when you've made it clear that you don't feel anything for me at all?" he shoots back.

"You could have been my future, instead of my past."

TRISTAN

SHE WAS SHIVERING, AND I WANTED nothing more than to pull her into my arms, surround her with my embrace, and will the night-mare of our lives to go away.

I took a risk and broke every rule just to experience a small ray of her light, letting it burn through my darkest places. I never expected to want and need her in order to breathe.

When you fall, you don't think gravity will actually ever pull you back down again, so when it does, it fucking hurts.

The minute I realized Zander had taken her out of our realm, and that she might be in danger, I thought I was slain, but I'm pretty sure I'll never recover from the words she just said to me.

"Leave me alone," she whispers hoarsely, and stumbles away from me, down the hall toward her bedroom.

A minute later, I watch Magali slide into Serena's bedroom and shut the door.

Zander walks into the living room wearing a solemn expression. "You okay?"

I pull out a cigarette and light it. "You almost wrote your death sentence tonight," I speak around the lit stick. "Don't ever fucking take her away from me again, Zander. Brother or not, I will end your existence if you interfere where she's concerned."

Zander chuckles. "You sound like a mated male protector." He gets in my face. "Serena isn't yours. Isn't that what this whole shitstorm is about tonight? You are already promised to someone, Tristan."

I inhale, and let the nicotine fill and burn my lungs.

His words have nothing to do with Serena, but everything to do with Freya.

This love triangle between Zander, Freya, and me has been ongoing for years. I'm sick of it.

"If you want Freya, take her," I state flatly.

Zander turns away from me, his face ashen. "It doesn't work like that, and you know it. You're the royal blood, not me. I just happen to be the adopted son," he barks out. "I've loved Freya since birth, but she isn't mine, Tristan. I know my place. It's time you learn yours."

"Fuck you," I snarl, and he doesn't turn around.

"I hope it was worth it." Zander ignores my outburst.

I rear back. "Worth it?'"

He faces me with a cold expression. "Sleeping with her. I hope it was good, because she's going to have one hell of a hangover tomorrow, and when the haze clears, and her world comes crashing down around her again, you'd better hope it's not too late for her to forgive you for using her."

"I didn't use her," I growl.

Zander flashes me a fake smile. "And there it is. You see, if you didn't have feelings for her, the satyr in you would have just used her."

That same smile stays firmly in place until he reaches the door, his fingers wrapping around the handle.

"If you love her, Tristan, I suggest you do something about it, before it's too late."

I stare at Serena's bedroom door for an eternity while I finish my cigarette before tossing it in the sink and grabbing what is left of the bottle of vodka.

I make my way over to her room, sliding down the wall, and sit outside her door. Regardless of this disaster, she's mine to protect, and I will do so with my last damn breath.

Something kicks my foot and I stir. I blink a few times, waking up, and look around. *Shit.* I'm still on the floor in the hallway. The bones in my back and neck ache from being stiff.

"Did you sleep here all night?" Serena's voice is harsh.

"Yes." I stand and look her in the eyes.

She looks up at the ceiling and crosses her arms. "Why?"

I jut my chin forward in challenge. "I'm your protector."

"Too bad you couldn't protect me from you," she glares.

I don't look away. "You okay this morning?"

"Are you asking because I drank my weight in vodka or because you slept with me while being engaged?"

"Vodka."

"I'm fine. A little headache, but nothing I can't deal with."

"Engaged?"

"How could you?" She trembles, and I reach out but she moves out of my reach.

"I'm sorry for the things I said last night. I never meant to hurt you, Serena. Truly. I thought we were on the same page. No feelings. Just . . . two beings getting lost in one another. I should have seen what was coming, when you stopped running. But I didn't."

All the fight leaves her face and her shoulders fall. I drink her in while she stands there for what feels like hours.

I open my mouth to say something, then close it, then open it again. "Say something."

"Asshole."

"What?"

She points to my forehead and I pinch my brows.

With an eye roll she grabs my arm and pulls me into the bathroom so I can look in the mirror. *Asshole* is written across my forehead in permanent marker.

Magali stumbles in and throws me a smug smirk.

I face her. "You do this?"

She signs yes and shoos us out so she can have privacy.

Serena stands in the middle of the hallway and I approach her back, leaning near her ear.

"I'm sorry," I whisper. "I wish things were different."

She shivers at my closeness. "I know."

After a moment, she steps away toward the kitchen. It takes every ounce of willpower I have not to follow.

"Oh, and Tristan?" she says without looking back.

"Yeah?"

"You're officially no longer my pretend boyfriend."

TWENTY-ONE
ALL I LONG FOR

TRISTAN

MY EYES TAKE HER IN AS she steps into class with Ireland and Ryker, laughing like she doesn't have a care in the world.

It's been a few months since the engagement announcement heard 'round the world, and we've fallen into an easy routine. Every day we go through the motions: an unbearable mundane pattern of class, training, and cordial living arrangements. Nothing more.

Rulf nods at me from the door, and I force a smile. I fucking hate that he gets to protect her and I have to watch from afar. Concern is written all over his face as he watches Serena compliantly take her seat before taking his leave.

He's been healed and back for two months. Surprisingly, he's unhappy that Serena has lost her rebellious edge. She's become agreeable. Compliant. Not herself.

I breathe in and start my lecture, forcing my eyes not to collide with the blue pair staring at me from the fifth row, second seat to the left.

My lecture is flat, my words forced. My heart isn't in it. I'm not even sure my heart exists anymore, and if it does, it's not mine. Without realizing it, I gave it away to Serena the night we were together in my cabin.

I made love to her in my bed, knowing that I'd only have that one brief moment in time with her. Though she never said it, I knew she felt it. I also knew the minute we were done, my future wouldn't include her, but an arranged marriage, an agreement that will prevent an ancient war between my realm and the water one.

All this time is passing by and I still can't seem to tell her how much I need her, want her.

Protector rules state that I can't tell her about the cessation. I'm not able to change our destiny. But she can. She can fight. Because there is a cessation and she's the key.

My eyes glide over the students before I let them fall on her. Her breath hitches in her chest as our gazes collide. I can tell she's trying to look away, but I hold her stare.

I'm not sure if she'll understand what I'm about to say, but I have to try. "If protector history has taught us anything, it's that the supernatural realms are all about power and politics. The power struggle between our realms is based on strategy—a game of chess, if you will. And even if you're the queen or king, you're simply a piece to be played for advantage," the words fall out of my mouth without emotion. "Yet, the queen is the most powerful piece, because, unlike the king, her movements are unrestricted. Her fate is her own. The queen has the power to end the darkness, and with the spring start a new beginning."

Serena chews on her lower lip.

Clearing my throat, I avert my gaze. The trust between us is gone, and maybe we need to move on, but I'm hoping the words resonate with her.

I turn to grab the bottle of water on my desk, but notice it ripple just the slightest bit. My eyes dart around the room and I still, focusing on my heightened hearing.

A low distant rumble hums in my ear. The same sound a group of horses would make as they approach. My heart rate picks up and I spin back toward the class.

"Class is dismissed," I state abruptly.

They students share confused glances, but don't argue.

"Serena," my voice is stern. "A moment."

She stills, her fight-or-flight response going into overdrive. Ireland and Ryker watch her before she dismisses them and makes her way over to me.

I wait until the rest of the class has gone. When we're the only two left, I snap my arm out and grab her wrist.

"What the hell, Tristan?" she snaps.

"Diablo Fairies." I state, and get ready to teleport us out of the classroom and into Chancellor Davidson's office.

I'm stopped when Rulf storms into the room looking like he's ready to light the world on fire. *Damn lapdog.*

"Serena," he barks at her, and I curb my desire to lunge at him and rip his throat out. "I've got this," he says to me, and grabs her by the elbow in a harsh manner.

I lose my shit. I knee him in the chest and catch him in the mouth with my elbow. He goes down quickly, which, given his protector assignment, has me furious.

"I'm starting to think you don't deserve to breathe the same air she does," I growl at him.

The sight of him touching her, in a disrespectful manner, set me off. Am I acting irrationally? Yeah, I am. But she's mine to protect.

He bends over in pain, and I grab his hair and slam him against the wall, pushing my forearm into his throat, cutting off his air. I watch him choke, clawing at my arm.

"Tristan!" Serena charges at me. "Stop."

I don't look at her. "I warned you, Serena, that under my protection, nobody lays a hand on you. I told you that if another being so much as looks at you disrespectfully, I will end their existence, without warning. That includes your royal guard."

"Let me go so I can protect her," Rulf demands.

I snort because he's doing such a great job of it. The thought ticks me off even more, and my fingers twist in his shirt, lifting him and slamming him again against the wall.

"She isn't yours to take care of," I spit in his face.

Rulf smiles wickedly before spitting blood onto the ground. "And she's yours?" he goads.

Fuck. He's right. Enraged, I roughly drop him onto the ground, his head bouncing off the floor as I knock him around.

"Leave him alone!" Serena pushes at me from behind.

I turn and face her. My expression is furious.

Her eyes quickly drop to Rulf, who is picking himself up.

"Are you all right?" she asks him.

"I'll live," he replies with a groan. "Can't say the same for your protector, though."

Her cold stare shifts to me. "He isn't my protector."

"Yeah? You might want to tell him that," Rulf seethes.

"What the hell is wrong with you?" Serena pushes at my chest, and the protector mark pulses, sending another irrational jolt of anger through me.

The Diablo Fairy army is getting closer and closer. I need to get her out of here, and the only way to do that is to get her away from her guard dog.

I curse under my breath, because I'm about to take this too far, but I need her to get worked up so I can teleport her. She won't go willingly at this point.

I look down at Rulf. He's pushing himself up off the floor, and I kick him hard in the ribs, causing him to fall back down.

"Sorry, man." I lean down and whisper in his ear.

Serena curses at me. "By the grace, I hate you!"

I stand and face her. "It's about fucking time," I push.

It works. Fire ignites behind her eyes, and she charges at me with her fists flying.

I grab her wrists and teleport us to Middle Lake, because it's easy to get to my realm from there if need be.

It's also what I told Rulf I would do when I whispered in his ear not to interfere.

"You are unreal." Her voice is cool as she comes at me.

"Serena—" I duck and grab her arms. "Stop it!"

"No," she jerks against me, tears streaming down her face. "I am not yours to protect!" she shouts.

My pulse beats faster, angry at her words. She doesn't see that regardless of what she wants, I am her bonded protector. I pushed too far and need to calm her down before we both do or say something we'll regret.

I pin her with her arms behind her back, and her chin juts out in defiance, exposing her neck. I curb the desire to run butterfly kisses down it just so I can hear her mewl.

Instead, I lean into her face. "While most areas of you and me are messy, when it comes to matters of your protection, I have not given you a reason not to trust me."

She closes her eyes.

"Look at me," I demand. "I need you to trust me—with only your protection right now. That's all I'm asking."

"I don't need your protection," she spits back, but some of the fight behind her words is gone.

"I disagree," I exhale. "Can you please just trust me?"

Her eyes open, and she stares directly into mine.

"Did you just say please?" she asks.

I hold her gaze. "I did. I'll beg if it will keep you safe."

"I trusted you more than anyone else I know, Tristan. Your lie destroyed that," her voice is hoarse.

"I swear to you that I will work twice as hard as anyone to regain it," I vow. "I just need a little faith right now."

Her eyes narrow. "I'm still pissed."

"I know." I release her. "I'm sorry."

She massages her wrists. "I know."

We take a seat on a rock near the water, and I text her clan and Henry. He informs me that the moment I got Serena off Academy grounds, the warriors retreated.

It's so odd.

Almost as if they're not even trying.

She's quiet for a while as I work through strategies.

"What are you thinking?" she asks.

"Asmodeus is slow to attack. It's strange," I say.

"How so?" she questions.

"It's as if the demon is playing with us. Testing us. These faux strikes feel more like a warning of what's to come," I sigh. "I don't like it. Something's off. Demons are coy, but not usually this messy. It doesn't feel right," I ramble. "And at this rate, his attacks won't be ending anytime soon."

"Is that what you want? For it all to end?"

"More than anything," I reply.

Silence falls between us for a moment before she shifts.

"What happens to us at the end of all this?" Serena asks.

I exhale. "I walk away. Not because I want to, but because I have to."

SERENA

LONG, RING-COVERED FINGERS CARESS MY CHEEK, making their way down my face with a gentle touch. At the soft caress, my lips part, and I stop breathing all together.

Tristan's hand flattens as it glides down my throat and over my collar bone, then stops over my heart. His eyes never leave mine as he inhales deeply and his hand slides across my breast and over the white lace fabric of my low-cut pajama top.

Bending at the waist, he leans down so his lips are a breath from mine. His gaze is intense while his hand moves lower, until two fingers run over the thin material covering my damp lower body.

Narrowing his eyes, he tilts his head, watching my reaction. I know this has gone too far, but I'm not stopping him. Skilled fingers slide up and down the cotton in a rhythmic motion, causing my body to tighten with pleasure.

I release a needy whimper as his lips brush the outside of my ear. "Is this for me?" Tristan whispers, cupping me. "Are you soaked with need to have me inside you, Serena?"

I swallow, unable to find my voice.

"Is it me that you want to take you higher, until it's my name rolling off your lips as you scream out in pleasure?"

At the rawness of his words, my body begins to tremble. Just when I think I can't take his touch for another second, he pulls his fingers away, bringing them to his nose and inhaling.

"You're so damn sweet," he growls into the dark room.

"Tristan." His name is a plea to finish what he started.

His lips tilt wickedly as he straightens to his full height and takes a step away from the bed.

Confused, I watch him, clamping my thighs together, desperately needing relief after his assault.

"You aren't mine to touch. And I sure as hell am not yours," he bites out, before turning and storming out of the room, as I'm left cursing his name.

I jolt awake with a gasp, and it takes me a minute to collect myself from my intense dream. I wipe the beads of sweat from my forehead with the back of my hand and look around my room.

Rays of the sun's light are peeking through the curtains, blanketing everything in a warm butter hue. Morning.

It's morning. And that was just a dream.

I will my heartbeat to slow down as I swing my legs over the side of my bed and stumble toward the bathroom. Throwing cold water on my face, I glance at the mirror. I look tired. Worn out. I miss the free-spirited girl I was a few months ago. I toss my hair into a bun and sigh, before brushing my teeth and padding my way toward the kitchen.

When I step out into the hallway, I stop in my tracks at the sight of a shirtless Tristan. Sipping on coffee. On the balcony. Half naked.

"By the grace," I mutter.

For the past few months we've managed to live together without too much drama. He's usually gone before I get up in the morning, and returns long after I've gone to bed.

After my dream this morning, though, my body is tight with the need for release, and seeing him here, with the sunlight beaming off his half naked body, makes me want to throw caution to the wind and ravish him.

I squeeze my eyes shut, then open them and focus on the coffee machine. Caffeine sounds good. I should get coffee instead of staring at Tristan's back. His beautiful corded back. My legs move me toward the balcony. To him.

Sensing me, he turns and offers me a sad smile.

"Hey." His voice sounds like gravel.

"Hi," I squeak out. "No class or training sessions today?"

"Nope."

"Why is that?" I give him a sideways glance.

"Your clan is coming in a few hours. We're meeting with them in Chancellor Davidson's office," he responds.

"Oh." I grip the railing, and my gaze roams over the Academy's campus. "I didn't know."

"The text came in this morning. Apparently, I need to explain my actions of the other day, when I teleported you off campus to Middle Lake without prior approval."

I bark out a laugh. "What?"

"Rulf wasn't too happy with the way I handled things."

"Rulf is such an idiot," I exhale.

"He's a necessary evil, to keep you safe," he states.

"And isn't that what this is all about? Keeping me safe so that I can fulfill my destiny and rule my race," I sneer. "The training, the protection, the strategy meetings."

"The best we can do, Serena, is be ready," he retorts.

"Ready?"

"For war," his tone is flat.

War. Is that really even a reality?

I don't trust myself to speak, so I simply nod my head.

I've grown up in the supernatural worlds. I know that war always lurks on the horizon; it's nothing new. Yet, to hear Tristan confirm it, as it relates to me, feels strange.

"It's almost summer," I change the subject. "Every year the Academy hosts the Solstice Gala. Will you attend?"

"No."

My heart sinks. I know I have no right to be saddened that he won't be there, but a small piece of me had hoped.

"Not a fan of dancing?" I jest.

Tristan turns to face me. "I'm leaving."

I stop breathing. "For the summer? I think we all are."

"Forever," he whispers huskily.

My stomach bottoms out. "What about me?"

Wrinkles appear in his forehead as he looks at me.

"I mean, I thought you needed to protect me to work off your sentence?" My throat is scratchy and tight.

"Oren has requested the ceremony with Freya be moved up. He's threatened to declare war on my mother's realm if we don't adhere to his new deadline. Given his threat and the fact that there are only few months of my service left, I've been fully absolved of serving the remainder of my sentence." His eyes study my face.

A piece of me dies inside. I lean against the railing for support and wait a few seconds to collect myself. As much as I want Tristan to be my protector, to give me strength, I know he can't. This is something I have to do on my own.

I just stand, like an idiot, staring at Tristan for the longest time. No matter how many breaths I take, I still can't breathe.

Leaving.

He's leaving.

To marry someone else.

Without a word, I turn and walk toward my bedroom.

I don't glance over my shoulder.

Not even when Tristan calls my name.

TWENTY-TWO
ONE LAST TIME

SERENA

I 'M HIDING. HIS ANNOUNCEMENT GUTTED ME. I can't face the fact that he's leaving. I have no right, but somewhere along the way, I fell for Tristan Gallagher. Hard.

Sobs break free from my chest, and I use my palms to wipe away the tears streaming down my cheeks. I'm devastated at the unfairness and cruelty of our world.

My door slams open and Tristan storms into the room, but immediately stops cold when he sees me.

"Are you crying?" he asks.

My heart disintegrates at the sound of his concerned voice, and I move a hand over my mouth to muffle another cry and turn away from him.

"Serena—"

I try to control my emotions and shaking.

"Look at me," he demands.

I don't. I can't. I don't want him to see my reaction.

Two warm hands grip my shoulders, forcing me to turn.

Tristan grips my chin between his fingers, lifting my face so he can look into my eyes. The intensity in his stare is unnerving. He's reading me, trying to gauge my response.

The way he's watching me forces me to attempt to control every breath and facial expression. I close my eyes and lean my head back, trying to get control.

It does no good.

He leans closer to my ear, his warm breath caressing the outside. "I like you," he whispers.

"What?" I hiccup.

"I like you, Serena," he repeats.

He moves back and our gazes collide.

"I like you too, Tristan," I whimper.

He swallows and cups my cheeks. "I want to keep you."

Another tear rolls down my cheek.

"I want to be kept by you."

"The bond will wear off soon," he assures me. "Then you'll stop looking at me like I'm one of your dad's cookies."

"I know," I sniffle, and hide a smile.

He steps back, runs his hands down my arms, and takes my hands into his. In silence we both stare at our hands.

The connection we have pulses through our palms.

"You need to stop looking at me with sexy in your eyes."

"What?" I rear back.

"You have sexy in your eyes, raindrop. We're not doing sexy anymore. You said it yourself, it was a one-time lapse in judgment," his tone has turned teasing.

I exhale, grateful he's trying to lighten the mood.

"As I recall, it was a multiple lapse."

"Yeah?" He smiles with pride.

I smirk. "Congratulations. You can give me multiple orgasms. You aren't the first, nor will you be the last."

My words were meant to be funny, but his face darkens.

"Know this. If I could, I would risk it all to be your last."

I suck in a sharp breath.

Inhale. Exhale.

He releases my hands and takes a step back.

"We're expected at the Chancellor's office in an hour."

I nod. "I'll get ready, then."

He doesn't look at me again. In one swift movement, he heads straight for the door, leaving me.

I've never in my life known this kind of sadness existed.

TRISTAN

I WAIT FOR SERENA ON MY bike. We could walk, but just once I want to feel her body pressed against mine as we ride. It's selfish, I know.

I wish things were different. That I could drive off campus with her and run away.

Seeing her upset like that knocked the breath out of me. It sucked all the strength from my limbs and stripped me of almost all of my resolve to walk away from her.

Serena St. Michael is it for me. Everything I've ever needed or wanted in another being. I never realized I was missing her in my life, until she stormed in.

Literally. In a rainstorm.

Saying goodbye to her—it's going to take me down.

The door to her dorm opens, and she steps out and smiles at me. Her mask is firmly in place. I roll my shoulders and do the same. This is how our world works. We're royalty. We don't have the luxury of feelings. We're here to serve, to protect, to safeguard.

I dip my chin as she approaches my bike.

"You want to take this?" she asks. "It's only a mile."

I shrug. "Safety reasons."

She smiles and straddles my bike like a pro. "Okay."

"Rulf is going to meet us there," I let her know.

"He mentioned." She wraps her arms around me and I close my eyes, basking in the feel of her. *Damn, I'll miss this.*

Too quickly, we arrive at the castle.

I turn off the engine and we both sit, unmoving.

A second later, she slides off my bike, takes off her helmet, and hands it to me without a glance. I'd give anything to be able to read her mind right now.

Hoping to appear calm, I try to think of something professional and protector-like to say. All I come up with is, "They're waiting."

In silence we make our way around the winding stone hallways, up the grand staircase, and into Chancellor Davidson's office.

Annabelle looks up from her computer and presents us with a warm smile. "It's nice to see you again, Mr. Gallagher and Miss St. Michael." She motions to the double doors. "You can go right in. They're all awaiting your arrival."

"Thank you," Serena replies.

I push open the doors and the room falls silent, as several protectors turn their attention to us, looking stoic.

"Serena." A warm, gentle voice greets.

"Mom!" Serena rushes into the waiting arms of Abby.

Abigail St. Michael can only be described as ethereal.

Her long, red hair falls over her shoulders as her tall form pulls Serena into a tight embrace. Abby squeezes Serena so hard, I can actually feel it through the bond.

Her sapphire eyes seek me out over her daughter's head. "Tristan," her mom acknowledges me with a kind smile.

"Hello, Abby," I reply. "It's nice to see you again."

Abby frowns. "You look tired." There is worry behind her eyes.

"I'm okay," I assure Serena's mom.

She nods and leans back, cupping her daughter's face. All of a sudden her expression falls. "Have you been crying?"

"No, Mom. I'm fine," Serena shifts.

"CALLAN!" Abby shouts, and in an instant he's there.

"What's wrong?" Callan's voice is lined with concern.

Abby grips Serena's face harder and shoves it at Callan. "You see it?"

Callan's brows droop over his eyes. He's squinting while studying his daughter's face. "What am I looking at?"

Abby sighs. "Her face, babe."

They both stare at her as if she's a newborn and they're awaiting her first word. It's awkward, and a bit adorable.

"It's beautiful," Callan plants a kiss on Serena's cheek. "Just like her mom," his grin widens.

"Not only did she just lie to me, but she's been crying," Abby points out, and murderous rage crosses Callan's features as he slides his eyes my way.

Yeah. I'm the cause.

Serena pulls her hand out of her mother's hands.

"Stop it. Both of you," she sighs. "I. Am. Fine."

Abby straightens. "You look blotchy."

Callan nods his head. "She's right. You do look blotchy."

"Blotchy means you've been crying," Abby continues.

"Remember those big red marks she would get on her cheeks when she wailed as a baby?" Callan looks at Abby.

"I do. It was so gross. And her snot would like drain out of her nose for hours without stopping," Abby shivers.

Callan shoots a look to Serena.

"You were literally a snotty, gross baby, pumpkin."

Serena exhales. "Thank you for that, dad."

"I second that," Rulf interjects, and my fists tighten at my sides so I don't kill him for insulting her in front of everyone. It's one thing when her parents joke, but not him.

"Miss St. Michael. It's lovely to see you," Chancellor Davidson greets Serena, and she gratefully steps away from her parents and offers him a quick hug.

"You too, Henry," she replies.

She turns to the rest of the clan, offering pleasantries to both her uncles. Suddenly the door behind the bookshelf opens up, revealing Serena's aunts McKenna and Eve.

"Stop it," Eve whines, batting McKenna's hands away.

"It's stuck and you're acting like an idiot," McKenna snips. "By the grace, don't struggle and I will fix it."

I'm man enough to admit that Keegan's mate, McKenna, scares me. Serena's aunt Eve—she's a different story.

"It wouldn't be stuck if you didn't push in into my hair in the first place," Eve counters, presenting a dagger.

"What are you doing, siren?" Asher asks.

With a quick flick of her wrist, the knife swooshes, the sound cutting through the air. Eve turns and faces Asher holding up a few strands of hair stuck together with gum.

"Kenna!" Abby scowls. "Did you put gum in her hair?"

Kenna shrugs. "I was planning to throw it out, but the blood of Eden bumped into me. It's her own fucking fault."

"Love you too, cupcake," Eve retorts, and throws the hair and chewed gum into the basket. Very queen-like.

"Is it always like this?" I ask Serena, stepping to her side.

Her shoulders sag.

"You have yet to experience a family dinner."

"Hi," Eve gives her niece a quick hug. "You okay?"

"I am," Serena uses her fake happy tone.

McKenna snorts. "Hey, it's the asshole."

"Excuse me?" I reply.

McKenna holds her phone up, showing me her screen saver. It's a photo of me, passed out, with the word *asshole* written across my forehead in permanent marker. No doubt Magali sent it the night they were drunk. Fantastic.

"Shall we get started?" Henry asks.

"We're waiting for one more," Asher says.

"Who?" Serena asks.

The double doors open, and in walks Gage.

TWENTY-THREE
BURN FOREVER

TRISTAN

I LOOK AWAY AS GAGE SWAGGERS into the room, cigarette hanging from his mouth. He nods his chin at me in acknowledgment before looking around at the rest of the gargoyles in the room.

"I guess the gang's all here. Like a bad episode of *Scooby Doo*," he inhales, and steps toward Eve, embracing her. "Hey, love. Good to see you again."

"You too, Gage," she smiles at him.

McKenna's eyes narrow at Gage. "What are you doing here, traitor?" she snarls.

Bored, he exhales. "I have a right to be here while you witch-trial Tristan for doing a job you asked him to do."

Chancellor Davidson steps in and starts the conversation, or argument, where these protectors are concerned. Almost immediately I find myself spacing out, as my eyes shift to the windows, my gaze focused outside. Every so often I catch the usual key words—responsibility, protection, reckless behavior.

"Tristan didn't kidnap me," I hear Serena scoff, and I quickly focus back in on the discussion.

What the hell?

"He did. From under my protection," Rulf barks.

"As I understand it, the Diablo Fairies were approaching. He teleported her to safety," Chancellor Davidson comes to my defense.

"He could have been the one who orchestrated the entire thing, for all I know," Rulf continues. "Regardless, he failed to keep her safe when he took her out of my safekeeping."

"I protected her," I shout, lunging for him.

Serena steps in front of me and places her hands on my chest, which is rising and falling heavily. "Tristan—"

"I keep her safe. ME!" I pause and correct myself. "I *kept* her safe. I took her away in that moment to protect her. I did what I had to do to secure her safety." I shove my hand in Rulf's direction. "You certainly weren't going to do it."

"I fail to see the logic of how taking her out of a heavily guarded protector environment, without permission, is protecting her," Rulf continues. "Unless there is something you two aren't telling us," he taunts.

My nostrils flare as I look at the blank faces in the room.

"Christ," Gage bites out. "You always were an ass, Rulf."

"Tristan," Abby says slowly. "Are you all right?"

"I'm fine," I grit, out of clenched teeth.

Asher and Eve watch us with understanding in their expressions. An understanding that I don't like. At all.

"The protector bond might be getting to you," Asher's tone is low. "It wouldn't be the first time this happened. Sometimes a blood bond clouds judgment, and—feelings."

"No, that's not—" I start.

"I think it's best that Serena continue here at the Academy for her own safety," Henry states. "Queen Ophelia has informed us of your obligations to your realm, Tristan, and we've agreed to release you of your sentence early."

My fight slips away. "Thank you."

Asher dips his head. "Gage explained the extenuating circumstances surrounding the royal guard's death."

I slide my gaze to Gage, who grants me a flat expression.

"We pardon you of all responsibility," the king decrees.

"Again, thank you," I reply.

Serena turns, standing in front of me. "I want him."

Callan's face turns baffled. "Excuse me?"

"Tristan is a protector, *my* protector, and I want to keep him on in that role," she explains.

"Serena," her aunt Eve approaches her as if she were a wounded animal. "Tristan isn't a full-on protector. He's also a prince with betrothal obligations," her voice is gentle. "Even if you, or we, wanted you to remain under his guardianship, it's simply not possible. He's obligated."

"But—"

"But nothing," Rulf steps in. "I will continue to watch over you as decreed by your aunt and uncle at birth."

"Tristan will be returning to his realm the day after tomorrow," Henry says. "With our respect and gratitude."

"So once again, I don't have a say?" Serena snips.

"It's not about say, honey. It's about royal duties," Abby interjects. "Ophelia was resolute about Tristan's."

The conversation eventually morphs into a strategy session with regard to Asmodeus and protection for the upcoming Summer Solstice Gala, as well as end-of-year preparations for Serena's protection when she returns home to London.

She and I watch the exchange like a tennis match.

"I have one more item of business before we disband," Henry says. "What about the protector bond?"

Neither Serena nor I respond. Nervously she twists her hair around her hand before placing in into a bun.

It's Gage who answers. "As long Serena and Tristan's bond hasn't been completed, it should fade within a few months." He would know. His faded when he lost Camilla.

My eyes roam over her neck.

That's when I see it, hidden behind Serena's right ear.

The Sun of Vergina.

My satyr insignia.

She's been marked as mine.

SERENA

I WATCH THE CLAN TALK AND discuss my fate as if I'm not even in the room. As usual, no one wants my input or opinion. They talk around me. Over me. Treating me like a child.

Warm fingertips brush lightly over the skin on the back of my neck and I shiver, ignoring the ugly feeling that keeps making itself known, because Tristan's leaving.

Forever.

"Serena?" My mom's voice breaks through my thoughts.

"Sorry, what?"

"Dress shopping for the Summer Solstice Gala and ice cream. I was asking if you wanted both. Dad's buying," she wiggles her eyebrows.

"Sounds great."

"Just don't order watermelon." My dad jumps in.

I'm tired and emotionally drained, and I just don't have the energy to argue that fruit-flavored ice cream is a dessert.

I turn and look at Tristan.

His expression is equally sad and remorseful. His gaze roams my face and there is a deep pain behind his eyes. One glance at the torn look on his face makes everything—everyone—else just fade into the background.

"I'm sorry for all of it, raindrop."

I close my eyes and let myself believe that it was months ago, and we were just two friends giving each other a brief moment of reprieve and comfort from all the dark in world.

Warm lips kiss the top of my head, and I open my eyes just in time to see Tristan turn and leave, taking my heart with him.

TWENTY-FOUR
THE DIABLO FAIRIES

TRISTAN

MY HEART JUST ABOUT BURST OUT of my chest at the sight of my mark on Serena. It can only mean one thing: the prophecy is true. The cessation is real. There is hope after all.

I make it halfway down the hallway when a tingling sensation crawls up the back of my neck, causing me to still and listen. All my supernatural senses kick into overdrive.

The Diablo Fairies.

I can hear them on the lower level of Domus Gurgulio, searching. Doors are being thrown open and then slammed shut. Voices are rising with each empty room discovered.

Warrior chants bounce off the stone walls and float down the empty halls. They're violent and resolute.

A raw ache twists in my gut with the knowledge that Serena is in danger. Within seconds, I dart back down the hall and storm back into Chancellor Davidson's office.

Everyone's gaze shifts to me, and I prowl toward Serena.

"They're here," is all I say.

Every gargoyle jumps into action, snapping their gargoyle wings out and taking on warrior expressions.

While the London clan dons raven wings, Gage's and mine are a dark gray, and Henry's are a chocolate brown.

Asher and Keegan begin barking orders.

Chancellor Davidson walks over to a bookshelf. He tilts a leather-bound book and the wall slides open, revealing an impressive collection of cold weaponry.

He motions to the wall. "Take your pick, protectors."

We rush the wall and start arming ourselves.

Somewhere in the lower portion of the building, the floorboards groan with the weight of the warriors' steps, alerting me that there must be a large number of them.

"Henry, we will need reinforcements," I bark.

He nods and quickly sends out a campus-wide text that all protectors are to report to the castle, armed and ready. This is not an exercise. It's war.

I turn to Serena, who is strapping knives to the side of her thigh with steady hands and a calm demeanor.

Fuck, that is sexy.

Her unruffled gaze meets mine, and she smiles before cracking her neck and grabbing a gun off the wall.

She pulls back the safety and hands it to me.

Again. Fucking sexy.

I almost don't recognize the girl staring back at me. She's unafraid. Ready for anything. A true protector.

Inhaling deeply, I close my eyes and focus on the mission. Regardless of where today leads, I'll protect her, even if it takes me to my grave.

The sound of breaking glass yanks me out of my head. I look over at the window, and see that Keegan has taken an ax to it, busting it wide open. He motions to Asher to grab Eve.

"You, Henry, and Eve take the front," Keegan instructs. "McKenna and I will take the back and give instructions to the protectors as they arrive. Rulf, Abby, and Callan will hold off Kupuva up here. Gage, I need you and Tristan to teleport Serena to Paris and watch over her."

Serena crosses her arms. "Like hell they will."

"Serena," her father barks. "Not up for discussion."

"I am a royal protector, which means I fight," she states.

Asher mutters a few curses under his breath and grabs his mate's hand, dragging her toward the window while she snaps at him in protest. Henry follows along behind them.

Every sound in the building has ceased. It falls completely still and silent. Eerily so.

A whoosh of air whirls around us and suddenly dust, stone and plaster explode into the room with a bang. I throw Serena onto the ground with a grunt, covering her with my body as large pieces of rock fall around us.

Seconds later, we scramble to our feet and come face-to-face with Kupuva and the Diablo Fairy army.

Kupuva's soulless black eyes lock onto Serena, and I slide in front of her so she's protected from the glare.

Dust and debris float in the air around us.

In an instant, Rulf and Gage take places to my right. Callan and Abby appear to my left.

"Well, now. You've made a huge mess," Callan sighs, disappointed. "I'm going to need a card with your boss's name and address, so I know where to send the cleaning bill. This shit is not going to be cheap. Right, babe?"

"It's true. I don't think insurance is going to cover destruction caused by demon fairies," Abby replies.

"Really?" Callan glances at his mate. "We don't have a rider on the policy for that?"

Abby shakes her head, playing along. "Nope. Just flood."

"Hope you brought your checkbook," he taunts Kupuva.

"I come for girl," she states.

Callan laughs. "I feel like we've done this before."

Abby sighs. "I think we have. We need a vacation."

"I come for girl," Kupuva states again, more firmly.

"You'll have to go through me," I interject.

The leader slides her gaze between Serena and me.

"We Donga fight for her," the leader challenges.

"What the hell is a Donga fight?" Serena asks.

"It's a very serious and fierce ritual among the Suri tribes in Africa. A stick fight. It normally takes place in the name of love, so that young men can prove their masculinity and virility, show their courage and resistance to pain," Callan explains. "Settle conflicts."

Serena steps around me. "I can Donga fight for myself."

"No. Him." Kupuva shakes her stick in my direction.

Serena bristles. "Did you just say no to me?"

Callan releases a low whistle. "Lady, my daughter is like her mother. You say no and she'll kick your ass. Hardcore."

I grasp Serena's shoulder. "Donga fighting has to be done by a champion—on your behalf."

She snorts. "That is barbaric and archaic."

I pin her with a hard glare. "It's a respected ritual amongst warriors and tribes."

Serena falls silent in contemplation before I see the light bulb go off in her head. A small smile crosses her lips.

"You're going to fight for me?" she asks.

"This time, I am," I confirm.

SERENA

IN A STRANGELY RESPECTFUL AND CALM manner, we make our way to the quad. My uncles and aunts, as well as the protectors that were called in for reinforcement, have all appeared behind us and have been informed of what is taking place.

This is by far the oddest thing I've ever seen.

And that's coming from a gargoyle who grew up in a supernatural world filled with vampires, nymphs, goblins, sorceresses, and other creatures most only dream of.

If there's one thing to be said about the supernatural realms and the beings in them, it's that we respect traditions and rituals.

No matter what we're fighting for.

Even love.

I watch as the decorated warriors slide fingers full of clay on their bodies in preparation.

Kupuva motions to Tristan that he should do the same, and with a heavy sigh, he takes off his shirt and necklace, throwing them both to the ground with annoyance.

A Diablo Fairy steps up to me and hands me a stone bowl filled with the black dirt. I look at it and after a moment, the fairy pushes it toward me, ordering me to take it. I do.

"Since I am fighting for your honor, you'll need to decorate me with the clay," Tristan whispers.

I catch his eyes. "This is ridiculous."

"You're lucky I don't have to wear the string of colored beads around my genitals," he replies, and I laugh.

I dip two fingers into the cool mud and scoop some up, then step closer to Tristan's bare chest, holding his eyes while he looks down at me with a fierce expression.

The minute the clay touches his stomach, his muscles twitch and he flinches under my touch.

"Sorry. Is it cold?" I use a soft voice.

"No," his voice cracks.

Placing more clay on my hand, I move toward the protector mark over his heart. At my touch, Tristan braces his hands on my hips, exhaling a hiss before his eyes darken.

I still my fingers and we just stare at one another.

His jaw is tight as he works it back and forth.

"Keep going," his voice is gravelly.

Once I finish, he looks down.

His lips lift on the sides when he sees the raindrop around the protector mark and the *S* I made on his chest.

"Really?" he questions. "Superman?"

I shrug. "Superman is hot. But that *S* stands for Serena."

He closes his eyes briefly before he opens them again. "I protect what's mine, Serena. You are mine. Trust me."

I swear the universe shook around me at his declaration.

"I do."

We face the warriors, who are carrying a man, dancing, and singing in chant. Kupuva hands the man her stick, and he is placed on the ground before taking a fighting pose.

Magali runs over to Tristan and hands him a stick.

"You have a Donga stick?" I ask.

She rolls her eyes. "My family is South African. It hangs on the wall in our family room. It's more of a decoration."

"Thanks," Tristan nods, and steps forward.

So does the warrior they've chosen.

Without warning, Tristan snaps his stick out and lands a hard blow to the Diablo Fairy's back. The warrior grunts.

In the next second, he returns the blow to Tristan.

When Tristan growls, I take a step forward to stop this, but am grabbed from behind by Gage, who pulls me to him.

"Do not interfere, Serena. This is custom. They're testing one another to see if they're worthy opponents."

"You want me to just stand here while they torture and beat on him?" I seethe.

Gages voice softens. "No. Watch as he fights for you."

Both warriors suddenly throw themselves into the fight. They hit one another over and over again with ferocious and fast strokes of their sticks. With each contact of the stick, they bruise and bleed, grunting and groaning in pain. It's violent, and my stomach roils at the sight.

Gage releases my shoulders and slides his hand into mine. I look down at our clasped hands and he squeezes mine as a form of reassurance that Tristan will be okay.

The demon fairy stumbles, and Tristan lands a hard blow to the back of his neck. The demon ducks and snaps his stick at Tristan's midsection, but Tristan moves out of the way and lands another blow to the demon's back, sending him sailing to the ground.

"It's forbidden to hit a being when they're on the ground," Gage explains why Tristan is circling the demon with heavy angry pants instead of ending him.

When Tristan's back is to the warrior, the demon stands and rushes at my protector. On instinct, Tristan twists and lands another hard blow to the side of the warrior's head.

Surprise flickers across the demon's face for a split second, before he's hit again with another smack to the other side, black tar-like blood gushing out of both holes.

Tristan pants as he faces the demon. His eyes shift over the demon's shoulder and land on me. With a loud roar, Tristan lifts his stick and knocks the demon's head clear off his body.

The warrior's decapitated body falls limply on the ground as silence falls around us, and I exhale in relief.

Tristan smiles at me, while blood and dirt cover him.

I shimmy out of Gage's grasp and with measured steps walk toward him. Just as I'm about to pull him into my arms, Kupuva steps in front of us and I yank out my knives.

"Serena, stop," Tristan grunts.

Kupuva's gaze falls to the weapons in my hands. She bends down, holding my eyes, and picks up her bloodied stick from the ground.

Wordlessly, she lifts it, and pushes my knives down with the tip so they're not pointed at her.

"Your champion won." Her voice is deep, authoritative.

"And you lost," I bite out.

"This round," she says, and points her stick at another demon. He places a beaded necklace onto it and she swings the stick at me, "Take the necklace. It is his right."

Confused, I slide it off the wood, while she faces Tristan.

Holding his side, Tristan lifts his stick to me.

Kupuva slides her focus to the necklace and then to Tristan's stick, telling me wordlessly to place it on the weapon. I do.

"CHAMPION!" she calls out, and her army retreats.

I watch in shock as they disappear.

I turn to Tristan. "What just happened?"

"I won." He exhales.

"Won what?" I ask.

"Your love. You're mine," he says.

In the next moment he collapses in my arms.

TWENTY-FIVE
NO REGRETS

TRISTAN

I T'S FUNNY HOW AT THE END of your existence all you think about is the beginning. The things you never got to do along the way. I'd always wondered what it would be like to sacrifice yourself for love. Today, I found out.

Serena's smile flashes behind my eyes, and my heart squeezes. I don't know how it happened, but she managed to maneuver her way into the deepest part of me. She's destroyed me, and in the wake of my destruction, she's become my salvation.

I hear shouting all around me, but it sounds far away. A groan comes from my lips as my wet, sticky body slumps against the ground. Warm arms wrap around me, cocooning me in safety. My breaths are coming out in sharp pants, and there is too much pressure on my lungs to breathe.

Every gasp hurts like my chest is on fire. The pressure is choking me, pushing and tearing at my existence.

Serena's voice is at my ear. "I've got you. You're going to be okay," she assures me, as the blackness takes over.

Something soft and warm caresses my body in long, gentle strokes, leaving a wet trail in its path. A sponge, maybe.

"How is he, Ophelia?" Gage asks.

"The bruises are gone. His wounds have healed. Slowly, but they've healed," my mother replies. "His broken ribs punctured his lung, but that, too, has mended itself."

"That's good news," Gage exhales.

A soft hand brushes across my forehead. "It is."

"He protected her, with his life," Gage states.

"I know, Gage." My mother's tone is sad.

"He loves her, Ophelia," Gage continues.

"Sometimes in life, love must be sacrificed for peace."

"The princess I used to know would have chosen love over her royal obligations, Ophelia," Gage points out.

My mother sighs. "The queen sitting before you knows better. Love doesn't bring peace. Love doesn't save realms. Treaties do. Power does. Sacrifices have to be made. Tristan understands and respects the way of our world. After Camilla, Gage, you should understand how deadly and foolish it is to choose love and forsake all else."

Silence fills the air.

"Even if it meant war, I'd sacrifice everything to have one more minute with Camilla. To tell her that I love her. To hear her laugh. See her smile. To feel her touch. Or taste her lips. I'd choose those sixty seconds over a lifetime of peace," Gage's voice cracks. "Any day of the week."

"Why is that?" my mother whispers.

"Love is peace. Death is war," he replies, and I hear his footsteps retreat.

A little while later, my mother kisses my cheek and moves her mouth closer to my ear so she can whisper.

"This isn't the end of your story, it's just the beginning."

SERENA

I SLOWLY MOVE THROUGH THE LARGE tent, pretending that breathing is easy. The façade of happiness is firmly etched across my expression as the eyes in the room follow my every move with morbid curiosity.

Huge white flowers hang from the ceiling, draping the entire gala in an elegant white canopy.

The tent's walls are open, allowing for the warm breeze to float through. With each light gust of wind, the hanging vines sway as though they're dancing with one another.

Strewn about the gala are large vases and balls made of white flowers classily highlighted by crystal chandeliers.

This year's Summer Solstice Gala has a white party theme, and it's simply breathtaking.

"Hey, Princess," Ethan whispers in my ear, and I turn.

He and Lucas are dressed in matching white tuxedos.

"Don't you gentlemen look dapper this evening?"

"Save us a dance?" Lucas pouts adorably.

"I always do." I return his pout with a seductive wink.

"Where is Magali?" Ethan asks.

"Dancing with her date." I point to my best friend.

Zander dips Mags for the third time, and she giggles. From her upside-down position, she waves at us. I smile and shake my head at how silly they are together. Over the past month, they've gotten really close.

It's nice to see her so happy.

Ireland and Ryker join us, and Ryker hands me a glass of champagne so that we can toast to summer.

I take a sip and continue to scan the room for the one being that I need and want to see more than breathing.

On cue, the lights dim, infusing the tent in an amber hue.

I lock eyes with Tristan as he makes his way toward me.

Everything fades away and suddenly, it's just him and me. His grin is wide and unapologetic as he approaches. I love the way his eyes darken when he looks at me. A lazy, seductive look crosses his face, the one that always makes me weak in the knees.

"Hi," he says in a hoarse voice.

"Hi, yourself." I try not to burst into tears at the sight of him, standing and completely healed.

"I notice you're without a date this evening."

"It's a long story. I was supposed to come with this guy, but he got into this incredibly brutal fight a few days ago. He went all alpha caveman and beat some dude with a stick. He's been on bed rest since then, healing."

Tristan grimaces. "Sounds like an asshole."

"Oh, he is," I laugh.

"You should up your standards," he suggests.

"Did I mention he's also engaged?" I add.

"Definitely not fake boyfriend material," he teases.

"Nope. That means I'm free. If you'd like to dance."

"I would be honored," he holds his hand out.

I take it and let him lead me to the dance floor. Tristan pulls me closer, and we sway to the music.

"You look beautiful," he says near my ear.

"Thank you," I whisper into his shoulder.

"Have you ever walked through someone's personal space and looked at their framed photographs?" he asks.

I look up at him. "Yes. Why?"

"It's rare to see rain in a photo," he surmises.

"I never thought about it." Until now.

"There's always a storm, Serena. The rain will always come, and when it does, I'll think of you now. The rain is my framed photo of you. With every drop of water, I'll close my eyes and remember our first encounter. The one where you were twirling across emerald fields, with your hands out, in the rain. That's how I'll remember you. Free," he whispers.

A hard lump grows in my throat, making swallowing impossible. "That's a beautiful memory."

With his head, he motions to the back of the tent, clasping our hands together and weaving us through the bodies on the dance floor.

We step out to the patio, and I take in the sunset. The warmth of Tristan's body presses against my back, and his scent wraps around me. He places a small kiss behind my ear and I shiver at the contact. Slowly, I turn and face him, rendered speechless at how handsome he looks in his white button-down shirt and black dress pants.

"Promise me something?"

"Anything," he vows.

"Promise I'll see you again." I hold my breath.

"Even if it's only in our dreams, I swear," his tone firm.

I try to fight back tears, but one escapes.

The back of his knuckles brush over my cheek, wiping away the tear, and he grants me a small smile.

"Listen to me carefully. Tonight, I'm going to let you go. Not because I want to, but because I have to. I will take care of you. Even if it's from afar. I'll dream of you every damn night. I'll remember you, always," he says slowly.

My heart thuds against my chest.

"I will never regret you, raindrop."

I search his eyes. He may as well have said he loves me, because his words have the same effect on me.

He takes my hand and turns it over, placing the necklace he won in the battle in my hand, and then closes my fingers around it. He leans forward and presses his lips to my forehead, then drops his hands and backs away from me.

With every inch of space that he puts between us, I feel my heart crumble. I swear I can hear our hearts shatter at the same time as the universe rips us apart. As much as I know that he has to leave, that he isn't mine, I'm a breath from falling on my knees and begging him to stay.

I wait until he's gone to whisper, "Choose me."

I wait until he's gone before the tears fall.

I wait until he's gone before darkness descends.

My hand tightens around the necklace I'm clasping, and a small pain pricks my finger, causing me to drop it.

I look down at the beads lying on the floor, and notice a small piece of paper hanging from the string. It's folded origami in the shape of a lion.

As I undo each fold, the tiny mark behind my ear burns.

Like it's coming to life.

When I've finished, I flatten the small note out in my palm and read Tristan's words.

The Sun of Vergina is our cessation.

EXCERPT FROM AEQUUS

SERENA

THE DARK TEMPEST LURKS ON THE horizon, casting a shadow over the cloud-filled sky. Heavy gusts slice through the atmosphere in quick, angry bursts. With each surge of air, the ache in my chest recedes, allowing me to breathe.

I've always envied the currents. Wind is the epitome of strength and power, and has the ability to move freely throughout the world. It can't be captured. Or tamed.

I'm an elemental gargoyle, which means the air strengthens my spirit, making it vitally important in order for my protector energy to flow properly. Controlling the unseen currents reminds me there's so much more to this world than what we can visually see.

I continue to manipulate the wind's speed until I'm exhausted. I'm hoping the directional streams will bring the rain. You see, how the air floats between the clouds or trees determines whether or not a storm will appear.

The air currents grow and change—as the world does.

They can create calm and peace.

Or chaos and destruction.

I drop my hands and everything around me stills.

When Tristan returned to his realm, he took the rain, and in its place, the winds arose in my dominion.

Tristan Gallagher.

The ache in my chest spreads at the thought of my protector, the prince of the woodland nymphs. It was only months ago that, like the wind, he blew into my life, bringing with him the calm, and then the storm.

Tristan is half-gargoyle. In order to avoid a sentencing of stone petrifaction, my family assigned him to protect me from a possible attack by the Diablo Fairies—a legion of ancient warriors who practice black magic. They're a new breed of supernatural creatures, created by Asmodeus, the king of the Nine Hells, in order to end my existence.

After the death of his mate, the demon lord declared revenge on my family, the London clan of gargoyles, and the entire protector race. Unbeknownst to me, Asmodeus blamed my clan for his mate's demise.

He's made it clear that I'm his primary target. As such, my family felt it necessary to add more protection to my royal guard. Hence the introduction of Tristan into my world. Successfully ending my existence will ensure I can't take my place as the next leader of the gargoyle race—a distinguished title within the supernatural world, which, to this day, my uncle Asher proudly assumes.

If Asmodeus were to succeed in destroying both my uncle and me, it would leave the protector world open to attack.

Kupuva, the leader of the Diablo Fairy army, recently challenged Tristan to a Donga fight—a barbaric and archaic competition and ritual known among the Suri tribes in Africa. Its primary purpose is to settle conflicts.

A champion is chosen on your behalf to fight for your honor—and love.

Tristan was chosen to fight for me—and won.

The Diablo Fairy army has backed off, for now, but the victory was short-lived because Tristan is also half-satyr, a male nymph. His mother is Queen Ophelia of the Woodland realm, which makes him a prince.

For centuries, the wood and water realms have been teetering on the brink of war, locked in an ancient power struggle. To solidify their alliance, Tristan was promised in marriage to Freya, the princess of the water realm, and someone he doesn't love.

Shortly after his triumph against Kupuva and her army, Tristan returned to his realm to fulfill his oath and secure peace for his kingdom and kin.

Leaving me alone.

With a broken heart.

I look up at the gray clouds and, with a quick flick of my wrist, attempt to force the rain to fall from the sky.

The wind releases my fury. But the rain? The rain calms me. Since Tristan left, it hasn't rained.

"If you keep doing that, champ, you'll cause a hurricane."

I throw Zander, Tristan's half-brother and best friend, an over-the-shoulder annoyed glare.

"So be it." My voice is empty.

His steps are measured as he approaches me.

"Angry much these days, Serena?"

I bark out a laugh. "How can you tell?"

"Call it a satyr hunch," he banters, stepping next to me, and lowers his voice. "The tornado you're conjuring has spilt over into the woodland realm. The trees are bending and the leaves trembling as if something dark is on the horizon."

My response is a one-shoulder shrug. "Maybe it is."

Zander watches me with his stormy jade eyes and inky rock-star hair. He looks nothing like Tristan.

Tristan's hair is a warm caramel color, longer on the top, and messily styled. The flecks of gold in his serious cognac gaze are deep.

Tristan looks like the calm before the storm, whereas Zander looks like the darkness that will overtake you.

Appearances can be deceiving, though. Where Zander's personality is lively, warm, and inviting, Tristan's is full of darkness, haunted coolness, and impassive indifference.

Except with me.

"Would this tempest be about my brother's upcoming nuptials to a certain nymph princess?" he watches me.

At his words, rage consumes me.

The reality of my situation hit me full force ten seconds after Tristan walked out of my life. Since then, the gloomy days match my dark mood.

Male protectors should come with a warning label. They aren't good for the heart. Period. The End.

My attention snaps to Zander's face as the thunder rolls in and lightning strikes over the lake multiple times.

Zander's gaze roams to the sky. "You need to get past this, Serena. Let him focus on his duties and oaths."

I scowl.

How am I supposed to get past this? How can I move on from Tristan, when he is tied to me by a blood bond?

Ever since Tristan came into my life, I was given a taste of freedom, something I'd never had before. My free will isn't unrestricted; it came at a price—the loss of my heart.

In order to safeguard me, Tristan's protector mark was infused with my blood. A blood bond is the only way a gargoyle can truly protect their charge. Once it's broken or begins to fade, the gargoyles become short-tempered and sullen. I've been told that with time, it will fade.

Just like my memories of Tristan.

I shiver, out of loneliness and rejection.

"The bond we share doesn't leave me a choice," I snap.

Zander doesn't get angry at me for my outburst. Instead, his demeanor becomes softer, understanding.

"You do have a choice, Serena," he pacifies.

Chaos reigns around me and then suddenly, everything stops. "Wrong," I state sharply. "If I really had a choice, I would have chosen Tristan. He would have chosen me."

Zander swears under his breath and pinches the bridge of his nose. Dark circles frame his eyes and his lips pull into a tight smile, across his straight white teeth.

"You think he likes this, Serena? Do you think Tristan isn't hurting in the same way you are?" he grunts. "My brother is miserable. If you thought he was dark and broody before his time with you, he's worse now."

Words become caught in my throat, and my shoulders fall in defeat. I know Tristan feels this too. How can he not?

Maybe I should move on. At the thought, the small mark behind my ear tingles, reminding me it's there.

My hand lifts and rubs at it, trying to soothe the burn.

Zander's forest-clouded focus narrows in at the motion.

"Have you told him, yet?" he asks.

"About what?"

Rolling his eyes, Zander folds his arms across his muscular chest. "The mark. Behind your ear, Serena."

I look away. "Why would he care about a freckle?"

"A freckle in the shape of his insignia," he counters.

As the prince of the woodland nymphs, Tristan wears an emblem around his neck, the Sun of Vergina.

It marks him as nymph royalty.

Oddly enough, the symbol, his mark, is on my skin.

Sighing, I slowly turn my head.

The minute my eyes meet Zander's, I lose the ability to argue anymore. Instead, I swallow the dryness in my throat.

"I have no idea why it's there, Zander. Until I do, I don't think Tristan needs to know. Not now, anyway. You know, with everything else he has going on," I whisper.

Zander shakes his head in disagreement. "There is a deeper meaning behind it. It isn't just a coincidence."

He's right. Before Tristan left, he handed me a note, which read: *The Sun of Vergina is our cessation.*

His words contain a hidden meaning that I can't decipher. I've been going over and over them again in my mind, trying to figure out their meaning. Exactly how, or what, the insignia will stop or end, I have no idea.

"Do not tell him, Zander. Until I understand it, Tristan doesn't need to be made aware," I demand.

"He'll kill you when he finds out," he scoffs.

I snort. He won't. Tristan wouldn't ever hurt me, I lie to myself, as the ache in my heart makes itself known again.

"I'm not afraid of Tristan. Or his wrath," I mumble.

"You really have no fears, do you?" he mocks.

Slowly, I raise my head and lock eyes with Zander.

"I fear what my life will be, without him in it."

And damn it if I wasn't going to do everything in my power to prevent that from happening.

"Well, then, I guess your fears are about to become a reality. I'm here because his ceremony is in five days. Freya's father, Oren, has moved up the date. Again. I wanted to personally let you know, before you found out another way. Given how you took the news the last time."

I school my features, pretending not to have heard him.

"Serena?" he questions, at my quiet state.

That's it. I'm done letting fate decide our futures.

"I need a favor, Zander," I state.

"What now?" he asks, with caution lining his tone.

"I need you to sneak me into your realm," I say.

"What?" Zander laughs out loud.

"You're the second in command of the army that guards the woodland realm. I need you to sneak me in."

Zander falls silent as he studies my features. After a moment, he sighs. "Why? What are you going to do?"

"Stop a wedding."

"You're serious?" he exhales. "You'll start a war, Serena."

"He's worth starting a war for."

"So you're saying it is the crazy, obsessive, *I will die for you* kind of love?" he responds, pinning me with a look.

Zander once asked me if I felt that way toward Tristan, and I lied and said no. But I do. Deep in my bones, I know.

"He's worth fighting for, Zander," I hiss.

"Just—" Zander runs his hand through his raven hair. "Be careful—he isn't yours."

"Trust me." I step to move past him and lower my voice. "I'm well aware that he's not mine. Yet," I add. "That doesn't mean I can't—or won't—fight for him. Now, take me to the woodland realm, so I can save Tristan."

REVELATION

(THE REVELATION SERIES, BOOK ONE)

I'M RUNNING, *AND NOT VERY WELL*, *might I add. My lungs burn and my shallow breathing erratically bounces off the slick stone walls. I keep moving forward, forcing myself farther and farther into the dark underground passage. It's cold, damp, and smells like musk.*

"What the hell is following me?" I ask myself, as confusion sets in. The only thing I'm certain of is that I'm bone-chillingly terrified, down to the core of my very soul. I'm frightened that whatever is chasing me will catch me, because when it does, there's no doubt it will kill me. Its hatred and anger rolls off it in waves, crashing through me like a sharp gust of wind, suffocating me. I'm positive it's pure evil.

Just as I reach the end of the tunnel, I hit a solid wall, ceasing my progress and ending my futile efforts at escape. "Shit," I whisper out loud, while I strike my palms against the water-slicked stones. Feeling defeated, I place my forehead to the damp wall and release a soft whimper.

I need to figure out my options, quickly. I sense its presence closing in, dropping the tunnel's temperature from cool and damp to downright frigid, the glacial air settling around the passageway. My breath comes out in a cloud in front of me. My heart rate increases as I stifle the gag reflex being challenged by the rancid smell of sulfur and sour milk.

"Eeeve," it hisses, mocking me. Sensing my deepest fears, it begins to play with me by using those emotions against me. "Oh God," I exhale, as I close my eyes and rub my temples, trying to ease the dread rising in my throat.

Panicked, I start talking to myself. "Think, Eve." I turn around, allowing my eyes to scan over the dark enclosed area. All I can see in front of me is black. Blowing out a harsh breath, I begin to pray for a miracle as I wait for it to manifest.

"Nope, nothing," I say dejectedly to no one.

I twist back to the wall. In a frantic state, I push and pound on the large, dark gray stones, trying anything. I'm desperate, and there's an off-chance that located somewhere is a hidden opening that could grant me freedom.

Then I hear it. The thing I fear most. I spin and freeze, fixed in my spot at the hissing sound of slithering snakes. Oh shit, now I'm really afraid. My heartbeat echoes in my ears as a severe chill runs down the length of my spine. My lips force air out sharply in a frenzied state, causing strands of fallen hair to jump away from my face with each irregular breath.

Without warning, the tunnel goes silent. The only sound ricocheting off the wet stones is my strained breath being forced into the dark abyss. I remind myself to inhale before I suffer from a full-blown panic attack. With great slowness, I rotate to face my attacker.

No one is there.

As I swallow hard, my eyes shift down to the floor and take in the dark tendrils of smoke that crawl around my ankles, rooting me to the ground. What the hell? My eyes dart around wildly, searching for the point of origin of the wisp, but there isn't one.

With my back pressed flat against the cold concrete wall and the dampness seeping into my shirt, I've resigned myself to the fact that this is how I'm going to die. I close my eyes in acceptance and attempt to steady my breathing, listening to the droplets of water hitting the ground.

Drip.

Drip.

Drip.

I try to convince myself it will be okay as the dark cloud works its way up my body, wrapping forcefully around my neck and cutting off the oxygen supply sustaining me.

Black spots form behind my closed eyelids as I become light-headed and dizzy. The lack of oxygen begins to take hold of my body, and I start to lose consciousness. Crap.

"Dimittet eam, Nero," I hear a strong male voice order, in a calm yet deadly tone.

I can't see my savior. Everything is shrouded in darkness. Maybe he isn't even here, and I'm hallucinating in my final moments of life.

The black mist loosens its choke hold on my neck while hissing angrily. "Deus tuus, ibi est filia eius."

A putrid gust of air blankets my face with each seething mock. Changing its mind, the evil smoke cackles, wrapping around my throat again and gripping firmly, causing me to wheeze. What the fuck?

"Dixit mittam tibi pergat ad profundum inferni, sive," my liberator says heatedly in Latin.

Nero releases me, then turns to my rescuer, morphing into the outline of a man. At the discharge of its hold, my body slides down the slick wall, landing harshly on the glacial, water-soaked stone floor. I begin coughing and gasping for air as I place my head between my legs, willing air into my lungs.

"Et subdit quod me putesssss?" Nero hisses.

"Yes, you repulsive excuse of an existence, I do think I can send you back to the depths of Hell," my protector replies calmly, yet cockily.

"Et veniunt ad me ut, gurgulio," Nero states, in a final slithery tone. At that command, my savior pulls out a long, black, granite sword that reflects the water cascading down the passage walls.

"Delectabiliter," the dark knight replies coldly, before he attacks.

Even wrapped in blackness, I can sense he's a trained warrior. His body moves with ease and agility as he engages Nero. I hear each whoosh the sword makes as it slices effortlessly through the air, making contact with each thrust.

I can't make out any of the warrior's facial features, but I know he's large and moves fast and efficiently. I close my eyes for a brief second, only to throw them open in alarm at the high-pitched shriek coming from the thing called Nero, as it bursts into blue flames and vanishes.

That's when I officially lose control over my emotions and begin to shake uncontrollably, with tears flowing down my pale cheeks. The blackness engulfs me, choking me. I shut my eyes, wishing that everything would just stop, and that I was anywhere else.

All of a sudden, I feel warmth and calm flow through my veins, as my guardian kneels down next to me and pulls me into his safe embrace with gentleness. He strokes my hair, trying to pacify me as I cling to him for life.

The masculine scent of smoky wood and leather fills my nose, as his deep voice whispers in my ear.

"Hush. It's all right. You're safe. No harm will come to you. I've got you." His tone is slow and soft, as if speaking to a wounded animal, lulling me into a state of calmness.

With great tenderness, his large, warm hands cup my cheeks and lift my face to meet his, wiping the tears away with his thumbs—a pointless effort, since the flow increases with the kind gesture.

My gaze lifts and connects with a pair of glowing indigo eyes. They're staring at me with such intensity and affection that his look creates an ache deep within my chest, as my body draws itself to his of its own accord, like it knows him.

The voice belonging to those eyes speaks with a firm vow. "I will protect you . . . always."

Gasping for air, I abruptly sit up in bed and swallow down a scream. My fists clutch my blanket in a severe death grip, as pieces of my light brown hair fall from my ponytail and stick to the sweat on my face and neck.

I drop my head into my waiting hands and realize my cheeks are wet, most likely from the tears that escaped my hazel eyes during my nightmare.

The dampness causes my long, dark lashes to stick to one another while I rub them. The lids open, then close again, and I order myself to take even breaths to calm my erratic heartbeat. As I slowly open them for the final time, my heart rate picks up once more, at the realization of what's coming next.

I turn to my left and steel myself.

"What. The. Hell. Eve!" Aria, my roommate and self-appointed best friend, screeches, and I wince from the high-pitched octave. *Crap.* I woke her up, again.

She's sitting on her bed, looking like a pissed-off fairy. Her normally cute pink, pixie-cut hair is suffering a major case of bed head, sticking up in all directions.

"Are you okay?" Aria asks, with an irritated yet concern-laced voice, and her petite hands on her curvy hips. She's staring at me, waiting for an explanation as I open and close my mouth like a gaping fish, trying to form intelligent words.

"Sorry, I um, bad dream," I mutter inarticulately.

"No shit," she says, with sarcasm dripping from her lips. "Same one?" The question is thrown out along with some serious stink eye radiating from her round chocolate orbs.

Arianna "Aria" Donovan dislikes being woken up in the middle of the night. I know this because we've been college roommates for all of one month now. Which means I've woken her up more times than I care to count.

We met over the summer during freshman orientation, and according to Aria, it was "friendship at first sight." As new students, we were placed into groups of ten and forced to play this ridiculous get-to-know-you game where each person had a photo of a particular cartoon character taped to their back. The goal was to ask the group questions in an attempt to gain enough information to guess who your character was, so you could partner up with your match for the rest of orientation.

Aria was *Bert* and I was *Ernie*. We've been inseparable ever since, even requesting to room together this semester. Well, in truth, Aria demanded we room together, and since I'm pretty easygoing, I didn't put up a fight, figuring it would be nice to know someone.

At the moment, I'm thinking she's second-guessing her choice in roommates.

She sighs and prowls to the minifridge, grabbing a bottle of water and shoving it in my hand before turning on the crystal-embellished lamp on the pink thrift-store-revived table between our beds.

Our dorm room is a decent size. We got lucky in the housing lottery and managed to snag a suite. Unfortunately, that means we share it with two other roommates.

The space consists of two shared bedrooms, a common lounge area, and an attached bathroom. Overall, it's your typical college dorm room, amped up with Aria's thrift store finds reincarnated into amazing pieces of art, because she is an eternal optimist and believes everything can be redeemed.

Her décor style matches her schizophrenic personality to perfection—Barbie meets Marilyn Manson. She's the only person I know who can pull off pink combat boots, black nail polish, and dark black smoky eyeliner with a pink sundress, and have it look adorably sexy.

I like her one-of-a-kind style. It offsets my average, girl-next-door fashion sense, which usually consists of skinny jeans, knee-high boots, and a cotton long-sleeved shirt. I suppose it's what originally drew me to her—opposites attract. I also presume that's what makes our friendship fun.

The cousins, our other two suitemates, are a different story. Speaking of which, I need to take cover as the door to our room crashes open in dramatic fashion and both Abby and McKenna enter the room like a Victoria's Secret pajama commercial.

Abby, the younger of the two cousins by only a few months, smiles with her delicate arms folded, allowing her long red hair to cascade over her refined shoulders.

"You okay, Eve?" she asks with concern.

Even at three in the morning, Abigail "Abby" Connor is ethereal looking. She's wearing her black flannel pajama bottoms and a cute green T-shirt that says, *Kiss Me, I'm Irish*. The green brings out the flecks of shimmer in her crystal-blue eyes.

I force a casual shrug. "Yeah. Just another bad dream. Sorry to wake you guys up again."

She responds with a warm smile.

On the other hand, McKenna just grunts. I've deduced it's simply because she hates talking to people.

Now that I think about it, McKenna "Kenna" McIntyre just dislikes people in general. She's always ranting about the "human race" being inferior. Inferior to whom, she's never clarified. Most of the time, her off-handed comments go in one ear and out the other, because they're so frequent.

I exhale and take a sip of water, the cool liquid hydrating my dry throat.

McKenna narrows her sapphire eyes, outlined with lush black lashes, at me. "Seriously, Eve. I'm tired of waking up to your fucking screaming every night," she comments in a harsh tone.

I grimace. "Was I screaming? Sorry, I had no idea," I offer. Of course I was screaming. I was being choked to death, for God's sake. The shrieking might also be why my throat feels like sandpaper, making it painful to swallow or talk.

Turning like a graceful but angry swan, McKenna heads toward the doorway, stopping just before making her dramatic exit. "You look like shit, by the way," she snarls, and flicks her long, platinum-blonde hair over her shoulder to enhance her point. With that, she storms out, fuzzy slippers and all.

Most of the student body on campus is terrified of McKenna. It would be wishful thinking to assume they're put off by her "sass" and "straight shooting" attitude.

I think she just gets off on intimidating people. She also has no filter, a vocabulary rivaling any truck driver, and can make even the strongest person fold into her- or himself with her malevolent stare.

Needless to say, the jury is still out on our friendship. It's only been four weeks. Abby, on the other hand, is extremely likable, and is becoming a good friend.

"Sorry," I mutter, for the fourth time this week.

The nightmares began on my eighteenth birthday. Each time, I wake up in a cold sweat, gasping for air, crying and screaming from being terrified and tortured in the outlandish dream. It's been rough, to say the least.

Lying back on my pillow, I put my arm over my eyes, willing my body to calm itself down, as the adrenaline still pumps wildly through my veins. I try using the breathing techniques I've learned through years of studying yoga. It's not working.

Abby fidgets with unease. "Kenna doesn't mean to be bitchy. She's just tired," she excuses the poor behavior, a maternal habit of hers.

With poise, she sits on my bed, removing my arm from my hidden face. "Do you want to talk about it?" She offers a small smile. "It might help make it less scary and real if you say it out loud." Abby pauses before continuing. "You'd be surprised at my level of understanding when it comes to fear-provoking things," she says at almost an inaudible level.

"No. Thanks, Abby. I'm good. Just a bad dream," I say as persuasively as I can, for both our sakes, because if she knew what lurked in the darkness of the dreams, she'd have me committed.

Abby studies my face for a moment, searching for a hint of deceit. When she's convinced I'm all right, she stands to go back to her own room. "Okay, but if you change your mind, come and get me. I'm happy to listen, Eve. Night, girls," she utters in a sweet voice before leaving.

McKenna and Abby are both tall and built like dancers. While Abby exudes grace and regality, McKenna radiates fierce warrior princess. When they're together, it's intimidating.

Aria just stands there, staring at me, taking this all in while wearing her favorite pink T-shirt and matching boy shorts. All five feet of her looks both adorable and annoyed.

"Fine," she huffs, and relinquishes the idea that I want to elaborate on my nightmare-induced state. She crawls back into bed, pulls up her ruffled pink blanket, and turns off the light.

We sit in silence, the moonlight shining through the window, bathing the room in a blue glow and twisting the shadows on the walls. I turn my eyes upwards to the ceiling, focusing on it with immense concentration, wishing the terrifying dreams would stop so I could have a normal night's sleep.

After a few moments, Aria rolls over to face me as the night's silver light bounces off her features, masked in sympathetic concern. She goes to speak, but I cut her off.

"Please don't, Aria. I just don't have it in me tonight," I whisper, pleading for her to back off.

"Okay, but at some point we need to figure this out, Eve. I'm worried about you." She sighs, turns over, and goes to sleep.

I'm left to contemplate my dreams and their meaning while, once again, staring into the abyss of darkness.

2 ENCOUNTERS

OCTOBER IN MASSACHUSETTS BRINGS COOL FALL temperatures. Little by little, this charming New England campus, crammed with brick buildings and puritan heritage, is filling with warm autumn colors. I close the required reading for my Rhetorical Criticism class and take in a deep, cleansing breath, allowing the crisp air to fill my lungs while I sit on my favorite bench under an old oak tree in the campus quad.

I have an unusual connection to the tree. Perhaps it's the sheer size that comforts me, deceiving me with the sensation of being secure and sheltered. I've been on edge lately, as if a dangerous storm is coming—an illogical sentiment, since Kingsley College has been voted the safest college campus in the Northeast for the past ten years.

It's for that reason alone my overprotective aunt allowed me to attend in the first place, using some of the trust fund my parents left me after their deaths. Well, that and five forced years of studying Krav Maga. My beautiful and crazy aunt required I take it in high school and continue in college, because a girl can never be too safe or prepared. Her words.

Buried within a small town, the college epitomizes educational greatness and is steeped in rich academic tradition. At least that's what it says in the brochure. With a small community of just under six thousand students and flawlessly manicured estate-like grounds, Kingsley overflows with scholarly charm.

The entire campus sprawls out on three hundred acres, meaning you could walk from the west side to the east in under twenty minutes, or if feeling lazy, you can take the shuttle bus in five, which I'm sure I'll appreciate in the snow-filled months.

I'm currently on the west side of campus in the main courtyard. It has well-kept landscaping for miles, adorned with brick walkways, blooming fall flowers, and oak-tree-lined streets proudly boasting their warm orange, gold, and brown fall leaves.

My bench faces the centerpiece of the campus. Belmont Hall is an impressive brick building, showcasing four thick white pillars. Ten massive steps lead up to the large white double doors. It sits at the head of the quad like the queen of all university buildings. It's also the picturesque structure used on all the brochures to lure you into academic life here, promising exemplary education leading to a productive and fulfilling post-educational life.

I could sit here for hours and people-watch. Wrapped up in my reverie, I barely notice a small area near the trees harboring a soft blue glow. As my eyes focus on the illuminated area, my skin heats and warmth begins to flow through my veins. I'm having the oddest case of déjà vu.

I narrow my eyes, trying to get a better look at the radiance that has captured my interest, but whatever it was dissolves into thin air. As if nothing happened, I feel myself being released from the seize it had on me, leaving me empty and alone as coldness emanates through me, replacing the warmth.

"Great. Now I'm seeing glowing blue spots," I mutter under my breath. "I'm also talking to myself. Yep, Eve, it's official. You're starting to friggin' lose it." I seriously need a good night's sleep, or Aria's going to have me admitted to the psych ward.

My thought process is interrupted and my attention shifts to a group of giddy girls, whispering and giggling. Internally rolling my eyes, curiosity gets the best of me and I turn to see what the uproar is about.

Leaning on a classic black Wiesmann Roadster, in the parking lot near Lexington Hall, is a tall, lean, good-looking guy. He's smiling at his fangirl harem.

Smoldering hot guy is the type of male that females instantly drop their panties for. No doubt he makes every girl feel as if they're the only one on the planet. Damn if he didn't have the chiseled cheeks and blond scruff along his perfect jawline to solidify the cliché.

He runs a large hand through his golden hair, which falls to the midway point on his neck in a sexy cut, a stark contrast to his all-black outfit consisting of tailored dress pants, a V-neck T-shirt, a watch, and designer shoes that probably cost more than my tuition.

This guy's obvious love for black reeks of trouble. God, I need to stop gawking and drooling.

Lighting a cigarette, he turns, catching my eye with his. He gives me a slight nod as if he knows me. Then he shifts his sea-green eyes to the area I was just staring at in the courtyard, narrowing them while blowing out the nicotine-infested smoke from his mouth. He methodically rubs his lips with his thumb in contemplation.

Confused, I look back and forth between the quad area and him, but can't make out a connection or reason for his peculiar behavior. He refocuses his gaze back to me, bestowing a sexy but emotionally void smile.

Wariness runs over me. There's something aloof and conniving about him. He gives the impression of being standoffish, but it's too controlled, forced even. As if he knows what I'm thinking, the boy sneers at me and turns back to the scatterbrained girls vying for his attention. He says something that appears to be brilliant, because I swear they all swoon and blush simultaneously.

"Hey. Who's the hot guy?" Aria inquires, plopping down next to me, chomping on her pink bubble gum.

Is everything this girl touches pink?

"I don't know. He just appeared, looking all cunning and surrounded by his fan club," I say, feigning disinterest but keeping my eyes glued to him, watching his every move with an abnormal curiosity.

"Well, he's YUMMY. I wouldn't mind licking him up and down like a lollipop," she states with enthusiasm, wiggling her eyebrows.

I glance matter-of-factly at her. "Don't you think the other ten guys you're currently sleeping with would be upset if they saw you licking him in broad daylight, in the quad no less?"

"I'm not sleeping with ten guys," Aria fakes offense. "It's only three." She pretends to sulk.

I offer a smug smirk. "My apologies. I didn't mean to over exaggerate your promiscuity."

"Listen, I can't help it if the male species is drawn to my raw magnetic pull," Aria says. "I think it's the pink hair combined with my fishnets and combat boots."

"I imagine it's the short skirts, C-cups and open-door policy, but, hey, that's just me," I jest, and stick my tongue out in an adult fashion.

She pushes my shoulder with little effort behind it. "Jealous, Eves? If someone would let go of her virtue, someone might be less tightly wound," she adds in a dry tone. "Maybe your night terrors are caused by sexual frustration?"

She blows a pink bubble with her gum and pops it.

I exhale, tired. "Maybe." The girl has a valid point.

"In my professional opinion, a good orgasm is just what you need to help end the nightmares." Aria uses her fake psychiatrist tone to make me smile.

I stand and grab her, yanking her off the bench. "Come on, Freud. We're going to be late."

She bats her eyes prettily at me. "What? We're learning about psychosexual development in Psychology 101."

I bark out a short laugh. "That explains today's unfortunate probing into my nonexistent sex life."

We begin to walk over to the Art Center, and Aria grabs my hand, halting my movement as she looks over her shoulder. I follow her line of sight to a set of smoldering sea-green eyes.

"At least admit hotness has a really cool car," she purrs, and smacks my ass, causing me to yelp in surprise.

"Aria! Come on," I order. My tone is laced with annoyance as I glance once more toward the parking lot.

She's right. The car is smoking hot.

AS A COMMUNICATIONS MAJOR, ARCHITECTURE IS not a class I'm overjoyed to be sitting in this semester. However, it does fulfill my art prerequisite and it's the only afternoon class that fit into my schedule. So here I am, begrudgingly awaiting my instruction on "the fundamental devotion to the examination of the built environment," according to the first line in my textbook.

Professor Davidson is not known for easy grading or motivating lectures. As a matter of fact, he's notorious for his rather lengthy and tedious explanations, specifically his sermons focused on Gothic architecture during the medieval period. I hear they're as appealing as pulling out your own fingernails.

I'm planted in my normal seat in the back of the lecture hall, hiding in the throng of the hundred students suffering along with me, and internally cursing myself for not putting this credit off until the semester before graduation.

My eyes follow Professor Davidson as he walks into class, holding his beat-up old brown leather satchel and playing with his salt and pepper hair. His thick glasses and tweed suit add to the ensemble, topped off with a bow tie no less. I sigh. It's been a long month, meaning it's going to be an even longer semester.

Aria left me at the door to head to her design class. She's hoping to work for a large advertising agency, like her dad, when she graduates as a graphic designer, much to the dismay of her mom. As a doctor, she would prefer Aria join the practice. I envy Aria for her perfect family.

My mom and dad both died when I was a baby, leaving me to grow up alone with my mother's only sister, Elizabeth. Aunt Elizabeth loves to dress in long, billowy skirts, and is a bit scatterbrained, but she's warm, affectionate, and has loved me every day like I was her own daughter. She's also a very talented jewelry designer and owns a shop on Martha's Vineyard.

She never married nor had kids of her own, which surprises me, because she's quite beautiful; blessed with the same light brown, long hair as Mom and me. Her warm hazel eyes just draw people to her. I actually look so much like her that people tend to think she's my older sister instead of my forty-year-old guardian.

Smiling at thoughts of my aunt, I don't notice class has started and I should be taking notes. *Crap.* I turn on my iPad while Professor Davidson drones on and on about architecture's effect on art in the thirteenth century.

Midway through the lecture, I stifle a yawn, stretching my neck to the left, then the right, while my wandering eyes lock on a set of full, kissable lips. I lift my gaze to see whom said lips belong to. The very attractive owner is seated one chair over from me, looking every bit as bored and annoyed as I am.

Everything about him attracts me, especially his indigo eyes outlined in dark lashes that fan softly over his cheeks. He has dark brown hair, short in the back and sides, but longer and styled on top in sexy, messy pieces. I fleetingly contemplate what it would be like to run my fingers through his hair as I chew on the inside of my cheek, a nervous habit of mine.

His five o'clock shadow highlights a chiseled jawline that, at the moment, is clenched so tightly it's triggering a slight tic in his striking cheek muscle. *Odd.*

My eyes travel down the right side of his body, roaming over his forearm. A striking Celtic cross tattoo is displayed on the inside.

He has on a plain white T-shirt, worn blue jeans, and kick-ass black motorcycle boots. There are two thick, black leather bands adorning each of his wrists, adding to his masculine style.

Hotness crosses his arms, showing off his toned biceps and blocking the taut chest I've been staring at, hidden under his cotton shirt.

I lean closer, drawn to him like a magnet.

Suddenly, he narrows his eyes at me, with an intensity that could be construed as anger. At the force of his stare, my heart lurches and breathing becomes difficult. The warm sensation from earlier begins to run through my veins, causing me to shift uncomfortably in my seat.

Without me noticing, he's leaned over the empty seat between us. "See something you like?" his deep, masculine voice asks in a malicious whisper.

Those plump lips are now set in a hard line. Our eyes lock and hold one another's for what feels like an eternity, before I drop mine.

My cheeks flush with embarrassment as realization sets in. I was just caught openly checking him out. *Crap.*

Ignoring his question, I snap my attention back to the front of the lecture hall just as Professor Davidson ends my humiliation by dismissing us for the day.

Haphazardly, I throw things in my messenger bag and hurry to escape, only to find the six-foot-plus Adonis already blocking me in by leaning against the door frame in a casual stance.

I breathe out sharply, partly in surprise and partly in nervousness.

Shit, he's even hotter standing up.

He's also abnormally fast. I look back and forth between our seats and the doorway, wondering how the hell he got down here so quickly. *Eve, attempt to focus,* I internally scold myself.

I move toward the exit. Not trusting my voice, I release the breath I've been holding and give him an *excuse me* look.

He motions his hand, encouraging me to walk through.

"After you," he says, his smooth voice warming my cheeks again.

I walk through the door, rolling my eyes at his dramatics and my lack of vocal control. Once outside, the fresh air hits me, clearing my head and offering relief from the embarrassing exchange.

"No need to thank me. It's truly my pleasure." I hear his condescending voice come from behind me.

I spin around in front of him, causing him to stop abruptly to avoid walking into me. Not expecting my sudden movement, his hands grasp my upper arms to steady himself and prevent me from stumbling backwards.

Heat pools on my skin where he touches it. Against my will, I close my eyes at his close proximity.

His scent fills my senses—a heady, masculine combination of smoky wood and leather. I inhale and sway, slightly light-headed from the whiff, which ignites warmth in my veins.

The good-looking guy leans in closer and his lips softly brush my ear. His minty breath comes out in a cocky whisper, "Falling for me already?"

This snaps me out of my daze. I look up and give him my best *what the hell* look. He watches me for a second as confusion crosses his face, then he releases my arms abrasively, as if I burned him.

We study one another, each waiting for the other to say something or make a move. Both of us are in a defiant stance with our arms crossed.

I speak first, clearly a mistake.

"What the hell is your problem?" I bark, narrowing my eyes.

"The siren speaks," he says, feigning awe. "I was beginning to question your familiarity with the English language."

One side of his mouth tilts into a smirk. It's obvious he's pleased with himself and his lame answer.

"Charming," I reply, annoyed. "I happen to be well versed in the English language."

He places a long finger to his closed mouth in contemplation. "That's astonishing, considering that earlier, I caught you openly gawking at me." Indigo eyes scan my face as he leans in and lowers his voice to a sensual tone. "Pink lips parted, beautiful hazel eyes locked onto my chest, drooling as if I were a piece of chocolate." He pauses for effect. "Yet not a single word flowed through that pretty, pouty mouth of yours," blue eyes retorts, staring at my lips, waiting patiently for my response.

I swallow. Between his scent and his nearness, my body is overheating. "Shows how much you know. I prefer salty over sweet," I throw back at him, proud that my voice sounds strong.

It would be in my best interest to gather my dignity and just walk away. This infuriating guy is getting under my skin, distracting me with insults that appear to be compliments.

He snorts and gives me an insolent smile. "Yeah, I can tell sweet isn't your thing, sweetheart."

My jaw tightens. "I have a name, and it's not Sweetheart," I snap.

He crosses his arms, amused at my outburst, and gives me a crooked smile. "What would that name be?"

"Eve Collins," I offer in an even tone.

"Eve," he says in a husky voice.

The way my name rolls off his tongue does crazy things to my body. I secretly curse his good looks for causing my stomach muscles to clench and the butterflies to take flight.

"Eve," he repeats, as some form of understanding sinks in. "Without doubt, a suitable name for you."

The cute guy stands taller and puffs his chest out in some sort of proud posture.

"Meaning?" I question tersely.

"Wasn't Eve the mother of mankind? Of course, she was also seen as weak, allowing evil to succeed in tempting her to the forbidden." He challenges me with his eyes.

I pull my brows together, confused by his bizarre statement. "Are you implying I'm weak?" I question, with a slight octave change.

He just stands there, calm and unfazed by my growing temper. For some reason, his lack of reaction makes me even more irate.

"I can assure you that's not the case," I say. "As a matter of fact, I could punch you right now and you'd be seeing stars for weeks, followed by a plastic surgeon to reset your nose, pretty boy."

Clearly unaffected by me, he laughs deeply, placing his hands up in mock surrender while backing away from me. "There's no need for threats of physical harm, Eve."

His gaze locks onto mine, assessing me, probably waiting to see if I'll actually punch him. I angle my head to the side in annoyance and continue to watch him watching me.

As soon as he finds what he's searching for in my eyes, he nods, seeming to have had some sort of internal dialogue with himself. His face turns impassive.

"Your lack of knowledge with regard to your name means nothing," he says, casually shrugging me off.

I feel a migraine coming on. This conversation is nonsensical and it needs to end. "I don't think this is working." I motion between us while giving him an irritated glower.

A mischievous grin forms on his face. "Do we need couples therapy already?"

My frustration is now off the charts, so I exhale loudly, hoping he'll get the hint. "That's not what I meant."

He leans into my personal space and narrows his eyes, attempting to intimidate and fluster me more than he already has, and for the love of God, it's working.

"Would you please stop? I can't think with you in my face," I grumble.

At this, he leans away. "I make you nervous?" It's a question with a hint of curiosity.

"Ah, no. Far from it," I answer, still a bit shaken.

"Your unconvincing tone says different," he retorts.

I'm just about to offer my witty comeback when his eyes snap up, quickly scanning the area behind me before redirecting his focus back to me. He frowns.

Before I can glance at what caught his attention, blue eyes speaks, ending my inquisitiveness.

"As delightful as this conversation has been with you, I have somewhere I need to be. Try not to walk into anyone or anything," he mocks, as he begins to walk away.

"Whatever," I mutter, and add under my breath, "ass."

He stops and turns back toward me, stalking me slowly, like a predator. "Tsk. Name-calling is very unbecoming of you, Eve." My name comes out like a dig. "Perhaps you should consider your choice of words within the English language with more care when conversing with others."

I just stand there, glaring at him, racking my brain for a smart-ass response. Unfortunately, he has me all tongue-tied and at a loss for witty repartee.

Hotness, of course, wastes no time conquering the silence. "I'll be anticipating your retort, siren.

TRANSLATIONS

Eímai Tristan, gios tou Ofilía. Evlogíes sti gi, to neró, kai ton ouranó pnévmata. Tha akoúso, odigós mou. Anoíxte ta chéria sas kai na kalosoríso mou spíti." (Greek): "I am Tristan, son of Ophelia. Blessings to the earth, water, and sky spirits. I will listen, guide me. Open your arms and welcome me home."

ABOUT THE AUTHOR

RANDI COOLEY WILSON IS AN AUTHOR of paranormal, urban fantasy, and contemporary romance books. Randi was born and raised in Massachusetts, where she attended Bridgewater State University and graduated with a degree in Communication Studies. After graduation, she moved to California, where she lived happily bathed in sunshine and warm weather for fifteen years.

Randi makes stuff up, devours romance books, drinks lots of wine and coffee, and has a slight addiction to bracelets. She currently resides in Massachusetts with her daughter and husband.

She loves to hear from readers. Please reach out to her at: randicooleywilson.com or via social media outlets:

Twitter: @R_CooleyWilson
Facebook: www.facebook.com/authorrandicooleywilson
Goodreads: www.goodreads.com/RCooleyWilson
Randi's Rebels: www.facebook.com/groups/randisrebels

ACKNOWLEDGMENTS

THERE ARE SO MANY PEOPLE TO thank who are a part of this amazing journey I'm on. A simple thank you to them for encouraging and supporting me just doesn't seem like a strong enough show of gratitude on my part.

To my husband and daughter, thank you for loving me and sharing your time with the characters I write.

Hang Le, I could hug you all day long for the amazing Royal Protector Academy covers, logo, and series promos. Thank you for visually capturing my stories.

Sarah Hershman and the team at Hershman Rights Management, thank you for your ongoing support.

Rick Miles and the entire Red Coat PR team, thank you for allowing me to be part of your author family.

Maggie Mae Gallagher, thank you for coming into my life and taking care of business so I can focus on writing.

Kris Kendall, I love you. Enough said.

Janelle Rhiannon, you're an amazing critique partner.

Liz Ferry, thank you for polishing this story so it shines.

Perfectly Publishing, thank you for making the interior of *Vernal* look as cool as the exterior.

A HUGE thank you to Randi's Rebels. Y'all are the best reader group a girl could ask for. You keep me sane when I need it, provide me with endless book recommendations, and fill my days with man candy and laughs. Rebels Rock!

A special shout out to Christine Petrey, who got to name Zander, and Tabitha Hulsey, who named Freya.

Thanks to my family and friends, I love you all.

To the readers, thank you for reading my stories. Thank you, for taking a chance on me. Thank you, for trusting me with your imagination. I'm honored to be part of your literary world.

Printed in Great Britain
by Amazon